WHAT WAS THE TRUTH ABOUT THE TWO MEN EMMA LOVED?

One was her father, Jack Tremayne, so handsome and dashing, and so secretive about his past and present activities. The other was the attractive, maddeningly elusive Lucien de Fontenay, who offered Emma his love but not his confidence.

Now Emma could no longer escape the suspicion that her father was a murderer and philanderer, and that Lucien was little more than a brigand, and the lover of another woman. But it was too late for her to turn back from the path she had chosen. For better or for worse, Emma was on the side of these two men as they defied a brutal, cunning power in a gamble that would decide not only their personal fates but the destiny of Europe. . . .

"Some of the most fascinating characters you are likely to meet between the pages of any book!"
—Springfield News & Leader

"An engrossing, romantic, drama-filled novel which beckons a one-sitting read, so captivating is the plot!"
—Lewiston Journal

Big Bestsellers from SIGNET

The
Place
of
Stones

By
Constance Heaven

A SIGNET BOOK
NEW AMERICAN LIBRARY
TIMES MIRROR

COPYRIGHT © 1975 BY CONSTANCE HEAVEN

Library of Congress Catalog Card Number: 74-30595

This is an authorized reprint of a hardcover edition published by Coward, McCann & Geoghegan, Inc.

SIGNET, SIGNET CLASSICS, MENTOR, PLUME AND MERIDIAN BOOKS are published by The New American Library, Inc., 1301 Avenue of the Americas, New York, New York 10019

FIRST PRINTING, JUNE, 1976

1 2 3 4 5 6 7 8 9

PRINTED IN THE UNITED STATES OF AMERICA

For CASPAR and MARIE

Author's Note

A bibliography of the memoirs and travel books consulted would be pretentious in a romantic novel such as this, but I owe a large debt to *The Counter Revolution* by Jacques Godechot (Routledge 1972), a fascinating study of the rebellious underground and the English agents operating in France during the revolution and the Consulate; also *Aspects of the Revolution* by Richard Cobb (Oxford University Press 1972), which includes grim details from the reports on captured rebel groups unearthed from police archives.

'Princesses of Les Baux . . . who throned it on high upon your rocks of gold . . . the tempest still howls in all its mighty strength between your ruined halls and down your desolate battlements . . . the Rhône-wind riots through your walls of stone . . .'

Frédéric Mistral

Chapter 1

It began, the whole tangled story, on the day I saw Lucien for the first time though then I did not know his name or where he came from or indeed anything about him. I had been out early, riding Rufus across the moor. He had been skittish that morning and without any warning stopped short at a low hedge that he had always taken in his stride. I went clean over his head and landed in the soft grass and mud. I was not hurt, but it took me some minutes to recapture him and so, still a little bruised, I came up through the wood leading him by the bridle. It was then that I saw the young man.

He was standing absolutely still, his eyes fixed on the house, the sea wind playing wildly with the thick brown hair. I halted and watched him curiously from the shelter of the trees. Goodness knows Trevira House was not all that remarkable. It had been built in the seventeenth century and the mullioned windows, the ivy clambering up the old stone walls, did have a certain charm, though it was crumbling badly in places.

I had always regarded this stretch of cliff and the rocky cove below washed by the Atlantic breakers as our own private property. Not even the villagers came up here. To find a stranger standing there was unusual to say the least. I stepped out resolutely from behind the trees.

'Are you looking for someone?'

He swung round, his eyes running over me. 'They told me if I followed the cliff, I would come upon a path to the shore.' His voice was husky but pleasant, with a distinctly foreign accent.

I frowned. No one ever used the cove for any purpose without my father's permission.. The stranger wore the heavy boots and rough frieze jacket of a seaman but the

9

long brown hand that held the fisherman's stocking cap
was certainly not that of a sailor. There was too something
very distinctive about the finely cut features, the high-
bridged nose and clear olive skin. His casual easy air irritated me.

'Who told you?' I said indignantly. 'This does happen to
be private land.'

'Is that so?' An amused smile played around his mouth.
'You really need not concern yourself, boy. I have not
robbed your master of so much as a blade of grass.'

I blushed a little under his steady gaze. I was wearing a
pair of old breeches, my frilled shirt was none too clean
and my brown leather waistcoat had seen better days. It
was little wonder if he had taken me for one of the stable
lads. I said slowly, 'There is a path but it's very rough . . .
and it's slippery after the rain. If you are not used to climbing, you could break your neck.'

'*Tant pis*,' he shrugged his shoulders with a little foreign
gesture. 'So much the worse for me. All the same I fear I
must risk it. Here, boy,' he dug into a pocket, 'take this for
your pains.' He tossed me a coin before turning his back
and walking rapidly along the cliff.

I watched him disappear over the edge before I looked
down at myself ruefully. Mud plastered my boots, and the
wind had blown my short hair into a sorry tangle. Rufus
snorted and pushed against me impatiently. I gave him a
sharp tap on the nose.

'Brute! You can wait for your breakfast!'

I bent to pick up the coin. It was not a shilling as I had
expected. I turned it over curiously. One side was clearly
stamped with the dull heavy features of Louis XVI, Louis
Capet who had died under the guillotine ten years ago.
How odd to meet a Frenchman on Trevira Head at eight
o'clock on an April morning even if England had been at
peace with the new French republic for nearly a year.
Cornish villagers still looked suspiciously at all foreigners
even though, with the beastly guillotine lopping off heads
by the dozen, there had been a flood of refugees fleeing
from the Terror in Paris and seeking safety in England.
Perhaps the stranger was another émigré come over in one
of the fishing boats as they still did sometimes, though he
did not look in the least like one of the weary care-worn

aristocrats I had met in London eking out a precarious living as tutors or governesses or even as cooks and seamstresses, and perpetually bemoaning the cruel fate that had deprived them of wealth and loved ones.

I dropped the coin into my pocket and dismissed the mystery with a shrug. The wind was cold, it had begun to rain once more and the thought of hot coffee was very tempting. I went across the grass, led Rufus round to the stable block and entered the house by way of the kitchen.

Deborah was busily kneading dough and waved a floury hand. 'The master be down already, mistress. He's been askin' for you.'

'All right, Deb. I'm on my way now.'

I paused for a moment in the doorway of the morning room. My father was already tackling his eggs and kidneys. Jack Tremayne at forty-three was still a good-looking man. The crisp red-brown hair had no touch of grey and the excellently cut blue coat fitted his broad shoulders to perfection. I looked at my charming elegant rakish father with deep affection before I came across to him and kissed the top of his head.

'Good morning, Papa. I'm sorry I'm late.'

He leaned back in his chair and looked me up and down with strong disapproval. 'My dear Emma, do you have to go about looking like a disreputable gutter rat? No wonder our neighbours look down their well-bred noses at us. What have you done with the splendid allowance I give you? Spent it on those damned horses, I suppose.'

'It's not as splendid as all that, Papa,' I said calmly, pouring myself a cup of coffee and bringing it to the table. 'Fashionable gowns are very expensive and you've never cared a rap what people think, so don't pretend you have. Besides Rufus threw me this morning.'

'Good God! Are you hurt?'

'Of course not. I know how to fall off. You taught me. Don't you remember?'

'I'm beginning to realize I taught you all the wrong things,' complained my father, watching as I reached out for an apple and began to peel it. 'For heaven's sake, girl, eat something sensible. You peck at food like a chicken. How am I ever to marry you off if you go about looking like a starved kitten?'

11

'I don't,' I exclaimed indignantly and then met his eyes across the table. 'Besides you don't really want to get rid of me, do you, darling?'

'I must admit the prospect has its charms,' sighed my father going back to his kidneys. 'I have nightmares sometimes wondering what is to become of you if something kills me off one of these days. What on earth does the future hold for a young woman of twenty-two with few social graces except an outspoken tongue and the ability to ride horses like a jockey and whose only inheritance is likely to be a ramshackle house, a few acres of Cornish bog, half a share in a derelict tin mine, and who is as thin as a scarecrow into the bargain? Men like their women with flesh on their bones.'

'Do they?' I grinned at him. 'Well, you ought to know.'

He raised his eyebrows. 'That is not a nice remark for a daughter to make to her revered father.'

'We're not nice and anyway you're not going to be killed off, are you? Besides it is fashionable to be thin. They say that in Paris Madame Bonaparte wears her muslin gowns damped to show off her lovely figure. Think how dreadful it would be if she bulged.'

'Horrible,' agreed my father pushing aside his plate. 'All the same it sounds deuced unhealthy to me. However if you really want to catch your death of cold in this fetching manner, you will have every opportunity in a day or two.'

'I will?'

'Certainly. Is there any of that marmalade you made so badly last year?'

I put down my half-eaten apple. 'Oh, don't be aggravating. What do you mean?'

'What I say and don't gape at me, it is most unbecoming. Pour me some more coffee instead.' He smiled at my impatience, taking the cup and sipping it before he said casually, 'How would you like to come to Paris with me?'

'Paris!' My mouth really dropped open this time. 'But how? Why? When? Papa, can we?'

'I don't see why not. It's true the peace treaty is wearing a little thin and no one seems to know which way that damned fellow Bonaparte is likely to jump, but a great number of my acquaintances have been running backwards and forwards across the Channel in the last few months.'

'It would be wonderful, only . . .' I hesitated, 'only . . . can we afford it?'

He made an airy gesture. 'You can always find funds for what you really want to do.'

'Yes, I know but . . .' I put out a hand and touched his. 'Father, what is it this time? Business or pleasure?'

He was silent for a moment. There had always been a far deeper love and understanding between us than any I'd known between other fathers and daughters. His fingers curled up and enclosed mine. 'Both, my dear, but that needn't worry you. I have a number of friends in the embassy over there. You won't be lonely. I can promise you that.' He withdrew his hand. 'Besides Victor will be coming with us. He will take care of you.'

'Oh no, not Victor Jarrett. You can't mean it. That will spoil everything.'

'Why?' asked my father humorously. 'Because he wants to marry you?'

'Oh it's not that,' I replied scornfully. 'I can always stop him proposing, or nearly always, but he'll be there, under my feet all the time, and he is such a deadly bore.'

'He's not the liveliest of company, I grant you that, but you might do worse than accept his offer, Emma. He has money and he is eminently respectable.'

'I don't care if he is richer than . . . than the king of England. He's still duller than dull. I'd rather be dead,' I said vehemently. 'You can't really want me to marry him. Just think what it would be like to have him here . . . always!'

'The idea is a little daunting, I must admit, but he has a fine house of his own, you know. Be nice to him, pet, just to please me,' said my father lightly. He stood up, a tall man, lean and powerful. 'Now I really must be off. I'm riding into Penzance. You might see that the trunks are brought down from the attics and get Deb to help you with the packing.'

'When do we go?' I called after him as he went through the door.

'Tomorrow. I've booked our passage already.'

I watched from the window as he took the reins of his horse from Silas and vaulted lightly into the saddle. He turned to wave before he rode away. It was foolish, I knew, but I never saw him leave me without a faint tremor of anxiety. He came back; he always came back, but supposing one day he did not . . . I shut my mind quickly against such a frightening thought, yet try as I would, I could not easily dismiss it; intangible, I could never quite put a finger on it, but it was always there, an element of danger that was in the very air he breathed. He had never been quite like other fathers, like the solid dependable men who came to fetch my friends from Miss Faversham's high-class school. I did not want him to be like them, I was proud of his difference, and yet sometimes, when I was very tired, I wished I did not love him quite so much.

Deborah had come in to clear the breakfast table and I turned to her. 'Do you remember where our trunks were put, Deb? Are they in the attic?'

'Aye, that they be, Miss Emma, and a fair dirty place it be up there too. I keep meanin' to lay me 'ands on it, give it a good clean-out, but there's never the time. What are you wantin' with them ole things?'

'Mr Tremayne and I are going to Paris, Deb . . . tomorrow in fact.'

'Paris, never!' Deb raised her hands in horror at the very idea. 'Not with all them Frenchies! Why, it be like goin' in the lions' den. They'll 'ave your 'ead soon as winkin' if you don't look out.'

'Don't be silly, Deb. That was years ago. There's no danger now. I'm going to change. Tell Silas to fetch the trunks down later on.'

'Aye, I'll do that. Don't you go rummagin' up there on your own now. You might come to some 'arm. Goin' off sudden like that . . . tomorrow of all things! You'll be wantin' your clean shifts, I suppose, and the Master's shirts not yet laundered . . . I've only one pair of 'ands, Miss Emma . . .'

Deborah loved a good grumble. She went on piling plates on the tray and muttering to herself while I went up the stairs. My father had always enjoyed springing surprises on me and I had long learned to cope with them. When I had stripped off my muddy breeches and washed my face, I remembered what Deb had said about the dirt and dust up in the attic and hunted through my wardrobe for my oldest gown.

I smiled as I took out the blue merino with its narrow bands of black braid. I was sixteen when I had it and so proud, my first really grown-up dress, and I had worn it on the never-to-be-forgotten day when my father came to fetch me from school and I left the great gaunt building for the last time. The extraordinary thing was that it still fitted me. It hooked easily round the waist even if the bodice had become a little tight. I brushed my tangled hair and looked critically in the mirror. Perhaps Papa was right. Perhaps I was too thin. 'Twenty-two and still without a beau!' How the girls at school would have giggled over that. I was nearly as old as poor Miss Graham who taught geography and deportment and had already been condemned by the cruel wit of rich young women as fit only for a life of sad resignation in a lace cap and mittens.

Then my sense of humour came to my rescue and I laughed at myself. A thin streak of watery sun lit up the red-gold tints in my hair. I remembered the young man on the cliff top and Paris seemed suddenly a very delightful prospect. I had no wish to exchange my life with anyone. It was only just occasionally that I wished my father and I were not quite such lonely people. There were no aunts or uncles, no cousins to share girlish secrets with. My mother had been an only child, running away from this very house to marry the dashing Lieutenant Tremayne, barely twenty, and just returned from fighting with Cornwallis in the American War of Independence. She had died the following year a few days after I had been born.

Until I was eleven, I had lived an odd up-and-down life with a succession of nursemaids and governesses, sometimes in very peculiar lodgings with a god-like father who would appear unexpectedly with a pile of expensive presents. He would horrify my nurse by buying me far too many sweets and ices and carrying me off to unsuitable places like Vauxhall Gardens and the circus which I adored, and he once bought me a puppy that was stolen the very next week.

Then there had been school, five hateful years when I had never seen him at all; my only link the infrequent letters, stained, creased and dirty, handed to me by the head-

mistress with a disapproving sniff. I read them rapturously
and kept them in a locked box beside my bed in the long
dormitory. The months had seemed endless until the
morning I was summoned to the parlour and he was there,
taller, handsomer and even more wonderful than I remembered him, and he put his arm round my shoulders and
smiled charmingly at the scandalized headmistress.

'My dear Madam, I must have my daughter. I need her
to keep me in order. I hope to God you've taught her the
right things. The wrong ones we shall doubtless learn together,' and so we had.

I tied a neat silk scarf over my hair and went up the
creaking wooden stairs to the attic. Deb was right. The
floor was velvety with black fluff and the raftered room
was crammed with discarded furniture, old bedsteads, broken china, childish toys, the debris of a lifetime, several
lifetimes perhaps, all perilously stacked on top of one another. I nearly choked when I pulled incautiously at what
looked like a damask curtain and a pile of moth-eaten garments fell smotheringly on top of me in a cloud of ancient
dust.

I found the trunks easily, the big one I had taken to
school and a military chest battered and brassbound with
James E. Tremayne painted on the lid. Tucked at the back
between the legs of a spotted rocking horse, there was a
curious bag of thick brown canvas bound with leather, a
kind of knapsack such as a climber or walker might carry,
the very last thing I would have associated with my elegant fastidious father. It must have come with the rest of
our possessions when we moved from London to Cornwall. I pulled it towards me and unbuckled the leather
straps. They were stiff and hard. I broke my nail on one
of them. At first I thought it was empty, then my groping
fingers felt something soft and I drew it out. A ray of sunlight through the dusty window showed me a sash of tri-
colour silk, grimy now and stained, but quite unmistakeably the colours of the republic, the colours that must have
flashed before the unhappy king of France when they
brought him to the guillotine.

I had never known what my father had done during
those five lonely years except that he was out of England.
He had always avoided questions, putting me off with a

smile and a jest. Romantically I had sometimes thought of him gallantly risking his life to save the wretched victims trapped in the Paris prisons, but maybe he had been something else too, a spy, working for England, needing disguise.

I had never really been sure where our money came from. Until three years ago when a distant cousin of my mother had died and Trevira House came to my father, we had lived a hand-to-mouth existence on the fringes of society, sometimes rich, sometimes unable to pay the butcher's bill, but I had never minded. We had been too happy and school had taught me one or two useful accomplishments. I knew how to housekeep economically and I spoke fluent French.

'I could teach it,' I had said once enthusiastically in one of our more poverty-stricken moments, but my father had refused categorically.

'Not for the world! I'll not have my daughter at the beck and call of some overfed society bitch and her detestable children. We'll come round again, my pet,' and we always did.

My fingers touched something else in the bottom of the bag, something hard and trapped in the lining. I tugged at it and it came out with a jerk, a small book bound in leather, a coat of arms stamped in gold on the cover, but so faded I could not read it. It creaked open at a page and I saw why. A sprig of lavender lay in the crease, so dry and brittle it crumbled at my touch though a faint fragrance still lingered. Someone had marked the page. I had studied the lines at school. The stark agony of lovers' parting broke through Racine's classical French.

J'ai cru que votre amour allait finir son cours . . .

I believed that your love had deserted me, Now I know I am wrong, that you will love me always. . .

I sat with the book on my lap remembering vividly those first few months after I had left school, seeing them now with new eyes, realizing what I had been too young to understand. My father with all his apparent gaiety had been like someone recovering from an illness, tense, on

edge, taking me everywhere with him as if he needed me
desperately, as if he dared not be alone, so that people had
smiled at gallant Jack Tremayne playing the role of devoted Papa, only it had not been all pretence, it had been
real, I was sure of that now. I shut the book quickly with an
uncomfortable feeling that I was prying into a secret pain
that did not belong to me.

I pushed the bag and sash back among the other objects
all cluttered together and intended to do the same with the
book when I heard Deborah calling and went to the door
to listen. The maid came clambering up the rickety stairs.

'Mr Jarrett is here, Miss,' she said breathlessly. 'He be
askin' for you very urgent.'

Oh no, not Victor, prosing on and on about Paris. It
was too much. I couldn't bear it. 'Tell him I'm gone out,
Deb, say I'm on my way to Penzance with my father. Say
anything, but get rid of him.'

'You didn't ought, Miss Emma. He's a good man is Mr
Jarrett, him and his father. They've lived round these parts
for years gone past.'

'I don't care if they've lived here since Adam, I don't
want to see him and that's that.'

Deb went down again, grumbling under her breath, and
I followed, watching from behind the curtains at the land-
ing window. The stocky figure holding his horse in the
courtyard was reluctant to leave. I saw him glance up at
the house. He was arguing with Deborah. Then at last he
heaved himself into the saddle and rode away. I sighed
with relief.

Victor Jarrett had been the first of our neighbours to
call when we had come to Trevira in the spring of 1800.
He could not have been much more than thirty but he was
one of those men who are born looking middle-aged.
There could not have been a greater contrast to my father
and yet somehow they had formed an unlikely friendship,
chiefly perhaps because Victor owned a boat which he was
always willing to lend, something of which my father took
full advantage. I think it only amused him when Victor
formally asked his permission to propose to me.

'Ask away, my dear fellow,' he said with his arm round
my shoulders, 'but I warn you, Emma has a mind of her
own.'

That had been more than a year ago, but though I had refused him as firmly as I knew how, Victor had still not quite given up hope.

The sun had come out again, sparkling through the rain and I had a sudden longing for the salt smell of the sea and the fresh wind blowing away the cobwebs of the attic. The book was still in my hand. I put it on the dressing-table, washed the dust off my hands, picked up a shawl and went down and out of the front door. One of the spaniels sleeping in the hall got to its feet and lumbered after me across the grass.

At the top of the cliff, I paused. The narrow path climbed its tortuous way down through clumps of gorse and furze and young broom. It was a view I never grew tired of, the emerald green sea hurtling itself against the rocks in a flurry of white spray, the gulls with their harsh cry plummeting down for food and then soaring up again in effortless arcs. I had seen it first three years ago and felt I had known it in my bones for ever. Just within the shelter of the bay a small ship lay at anchor, rakishly built with long slim lines, and I wondered if this was what the young Frenchman had been making for. I was too far off to see the name, but I could make out figures moving about the deck and the tide was on the turn.

Victor occasionally brought his *Sea Witch* into the cove but I had never seen any other ship there. Curious to know what they were doing, I began to make my way cautiously down the rocky path. The spaniel was at my heels and I grabbed his collar in case he should fall. Then a stone dislodged by the rain rolled from under my foot. I lost my balance and released him to snatch at a branch and steady myself. To my horror, the dog jerked forward and unable to save himself went bouncing from boulder to boulder down the cliff. I screamed to him helplessly and out of the scrub of furze and gorse, someone answered. I went on scrambling down and met the man coming up, the terrified dog in his arms.

At first I thought it was the stranger whom I had seen earlier that morning, but as he came closer, I realized that though he was dressed in the same rough sailor's garb, he was older, nearer my father's age, the dark hair flecked with grey, a hawk-like nose in a tanned face. Tie a red scarf round his head and he could be a pirate, I thought, or a brigand chieftain.

'*Voilà*, Mademoiselle. Your dog, I believe.'

'Thank you. I thought he would be killed.' The dog was frantically licking my face as I bent over him.

The stranger laughed, showing white teeth under a dark moustache. 'He fell on top of me. Luckily I am strong or else we would both be in the sea, *n'est-ce pas?*'

'Is that your ship?'

'Not mine, but I sail in her. See, my friend waits with the small boat.' His bold eyes swept over me in a way that made me blush. 'I wish I could say *au revoir*, Mademoiselle, but unhappily I must leave you.'

I was almost sure that the man waiting on the beach was the young man of the morning and I sat on a rock with my arms round the trembling dog and thought how strange it was that on the very day my father told me that we were going to Paris, two Frenchmen should have appeared almost on our doorstep and were now sailing from our private cove. There could be a connection of course. We did sometimes entertain unusual guests at Trevira. Once or twice it had occurred to me that my father might be engaged in the smuggling that according to Deb was practised up and down the Cornish coast in spite of wars, the army and the revenue officers. But I did not really believe it. It was not my father's way. He had an aristocratic contempt for money. He would take risks at the gaming table or on the race course, sometimes losing, more often winning, but he would not soil his fingers with buying and selling.

It was later that evening after we had supped comfortably together and were sitting by the fire that some curious impulse impelled me to put the book I had found in the attic on his knee.

'Is this yours, Papa?'

He glanced at it without moving, but his mouth tightened. There was a wary look in his eyes and a long pause before he said, 'What is it?'

'It's Racine's *Bérénice*. I found it in the attic in an old canvas bag. I thought it might have been yours.'

'No, not mine. Racine was never a favourite of mine, too many damned heroics. "Men have died from time to time and worms have eaten them, but not for love," that's Shakespeare and he knew what he was talking about. It must have belonged to someone of your mother's family, my dear. Keep it if you wish.' He put down his brandy glass and rose to his feet. 'It's late, Emma, time for bed. We've a long day tomorrow.'

I got up obediently taking up one of the candles. 'Goodnight, Papa.'

'Goodnight, my pet. I'll just make sure everything is locked before I come up.'

I kissed him and went up the stairs. It was only when I was undressed and ready for bed that I remembered the book and came down in my dressing-gown to fetch it in case Deb tidied it away somewhere as she was so fond of doing. My father had gone and the fire was no more than a red glow, but though I searched everywhere, candle in hand, the book had disappeared.

Chapter 2

It was near midnight and the ball at the Tuileries was in full swing. When I looked round at the walls panelled in brocaded silk, the gilt sofas and chairs upholstered in golden satin, it was almost impossible to believe that only a few years before a howling mob armed with pikes and hatchets and screaming for blood had raged through the palace committing unspeakable outrages in these very rooms.

The heat from the hundreds of wax candles, the smell of perfume, the thronging crowds of perspiring dancers, the tables groaning under expensive food and drink, were almost overwhelming. I had seen the contempt on my father's face at the sight of the lavish gowns, the naked bosoms, the feathers and jewels, the gaudy uniforms. Bonaparte's reception had none of the restrained elegance of the best London society, little though I had seen of it.

We had arrived in Paris the evening before after an exhausting journey. The sea passage had been stormy. For one horrible moment I had thought my stomach would betray me, but fortunately it had passed off after a qualm or two. It was Victor who had succumbed, who had turned pale green and beaten a hasty retreat. It was not that my father would have been unkind if the same fate had overtaken me, he never was, but I felt it would have been letting him down to be like the other women passengers, crowded into the tiny stifling cabin, moaning and groaning, waving scented handkerchiefs and wishing loudly that they were dead. I wondered sometimes if he had any idea of the high standard he demanded from me.

It was like the first time we had gone hunting together. I had deliberately taken the fences beside him and when inevitably I was thrown, I had laughed at the bruises, gritted my teeth and let him lift me back into the saddle and ride on as if nothing had happened. He had taught me to fence and shoot as if I were a boy, the son maybe that he did not have, and once or twice he had demanded that I show off my skill to the admiration of his sporting friends. 'She's a good plucky 'un, your gal!' they exclaimed and clapped me on the shoulder. I was happy then, sure of his love and his pride in me. But all the same it could be a strain. I used to wonder sometimes what it felt like to be cosseted and spoiled, fussed over as if I were a rare and valuable piece of porcelain, like Dorothy. She was the daughter of one of the ambassador's staff and had cheerfully confessed to me that morning that she loathed horses and had no accomplishments whatsoever except an ability to sing a little and let her hand stray across the strings of her harp to show off the full curves of her beautiful bosom.

I could see Dorothy now surrounded by a laughing group of young officers. She had danced the entire evening whereas my own card was woefully empty except for the scrawled name of Victor Jarrett. I sat straight-backed on the hard sofa and tried not to feel envious. My father had left me with the acquaintances I scarcely knew and gone off cheerfully to the card room, never realizing how desperately lonely I felt. Well, I was not going to show it. I threw up my head with defiant determination, only to see Victor coming in my direction, square, stalwart and obstinately English, open disapproval of the raffish society around him written in every line of his face. I could not endure to dance with him again. It was impossible. Everyone would be expecting our engagement to be announced at any moment if I did. I looked around despairingly, seeking escape, and it was then that I noticed the young man who stood leaning back against the wall, arms folded, as isolated from the crowd as I was myself. There was no mistaking the face though he no longer wore the rough dress of a seaman.

'A gentleman should never be conspicuous by the cut of his coat!' my father used to say, but in this overdressed company the young man in his elegant black evening dress had an air of rare distinction. Victor had been halted by an acquaintance, but it was quite apparent that he was still on his way. I yielded to a reckless impulse. I moved quickly towards the stranger and put a hand on his arm.

'Pardon me, Monsieur,' I said in French, 'but would you do me a great favour?'

He turned to me and I saw the tilted eyebrows and the look of surprise. 'A favour, Mademoiselle? In what way?'

'Will you talk to me please?'

'Do we know one another?'

'Yes . . . well, no, not really.' Confusion overwhelmed me for an instant, then I leaned towards him whispering urgently. 'You see that gentleman coming across the ballroom. He wants to marry me. He has just proposed and I have refused him. It is not the first time and I cannot endure to do it all over again. I really cannot. So if you could just look as if we were old friends.'

'Ah I understand.' He smiled and the dark eyes glowed. 'It is difficult, is it not, to say no and again no . . . and yet I can find it in my heart to be a little sorry for him too.'

I knew I was blushing and hated it. 'You needn't be. It would be far worse for him if I said yes.'

'Truly? That I do not believe.' The dark head bent intimately towards me. When Victor threaded his way to us at last, it was to find us deep in absorbing conversation in the rapid French that I knew he found difficult to understand.

He said with exasperation, 'We are, I believe, engaged for the next dance.'

It was perfectly true, we were, but I lied with determination. 'Oh no, Victor, you are quite mistaken. I am promised to . . .' I paused, hopelessly groping for a name, and the young man took me up with a glint of mischief.

'I do not think I have the pleasure of your acquaintance, Monsieur. Lucien de Fontenay, at your service.'

Victor bowed stiffly in acknowledgement. 'I was not aware that you knew Miss Tremayne.'

'Neither did I until . . . until earlier this evening. Now I feel I have known her all my life. Excuse me, Monsieur,' and he held out his arm. I put my fingertips on it and allowed him to lead me towards the dancers.

It is not easy to continue a conversation while dancing a cotillion. As we bowed and curtsied, separated and came together again, Lucien said, 'I have told you my name and since it appears that we are old friends, may I know yours?'

'Emma . . . Emma Tremayne.'

'Emma,' he repeated lingeringly. 'It is enchanting.'

'It belonged to my grandmother,' I said prosaically. 'Most people think it very quaint and old-fashioned and I am not at all like that.'

'Maybe that is why. The unexpected is always delightful.'

'Do you always say pretty things?'

'Very rarely.'

When we came together again, he took my hand. 'I have not seen you at any of the other assemblies. Have you been some weeks in Paris?'

'Two days only.'

'Do you remain long?'

'It depends on my father. He has . . . interests here.'

'He is in France on business perhaps.'

He released my hand as the dancers swept me away from him. No doubt he thought my father one of the plump dull Englishmen hurrying to Paris to pick up the threads of trade lost during the years of revolution and war. For the first time that evening I felt happy about my gown. We had chosen it together in one of the most exclusive shops and dazzled by my father's charm the dressmaker had promised to alter it in time for the ball. It was ivory muslin over satin and dusted with gold stars.

'No jewels,' he had said looking at me critically, 'they are not your style. Just a few fresh flowers in your hair.'

I had been disappointed then, but now when I saw the admiration in a young man's eyes, I knew he had been right.

The dance was over. Lucien was leading me back to the sofa. 'You know, I nearly did not come here tonight.'

'Why?'

He looked around the room. 'Many reasons. I know very few of these people and I am only in Paris for a few days.'

'What made you change your mind?'

'It was changed for me. I was angry then, but now I am grateful.' He looked down at me, smiling. 'I should have missed meeting you. May I call on you at your hotel?'

I said frankly, 'I should like that very much, but you must meet Papa first.'

'Of course. I should be delighted. Is he here?'

'Yes.'

I was tempted to tell him about our first meeting on the cliff at Trevira but a rustle of anticipation had run through the ballroom and my father was coming towards us from the card room. He waved to me and there was surprise in Lucien's eyes. For an instant I saw Jack Tremayne as other people saw him; a gentleman undoubtedly, but an adventurer too, a man who even in a ballroom walked with the stealthy tread of a jungle animal who is aware of danger at every step. Eagerly I went to him.

'Papa, I want you to meet Monsieur de Fontenay. He has been so kind to me.'

He frowned as if he were displeased, but the next moment he was smiling, holding out his hand in English fashion and exchanging civilities with Lucien.

'Thank you for looking after my little girl,' he was saying smoothly. 'Of course we shall be pleased to see you if you can spare the time, Monsieur de Fontenay, but this is my daughter's first visit to Paris and we shall be out a great deal. There is so much I want her to see.'

He is putting him off, nicely but firmly, I thought miserably and this is the first young man I have ever really liked, but Lucien was not so easily daunted.

'Perhaps I may be of some use to you in that. I know the city well from a child,' and he smiled at me so that despite all common sense, my heart sang with joy.

It was the music that interrupted us. The orchestra broke into a stirring martial tune, the doors at the further end flew open and a little procession made its appearance.

'Bonaparte apes a king; it is a pity he doesn't look more like one,' whispered my father wickedly into my ear and I gazed eagerly at the extraordinary man who in a few years had swept to supreme power on the ruins of the revolution and seemed to hold the fate of France in his two hands.

He was young, not much more than thirty, and he did not look at all as I had imagined. He was small and thin, no taller than I was myself. His dark hair hung lank to his shoulders. He wore a plain dark blue uniform with white facings in striking contrast to the officers in scarlet and gold who crowded behind him. He walked rapidly down the room outstripping them, scarcely pausing to say a brief word here and there as he passed. Then to my utter amazement he halted in front of the young man beside me. The dark smouldering eyes in the sallow face scanned him from head to foot.

'So . . . you decided to show up after all, Citizen Fontenay.'

'Yes, General.'

'I'm glad you have so much good sense.' He peered up at the young man a head taller than himself, then prodded him in the chest. 'When are we going to see you in uniform, eh?' he went on raspingly. 'I can do with young men like you in my guards. We had to shoot your father as a traitor to the republic. Take care you don't follow in his footsteps. We cannot afford to waste bullets.' He uttered a short bark of laughter and strode on.

I saw the slow flush that surged up in Lucien's face at the rough jest and instantly hated the man who had turned it into a public rebuke. The young man was very still and I guessed at the anger that held him rigid for an instant, then he muttered something and walked abruptly away from us. I would have followed but my father's hand on my arm held me back.

'Let him go. An insult like that is enough to choke any man.'

'What a beastly thing to say!' I exclaimed indignantly.

'Yes, well, a soldier of genius doesn't have to be a gentleman, I suppose, but a little courtesy wouldn't come amiss. However we needn't concern ourselves with Napoleon Bonaparte for the moment. Have you enjoyed yourself, pet?'

'Oh yes, Papa, very much.'

'Good. So have I,' he grinned and slapped his pocket. 'I won too. You shall choose what fripperies you like tomorrow.'

My father kept his word. We went exploring into the fashionable and expensive shops in the Palais Royal and the girls who served us could not do enough for the handsome Englishman who paid them pretty compliments and was so lavish with his money. He bought me one of the new high-crowned bonnets trimmed with yellow roses and tied under the chin with wide satin ribbons, and to wear with it a summer gown of golden organza with a lime-green shawl every bit as extravagant as anything worn by Madame Bonaparte.

Paris, I discovered to my surprise, was a city of water and light despite its dark tortuous alleyways and the filth of the unpaved streets. From my hotel window I could look along the Seine, cool and silvery in the early morning and deep bronze green as dusk began to close in. When the carriage brought us back after the opera or an evening party, it was black as ebony, only the faint light from the flickering torches held by the servants resting here and there on the mysterious figures who haunted the banks by night.

I did not see Lucien for several days though he called twice and left messages. It occurred to me once that my father might be deliberately avoiding him, but our days were so crowded that I had little time for regret. It was horrifying and yet enthralling to stand on the edge of what had been the Place de la Revolution and recollect that here the guillotine had stood and, while the tumbrils unloaded their victims, the women knitted and counted the heads that fell into the baskets.

The English visitors stared up at the dark ugly house where a brave young woman called Charlotte Corday had stabbed the monstrous Marat to death and enjoyed every shuddering minute of it, but I preferred the delicious May mornings when my father hired horses and we went riding in the Bois de Boulogne. One afternoon he took me to the fair in the Boulevard du Temple where we saw the sword-swallowers and fire-eaters, the man who ate frogs and the dog that told our fortune by cards. Victor was disgusted but my father laughed at him.

'It is part of life, my dear fellow,' he said, 'and I want my Emma to see and know everything,' and we went on to the circus to gape at the Franconis performing incredible feats of horsemanship and the Foriosi who defied death high up on the aerial trapeze.

'France is balanced on a tight-rope too,' said my father grimly. 'It will be intriguing to see if Bonaparte can keep his footing on that slippery perch.'

I had begun to realize that he knew Paris intimately. He delighted in showing me places that other tourists knew nothing of.

'This is where Danton shouted his defiance at Robespierre on his way to the guillotine,' he told me one morning, pausing on the corner of the Rue St Honoré and pointing to the dark green door of the Maison Duplay behind which Robespierre hatched his murderous schemes.

'But Danton was a revolutionary, a murderer,' I objected.

'He was a brave man too. And he loved France. Do you know what he said when his friends urged him to flee out of Paris before he was arrested? "Can a man take his country with him on the soles of his feet?" '

'How do you know? Were you in Paris then?' I asked curiously.

'I had to go where my work took me,' he said lightly.

'Papa, what did you really do all those years when you were away?'

'Don't ask too many questions, little one. It is as well not to know too much. Just remember one thing. Never judge too rashly. There are always good men on both sides of a cause.'

Once or twice after the theatre or if a party ended early, he would suggest that we walked home instead of taking the carriage. He knew all the short cuts, all the ways that a hunted man might choose to make an escape and one night when we came down the dark narrow alley of the Rue du Chat qui Pêche, I could have sworn I heard footsteps following behind us.

'It's only the echo,' he said easily. 'Who would be interested in ordinary folk like us? All the same it is a fine place for an ambush. Plant a man at either end and you would have your victim trapped.' He patted my hand, but despite his reassurance I looked up at the tall shuttered houses and shivered. It was part of that element of danger that never quite disappeared from my thoughts.

Mostly, I was too happy to think about it and yet despite the ices at Frascati's, the balls at the Rivoli, the picnics and the excursions to St Cloud and Fontainebleau, Paris had a darker side and one night, accidentally, I found myself in the middle of it.

We had spent the afternoon watching a military review in the Champs de Mars. Together with a party from the embassy we saw the march past of the troops with their gold-laced commanders at their head. A sudden cannonade announced the First Consul riding a white charger among his guards and followed by the carriages of brilliantly dressed women. Afterwards we went on to the firework display in the gardens of the Palais Royal. Rockets shot up with their long tails of tinselled stars, golden rain lit up the trees and mimic battles flamed between giant set-pieces. The crowd was enormous and somehow in the crush I became separated from the others.

The paths were confusing. I walked up one and down another hunting for my father or Victor or even some other member of our party and after a few minutes I knew I was lost. Lanterns hung in the trees only cast a flickering light after the dazzle of the fireworks. Then to my relief I found myself amongst the arcades where a few mornings before we had been shopping, only now it was subtly different. The shops were closely shuttered, but there were people everywhere; women of all types, exotic, beautiful, their gauzy gowns scarcely concealing the bare flesh. There were men, too, in uniforms, in opera cloaks, even in rags. I realized with a sense of shock that this was the place I had heard mentioned in lowered tones among the men in the hotel, conversations that ceased abruptly when I drew near. I was not a fool. I knew their purpose and what happened in the lighted rooms up the wooden staircases. I walked boldly, head held high, and felt the eyes of the women bore into me, resenting me, hating me.

It was at that moment that a man crossed the path a little distance in front of me. It was difficult to be certain but I was almost sure it was my father. I recognized the blue coat, the easy swinging stride. I ran after him calling him by name, but he didn't turn his head and disappeared into the dark doorway of one of the shops. I stopped, bewildered and distressed, and then I heard steps behind me. I quickened my pace, but a hand was on my shoulder, a drunken voice was mumbling in my ear, wine-laden breath was hot on my cheek.

'I've not seen you here before, *ma petite*, where can we

go, eh?' I tried to run but he held me fast. 'Don't be shy. I pay well for untouched goods.'

In an agony of fear I twisted out of his grip, leaving my shawl in his grasp and running blindly up the avenue, pursued by a stream of abuse and the shrill scream of a woman's mocking laughter. Head down I collided with someone coming towards me. He took hold of me. I fought savagely but he would not release me. Strong hands captured my wrists in a firm grip and I looked up into the face of Lucien de Fontenay.

'I am sorry,' I stammered in confusion. 'I didn't know . . . I thought . . .'

'That you had jumped from the frying pan into the fire . . . isn't that one of your English sayings?' There was a hint of laughter in the dark eyes looking down at me. 'All the same, this is no place for you, Mademoiselle Tremayne. Surely you are not here alone?'

'We were watching the fireworks. I lost my father in the crowd and then I couldn't find the way.'

'I see.' People were staring at us and he frowned. 'I think I had better take you back to your hotel.'

'Please . . . it is not necessary. If you will point out the right path, I can quite well go alone.'

'No, it is not at all suitable,' he said with decision. 'We will take a cab. My friends can wait.'

But we had not gone more than a few paces when we ran full tilt into Victor, red-faced, perspiring and very much put out.

'Where on earth have you been, Emma? I've been looking everywhere for the past hour.' Then he saw Lucien and sounded angrier still. 'I'm sorry. I didn't realize that I was troubling myself unnecessarily.'

'I was on the point of escorting Mademoiselle Emma to her hotel,' said Lucien smoothly.

'Thank you,' said Victor with a touch of ice. 'You needn't concern yourself, Monsieur. I will take Miss Tremayne home.'

His manner irritated me so much that I turned deliberately to Lucien, holding out my hand. 'You have been very kind.'

'It was a pleasure.' He swept off his hat with a graceful

gesture and kissed the tip of my fingers. '*Au revoir*, made-moiselle.'

'Damned foreigners!' growled Victor looking after him. 'What is he doing here? That's what I should like to know.' He pulled my arm through his and hurried me along. 'You should be more careful, Emma. You didn't arrange to meet him, I hope.'

'No, I did not,' I replied nettled. 'But even if I did, I don't see that it is any concern of yours.'

'Everything about you concerns me, Emma. You ought to know that by now. This is no place for decent people. I told your father earlier. He should never have brought you here. He has no sense of what is proper.'

'Oh for heaven's sake, Victor, I wanted to come,' I said, up in arms at once at his criticism. 'It was my fault I missed you in the crush. Where is Papa?'

'God knows. I lost him too,' said Victor acidly. 'If you would only let me take care of you, Emma, nothing like this would happen.'

And how abominably dull it would be, I thought rebelliously, and then repented because he could really be very kind and reliable and I was more shaken by my unpleasant adventure than I was willing to admit.

He took me back to the hotel and much later that evening my father came in, looking unusually worried and out of temper. For once he spoke sharply to me.

'What the devil happened to you? I searched every inch of those damned gardens.'

I was about to blurt out that I had seen him and he didn't look as if he were searching for anyone, but I bit it back. Whatever he had been doing, he wouldn't want Victor to know. In some ways his anger pleased me. It showed how much he cared.

It was only afterwards that I remembered what Victor had said. I had met Lucien only a few minutes after seeing my father. Was he there for the same purpose? I would not believe it. I rejected it instantly, yet the little teasing doubt remained at the back of my mind.

Chapter 3

I slept badly that night, perhaps because I was overtired, perhaps because when my father kissed me at the door of my room, he said, 'I doubt if we shall be here much longer, Emma. Make the most of the next few days,' and I knew that, foolish as it might be, I did not want to leave Paris without seeing Lucien again.

After my restless night I woke much later than usual. When the chambermaid knocked, bringing me coffee and a crisp roll, I groped for my watch and saw that it was eleven o'clock already. The girl pushed open the shutters letting in a stream of brilliant sunlight. She came back to the bed, a beaming smile on her pleasant face.

'From Monsieur *votre père*, Mademoiselle,' she said and handed me a folded note.

I read it while I sipped my coffee. It was very brief. 'I am writing this since you are still sleeping and I am called out of Paris for a few hours. Victor will be happy to escort you to luncheon with Dorothy. Enjoy yourself, my pet, and we will dine together this evening.' He had signed it with the scrawled JT he always used to me. Involuntarily I remembered the moment last night when I thought I had seen him. Had he really been there with those women and was this somehow linked with it? Deliberately I pushed it out of my mind.

It was such a delicious morning and the sun was so warm that I put on the new golden dress, and tying the bonnet strings under my chin decided that it was a dreadful waste to wear it just for a morning with Victor and a sedate luncheon with Dorothy. I felt excited and restless. With only a little time left in Paris, it seemed a pity to waste even a minute of it.

Our hotel was an old one and my room was on the first

floor at the back of the building. At the end of the corridor was a door leading on to a flight of iron stairs going down to the quay. If I went that way, I could escape Victor. It only took an instant to make up my mind. Then I was trying the door. I found it open and slipped down the steps. I crossed to the other side of the quay to look up and down the river. An old woman with a basket of flowers at her feet thrust a bunch of sweet-smelling lilies of the valley towards me. I was hunting in my purse for a few sous when a voice behind me said, 'Allow me, Mademoiselle.' The flowers were bought and in my hands before I realized it was Lucien. It was so unexpected, such an answer to prayer, that I could say nothing, only smile with idiotic pleasure while the brown gnarled face of the old woman beamed up at us.

'I was coming to ask if you had recovered from last night's adventure,' he was saying.

I scarcely took in his words, only that he was there. I held out my hand. 'I've forgotten it already.'

'I must leave Paris soon. I couldn't go without saying goodbye.'

'I'm so glad you came.'

'*Vraiment?* I've come before several times, but always you were engaged.'

'I know, but today my father has been called away from Paris . . . and . . .'

'And what?'

'Nothing.' I decided to forget Victor and Dorothy. 'I was just making up my mind what I would do.'

'Will you permit me to make a suggestion? If you have not already visited Versailles, we could take a carriage. If it would give you pleasure, I should be delighted to show it to you.'

'It sounds wonderful.' I was not at all sure that my father would approve but I would have agreed to go anywhere on this enchanting morning provided that it was with Lucien.

He appeared to have no difficulty in finding a carriage and in no time we were driving out of Paris under the pink and white flowers of the chestnuts.

'They have lighted their candles already,' I exclaimed with delight.

'It is in your honour,' he replied lightly, and when I glanced up at the rather stern young face beside me, I could not imagine why I felt so happy.

By the time we reached Versailles, we were both so hungry that we decided to eat first and explore afterwards. We lunched in the open air outside Le Cheval Blanc. We ate an omelette aux fines herbes, followed by a creamy cheese on its straw mat and we drank a sparkling wine. It seemed odd to me that I who had always been so awkward with young men, should now feel so completely at ease with someone I scarcely knew. I don't even remember what we talked about while we ate, but when we had finished and he would have refilled my glass, I shook my head.

'No, I mustn't drink any more. Monsieur de Fontenay, you have quite forgotten, haven't you? You don't remember that we have met before.'

'Before the ball? Surely not. How could I forget?'

'Don't make pretty speeches when you don't mean them. I have something to prove it.' I felt in my little bag and brought out the silver coin triumphantly. 'There it is. It was in England and you threw it to me in a very high-handed manner indeed. Not at all suitable to the part you were playing.'

'I threw it?' he took it, frowning.

'You see how very easy I am to forget. It was on a cliff top in Cornwall and you were disguised as a fisherman while I . . .'

'But that was a boy in a muddy shirt . . . a scrubby little redheaded boy with remarkable dark blue eyes . . .' he broke off. '*Mon Dieu*, you mean it was you?' I nodded emphatically while he stared at me. 'Of course, I can see it all now. Surely there can never have been a bigger fool than I not to have recognized you at once, but you must admit . . .' and, he waved a hand at my golden gown, 'you didn't look quite . . .'

'Papa said I looked like a brat out of the gutter,' I admitted frankly. 'He is always scolding me about it, but Rufus had thrown me that morning and I often wear breeches to ride at home. They are so much more comfortable . . .'

'You mean that you live at Trevira?'

'Of course. I thought you must have realized that when you met my father.'

'No, I didn't know.'

'I saw your ship. I climbed down the cove and I saw you on the shore and another man who said he was sailing with you. He rescued my dog from falling down the cliff.'

'Ah I remember now. Pierre said he had met a little peasant who . . .' again he stopped. 'You must think me very foolish.'

'Why? I was wearing my oldest dress that morning. I'd been turning out the attic. Is he your friend?'

'Yes . . . in a way. He had been . . . visiting England.'

'Is that why you had come to Cornwall?'

He shrugged his shoulders. 'Not entirely. You see the ship once belonged to my father. As a boy I had sailed in her with him. Now it is sold, but when the Captain told me he was making the voyage, I decided to go with him for old times' sake.'

'I didn't think he was telling me the whole truth but to ask more questions seemed like prying into matters that did not concern me. I changed the subject.

'You said you were leaving Paris . . . where do you live, Monsieur de Fontenay?'

'Will you not call me Lucien?'

'Perhaps . . . if you will call me Emma.'

'With all my heart.' The look in his eyes frightened me a little. I dropped my own.

'Where do you live, Lucien?'

'In the south, in Provence, and I breed bulls.'

It was so unexpected that I could only gape at him. 'You breed bulls?'

He smiled. 'Well, not exactly. My stepfather does. He lives at Villeroy. It is between Tarascon and Arles and he owns grazing rights on the Camargue. He breeds the small black bulls that go to the bullring.'

'Do you fight the bulls?'

'No, no.' He laughed outright. 'That is what Louis longs to do. I work on the farm and in the vineyards. These few days in Paris have been partly on business for my stepfather.'

'Is Louis your brother?'

'Yes, he is only seven. Then there are Armand and Nicole. They are nineteen and twins, the children of my stepfather by an earlier marriage.'

'And is Nicole in love with you?'

His face changed. He said coldly, 'Why do you say that?'

'I am sorry. I didn't mean to offend you. It just slipped out . . . a little joke.'

'Nicole is far too sensible. But you don't want to hear the dull details of my life.'

'But I do . . . very much.'

'No, it is enough already. I would far rather talk about you.' He pushed back his chair. 'Besides I think we ought to go now if we are to walk a little in the gardens. We must return to Paris before dusk.'

Afterwards when I thought of that day, it was not the great palace I remembered. It was too ruined and desolate. The mob had ransacked it, smashing the windows and hacking at the fine furnishings. It was a tragic empty shell of something that had once been magnificent. Lucien hurried me through the gaunt echoing rooms and looking up at the stained walls and torn tapestries, I shivered and was glad to escape into the gardens. They were neglected and overgrown, the neat box hedges ragged and tangled with weed, but they were still beautiful with little grassy walks ending in hidden arbours. Flowers still bloomed and it was easy to see them as they must have been once when Marie Antoinette played the milkmaid and entertained guests in her days of happiness.

'Did you ever come here, Lucien, before the revolution?'

'Only very rarely. I was still at school.'

We were standing by a stone pool. There were no golden fish in the thick scummy water and the boy Cupid stood forlornly in the centre, his little bow broken. Lucien had taken my hand and there was silence for a moment. Then he sighed.

'It is all over now, all that life, and sometimes I think it is just as well, but it is not easy to find a new way.'

I did not understand him then. That was to come later. There was a sweet smell of spring, a scent of grass and early roses and heliotrope spilling out of cracked stone pots. I had never wanted a young man to kiss me before and had once slapped Victor's face when he grew too familiar, but now I wanted it with an intensity that frightened me. But Lucien made no move to take me in his arms. Instead he put my hand against his cheek for a second with a queer awkward gesture and then said abruptly, 'We should be going back. Your father will have returned and will be wondering what has happened to you.'

It took time to find a carriage and the journey took us longer than we had expected. It was almost dark by the time we got back to the hotel but my father had not yet returned. Lucien kissed my hand, holding it in both of his.

'I shall see you again.'

'Yes, yes, of course.'

His eyes held mine for an instant, then he bowed and had gone. I hurried up the steps into the hall. The proprietor came out of his office as I passed.

'Monsieur Jarrett has been in and out all day asking for you, Mademoiselle,' he said reproachfully.

I felt a little guilty. I had after all treated Victor very badly. 'If you see him, will you tell him I'm very sorry I missed him this morning, but now I'm going to my room. I've had a tiring day.'

'*Bien*, Mademoiselle. I understand exactly.' He gave me a sly grin as if he were quite aware of where I had spent the afternoon.

A group of English tourists were talking earnestly in the corridor as I went by. One of the ladies caught me by the arm. 'Have you heard the news, Miss Tremayne? They are saying everywhere that Bonaparte has had a violent quarrel with Lord Whitworth. He abused him quite shockingly in front of the whole diplomatic staff.'

'The fellow has no manners,' interrupted one of the gentlemen. 'I only hope our ambassador stood firm. These frogs need a lesson. It is time we showed them we're not prepared to eat humble pie to a jumped-up nobody like this Corsican. First Consul indeed! Ridiculous title! Who does he think he is? He'll be calling himself Emperor next, you mark my words!'

I did not take much notice. They were always gossiping about something or other. Papa would know all about it when he came back . . . if he did come back. The old fear suddenly gripped me. He was very late and I could not help wondering where he had gone. I was well aware that he was no saint and in the years we had lived together I had never enquired where he went when he disappeared for the odd day or so. A gentleman must have his pleasures and my mother had been long dead, but he had never at any time behaved in a way to provoke scandal.

I undressed and put on my dressing-gown. But when I was lying on the bed with the candle lit and a book on my lap, I did not read. Instead I lay thinking of Lucien. In a very few days now I would be going back to England and he would return to his distant home. We would meet and part like ships in the night as the trite old saying has it. I knew so little of him. Why, oh why did I have to feel like this about a man whom I might never see again?

I must have dozed off because I was suddenly wide awake, listening to heavy stumbling footsteps coming down the passage. I had no idea what time it was and I sat up, my heart beating. Someone was trying the knob of the door but I had turned the key before getting into bed, a necessary precaution, I had been told, in any foreign hotel.

The footsteps went on. I heard the next door open and a second later there came a crash as if someone had fallen, taking a chair or table with him. It must be my father and it sounded as if he were drunk, except that never, never had I known him not to be in complete control of himself however much wine he had taken. I hesitated only an instant and then was off the bed, not even waiting to put on my slippers. I picked up the candle, turned the key and hurried into the next room.

My father was lying face downwards on the floor, a small table that he must have clutched at to save himself fallen with him. I shut the door carefully. He would not want the whole hotel roused. I picked up the table, placed the candlestick on it and knelt beside him. He was not drunk. It looked horribly as if someone had tried to kill him. The thick brown hair at the back of his head was clotted with blood. As I touched it gently, he groaned and stirred.

He mumbled thickly, 'Is that you, Emma?'

'Yes. I heard you come in.'

'Help me to get up, there's a good girl.'

I put my arms round him and after a moment he made a supreme effort and with my assistance struggled to his feet. Clinging to my arm, he reached the sofa and sank down on it. Anxiously I knelt beside him.

'What happened, Papa? Did someone attack you? Should I send for a doctor?'

'No, no,' he said quickly. 'There's no need. It's deuced painful, but I'll be all right. Just give me a moment. It has knocked it out of me getting back here.'

'Where did it happen?'

'In the Street of the Fishing Cat,' he said wryly. 'You were right about that, Emma, and so was I. They couldn't have found a better place. If I hadn't a singularly hard head, I'd be dead by now.'

He managed a smile, but his bruised face, streaked with blood and dirt, was deathly pale. He leaned back with his eyes closed and I was afraid he would faint again. Somewhere I knew he kept a hunting flask of brandy. I searched for it in drawers and wardrobe and when I found it, filled the silver cup to the brim.

He roused himself and drank it gratefully. 'You're a sensible child, Emma. Some young women would have screamed the place down and woken everyone within hearing.'

'A lot of good that would have done,' I said scornfully, relieved to see a little colour creeping back into his face. 'Now I'm going to wash away the blood and put a cold compress on your head. It may help the bruising.'

I filled the basin from the water jug, brought a towel and washed the blood away gently to find the injury was not as serious as it had appeared at first.

'I shall have to cut away some of your hair, Papa. I hope you don't mind.'

'So long as you don't leave me looking too much like a shorn lamb,' he said humorously, but I saw how he compressed his lips against the pain. When I had finished, he held out his hand for the towel. 'Give it to me. Let me make myself look a little less like a gargoyle.'

'I will do it.'

He leaned back and let me wipe his face clean of mud and blood. There must have been a savage attack before the blow that had knocked him unconscious. Then I soaked the towel and held it against the bruised place.

'How do you feel?'

'A damnable headache, but I'll survive.' He smiled and sat up a little. 'Where did you learn to be so good a nurse? Put those things away, Emma, and come and sit here. I want to talk to you.'

'Shouldn't you go to bed?'

'Plenty of time for that. This is more important.'

But when I had poured the bloodstained water into the slop pail, wrung out the soaked towel and come to sit on the sofa beside him, he did not at once speak of what was in his mind. He took my hand in his.

'What did you do today, Emma, while I was out?'

I looked away. 'I spent the day at Versailles ... with Lucien de Fontenay.'

His hold of my hand tightened. 'You went with young Fontenay?'

'Yes. You aren't angry, Papa, because I didn't go with Victor and lunch with Dorothy?'

'Why should I be angry when in your place I'd probably have done the same,' he said dryly. 'All the same I'd rather you didn't get too fond of Lucien.'

'Why? What have you against him?'

'Nothing, but there's no future in it, my child. No doubt he is a very estimable young man, but he is the enemy.'

'Not now.'

'Soon, I'm afraid, England and France are going to be at each other's throats again.'

I stared at him. It had always been there, but no more than a possibility, something that might never happen.

'Is that all you have against him?' I asked in a stifled voice.

'Isn't that enough?'

'I thought you didn't like him.'

'Why on earth should you think that? Anyhow he is not important. Listen, Emma,' he went on gravely, 'I'd rather have kept you out of it, but there is something that you must know.'

'Because of what happened tonight?'

'Partly. It could happen again.'

'You mean ... it was not just thieves ...'

No, my purse is still intact and so is my watch.' He held out his hand with the one fine ring he always wore. 'They took nothing from me though I think they believed me dead when they left me. I don't know how long it was before I recovered consciousness and managed to crawl back here, but they must have had plenty of time if robbery had been their game.'

'Did you see them?'

'I thought I did, but it was very dark and I could not be sure.'

'Who were they?'

'I don't know.' He paused for an instant and then went on. 'You must know, my dear, that the years you were at school I spent in France, acting as an agent for the British government.'

'An agent? Do you mean you were a spy?'

'Not exactly. There were a great many royalists, you know, who did not emigrate at the outbreak of the revolution. They remained in hiding, men of all kinds, women too, and they banded together in Brittany, in the Vendée and the Midi to oppose the republic that had been forced on their country. England, for her own purposes, was willing to help them in their struggle, not only with gold, but with guns and ammunition brought in by ships and landed secretly. There had to be intermediaries, men who acted as a liaison between the royalists and our own country . . .'

'And you were one of them?'

'Yes.'

'It must have been terribly dangerous.'

'At times. It could be challenging too,' he said quietly, 'to outwit them, show yourself cleverer than your enemies, pay off old scores, exact revenge for a murdered comrade . . .' he broke off.

'But you came home . . . you gave it all up?'

'I had no choice. Besides there comes a time when murderous savage warfare, even in a cause you believe to be just, begins to sicken you. You are a man as well as a fighting machine and at times you are forced to recognize it. I thought I had done enough. I had served my turn.'

For some reason the words I had read in the attic flashed across my mind. 'Now I know I am wrong, that you will love me always . . .' Had it been then that the man had overcome the patriot and he had fled away from it?

'But that was seven years ago,' I said. 'Why should it affect you now?'

'Haven't you guessed? A few months ago the government approached me again. There has never been much faith in this treaty, it has only been a breathing space. The war department wanted an observer, someone who could pick up once more the links with the past . . .'

'And that is what you have been doing today and the night before last,' I said with sudden intuition. 'It was you, wasn't it, whom I thought I saw in the Palais Royal after the fireworks?'

'Yes, it was I. I heard you call but I dared not stop,' he said with a rueful grin. 'Were you shocked? You needn't have been. I was not indulging in a night of love, but it was an excellent place to meet, unlikely to be suspected.'

'But someone must have found out, otherwise why should they try to kill you?'

'Why indeed? Only it may not have been Bonaparte's secret police . . .'

'You mean they could have been the men you were working with, your former colleagues ... royalists? But why? It has no sense.'

'You're very young, Emma. You haven't learned yet that men's motives can be mixed; patriotism, loyalty, jealousy, revenge, hatred—they can all exist together.' He reached out a hand and touched my cheek. 'Poor child, it's a great deal to have to swallow in the middle of the night and I may be wrong in my suspicions, completely wrong, and in my case they have not succeeded. Here I am, very much alive and I intend to remain so. And now, my pet, I think you had better get some sleep and I too, if this vile pain in my head will permit it. I have an uneasy feeling that the next day or two may be difficult in more ways than one.'

'Are you sure you will be all right?'

'Quite sure.' I bent to kiss him and just for an instant I felt him pull me close to him. 'I'm sorry, my dear. I should never have brought you here.'

'Don't say that, Papa. I want to be with you . . . always.'

43

'My little Emma ... what should I do without you?' Then he gave me a push. 'Go on, off with you, and don't worry. I'm not got rid of so easily.'

He was right. I knew that. Like a jungle animal he had the gift of survival, but even a cat can come to the end of its nine lives and as I went back to my own room, the fear that had always been present seemed suddenly very close.

Chapter 4

I don't know what I had expected, but when my father joined me at breakfast the next morning he was elegant and debonair as usual with no visible sign of the brutal attack that had almost killed him, except for the dark bruise down one side of his face.

Victor frowned and remarked tartly, 'Fine company you must have been keeping last night, Jack.'

My father laughed and waved his hand airily. 'You're quite wrong, my dear fellow. Nothing more than an argument with a gatepost when I wasn't quite myself. You know how it is.'

'You should think of Emma.'

'I do, all the time, don't I, pet?'

I saw the contempt on Victor's face and knew what he was thinking. I longed to tell him he was wrong, but my father's hand on my arm kept me silent. I half expected Lucien to call that morning and I was not sure whether I was disappointed or glad when he did not come. Beside my father most young men had always seemed to lose their charm. My feelings for Lucien were still very private. I did not want to put him to the test.

One or two of the English visitors alarmed by the rumours flying about Paris had gone scuttling back to England in a panic, but a great many of them stayed on. No one seriously believed that the upstart Bonaparte who had suddenly made himself master of France would be willing to plunge his country into war again however high-handed England showed herself.

I don't think that my father was deceived, but he still had one or two ends to tie up before he returned and with his usual disregard of danger was willing to take risks, though Victor never stopped protesting against the folly of taking any Frenchman at his word.

'He's not a Frenchman, he's a Corsican,' said my father amused.

'He's a foreigner, and that's quite enough for me,' was Victor's stubborn answer and he said it again with a great deal more force two days later. We were just about to sit down to luncheon at Corazzi's fashionable restaurant. It was my father's birthday and he celebrated it lavishly by ordering champagne for everyone. We had scarcely begun when the party was rudely interrupted by the arrival of a Captain with two guards at his heels. He surveyed us grimly.

'I regret to inform you, Mesdames and Messieurs, that you must regard yourselves as prisoners of war.' He swept aside the outraged protests. 'I am sorry to interrupt your pleasures but since your British government has chosen to violate the treaty by seizing our ships without a shadow of legality, then the First Consul has no alternative but to take immediate reprisal. You will kindly return to your hotel without delay.'

There was no help for it. We were herded together and taken back under guard with strict orders to remain in the hotel. The Captain looked us over as we crowded into the dining-room.

'Tomorrow morning you will report to General Junot, Commandant of Paris,' he said. 'He will inform you as to where you will be interned.' He marched away leaving us looking at one another helplessly.

'Who the devil does he think he's talking to?' exclaimed Victor indignantly. 'This fellow Bonaparte must be out of his mind. He cannot treat us in this outrageous fashion.'

'I am afraid he can, Victor. The day they created him First Consul, liberty flew out of the window,' said my father thoughtfully. 'I wonder how long it will be before the French realize that for themselves.'

'I knew this would happen. I warned you. We should have left days ago,' persisted Victor.

'I quite agree,' replied my father calmly. 'But since we are still here, there is little point in reproaches.'

Some of the ladies had burst into tears and all around us was an angry buzz of conversation, everyone blaming everyone else for the awkward predicament in which they found themselves. My father took no part in it. He drew me quietly to one side.

'Go and pack for both of us, Emma. If there is a way out of this infernal country, then I shall have to find it.'

'What are you going to do?'

'Never mind. Do as I say, but quietly. Make no fuss about it.'

I did as he had commanded me, but while I folded shifts and petticoats and took the dresses out of my wardrobe, anxiety nagged at me. How would he contrive to get away from the hotel and if he were stopped, what would happen to him? If he were arrested and his present activities discovered, to say nothing of the past, he stood in acute peril of being shot as a spy. It had happened to others and I had no illusions. He would provide just the example of England's treachery for which Bonaparte was looking. I tried not to dwell on it. The prospect was too frightening.

By the time everything was packed, it was past six o'clock, but he had not yet returned. I realized that I had eaten nothing since an early breakfast and was faint with hunger. I rang for the chambermaid and asked for some coffee. Then I went into my father's bedroom. He had the habit of scattering garments and possessions everywhere, but now it was neat and tidy and somehow impersonal. The window was open and a fresh breeze blew in from the river. I had a curious feeling that it had taken him with it leaving no trace. I shook the sensation from me and took his dressing case from the wardrobe to pack the toilet articles first. As soon as I opened it, I saw the folded note. I knew a moment of sick fear before I took it to the window with trembling fingers.

'Forgive me,' I read in the fading light, 'if this seems like deserting you. Believe me, if there had been any other way I would not do it, but I know only one means of getting out of France and I must go alone. If I were to take you with me, it could mean danger for you and possibly death for me and those who will help me, and what I carry in my head could be vital for England's future. I have left you all the money I can spare. Trust in me still. Your loving Father.'

He had never signed himself that before and absurdly it brought tears to my eyes even though I rebelled against his decision. I understood his reasons only too well, but the very idea of separation from him for months—years perhaps, for who could tell how long a war might last?—was unendurable. The thought of Victor brought me no consolation. How could I stay here, shut up with a bunch of strangers in some vile prison ... all kinds of frightening rumours had been rife as to what Bonaparte intended to do with his English captives. There must be a way out, there simply had to be. Up and down the room I walked, forgetting about food, forgetting everything except the overpowering need to escape.

The idea leaped into my mind quite suddenly. There was Lucien. Surely he would help. I did not pause to consider difficulties. All I could think of was that he had owned a ship, or at any rate had easy access to one. Surely it couldn't be impossible to reach the coast and from there obtain a passage to Cornwall. I would go in a rowing boat if necessary.

The chambermaid knocked at the door. 'Oh there you are, Mademoiselle. I have been looking for you. The coffee is ready.'

I stared at her. The idea was beginning to take shape, but time was desperately short. I must act before it was too late, even if it meant taking a risk.

'Marie, is there any way I could get out of the hotel, just for a little while, an hour perhaps.'

'A way out, Mademoiselle?' she repeated doubtfully, then she broke into a smile, nodding her head. 'I understand. The handsome young man, the lover, Mademoiselle longs to bid him farewell. It is terrible to part and who knows for how long?' She paused a moment, then her eyes sparkled. 'I have it. There is the door to the quay. It is not often used and there is no guard there. I could leave it unlocked for Mademoiselle's return.'

'Oh bless you!' I could have kissed the plain round face and the romantic heart under the starched apron. 'You go and wait by the door now. I will come in a minute.'

When she had gone, I took the little purse of gold that my father had left in the dressing case and went back to my own room. I bundled a few necessities together, swung a long hooded cloak round my shoulders, peered out of the door to make sure no one was about and then stole along the passage. Marie was waiting for me. She held the door open and I slipped down the steps and then ran as fast as I could along the quay, up a side street and into the crowded Place de la Concorde.

I knew where Lucien lived. He had mentioned it that day at Versailles, but it took time to find a cab. At last, in answer to my frantic signals a decrepit vehicle pulled up and the surly driver took one look at me and demanded a fare twice what it should have been before he would consent to move.

The house when we reached it was tall and stately and had once seen better days, though now it was obviously divided into flats. The concierge put out his head as I went past but he did not stop me and nervously I knocked at the first door I reached. My courage was rapidly deserting me, but there was no help for it now. I had to go on. If he refused to help, I told myself, I could always go back to the hotel.

An elderly manservant, neatly dressed, opened the door. 'I am sorry, Mademoiselle,' he replied austerely to my anxious enquiry, 'but Monsieur le Marquis is not at home.'

I stared at him, wondering if I had come to the wrong address or knocked at the wrong door, but as if he had guessed at my bewilderment, he smiled faintly. 'Monsieur Lucien should return shortly. Will you come back or would you care to wait?'

With a gasp of relief I said, 'Could I wait please? It is very important.'

He stood aside to let me pass, taking my bundle out of my hands with old-world courtesy and ushering me into what must have been a library. While he lit the candles, I could not help noticing that the room still bore the marks of serious damage. Despite careful mending the brocaded walls showed where they had been slashed and torn. Axes had splintered the tall bookcases and yet, despite the ravages, the room retained still an atmosphere of grace and dignity.

'Shall I bring you some coffee, Mademoiselle?'

I shook my head. 'No, thank you.' I had not stopped to take anything at the hotel, but overcome by nerves I knew

49

I could swallow nothing. I must have waited for scarcely half an hour, but it seemed a lifetime. The evening was warm. I threw off the long cloak and, quite unable to sit quietly, I began to walk around the room, picking up objects and laying them down again. Over the fireplace hung a portrait. It had been split from top to bottom, but the canvas had been skilfully stitched and the proud pale face with the powdered hair gazing sternly out of the battered frame had a look of Lucien. I wondered if it was his father. There was little furniture in the room, but against one wall stood a desk untidily piled with papers. As I passed, one of them fluttered to the floor and I stooped to pick it up. I did not intend to read it, but I couldn't help seeing the signature and the last few lines.

'It seems so long without you. Come back soon, Lucien. Come back to your loving Nicole.'

I was still holding it in my hand when I heard his voice in the hall. He was saying something to his servant. I hurriedly put the letter down and turned to face him when he came in.

'Emma!' he exclaimed. 'What are you doing here? I thought that you and your father would have left France already.'

'No, you see we had not thought ... no one did ... it all came about so quickly . . .' Suddenly, maddeningly, anxiety and reaction choked my throat so that I couldn't go on.

He came to me at once, taking my hands. 'Don't distress yourself. Come and sit down. Tell me what has happened.' He put me on the sofa and sat beside me.

'I'm so sorry. It is stupid of me.' I pulled myself together with an effort. 'It was earlier today. It seems England has broken the treaty. We are being held as prisoners. You must know about it already, more than I do.'

'Yes, I know. Your ambassador is leaving Paris already. It is only a matter of time before war is declared, but I still don't understand . . .'

It was hard to say. I looked down at my clasped hands. 'My father has escaped. I don't know how he got away from the hotel but he did. He has gone.'

'Gone? Are you sure?'

'Oh yes. He left me a note.'

'He has left you here alone, but it is not possible. How could he do such a thing?' he said incredulously.

'There were reasons, important ones. I can't explain, but you must believe me. He had to return to England and he could not take me with him.'

He stared at me for a long moment before he said bluntly, 'Do you mean he is a spy?'

I looked away, unwilling to answer, suddenly realizing how little I knew of Lucien. I might well be betraying my father. I think he sensed my uncertainty. He put his hand on mine.

'Don't be afraid. Do you think that I would do anything to harm you or him? He will be in enough danger as it is.' His words echoed my own fear and I shivered. His fingers closed over mine. 'Why have you come to me?'

For the first time I knew the enormity of what I was asking from him. I said falteringly, 'I thought you might help me to get out of France. You said you knew the captain of the ship. There must be ways of leaving the country. I cannot stay here, I cannot. You must understand. I may never see my father again if I do.'

'And that means more to you than anything, more than your own safety?'

'Yes, yes, it does.'

'I see.' He looked at me for a moment, and then got up and moved abruptly away. 'You don't know what you are asking. How should you? I am the last person to be of any assistance.'

'But why? I thought . . .'

He turned to face me. 'You see I am on the suspect list myself . . . oh for many reasons. I cannot explain now . . . and you have a British passport. How in the name of God am I to smuggle you out of France with every port, every ship, every sea-captain alerted against people doing that very thing? Bonaparte is damnably efficient and he is furiously angry. He will stop at nothing to gain his own ends.'

'I'm sorry. I see now that I shouldn't have come. I'll go back to the hotel. It doesn't matter. I'll manage somehow. There is always Victor.'

'Ah yes, the good Victor, who wants to marry you.'

I managed a wry smile and got resolutely to my feet,

but the long day and the lack of food caught up with me. I swayed and took hold of the back of a chair to support myself.

'No, don't go,' said Lucien gently. 'You look exhausted. Joseph shall bring us coffee and some food. I need it and so do you. It won't be much. I don't usually dine here, but he will have something and while we eat, we will think.'

He went out of the room and, after a few minutes, came back smiling. 'Joseph never fails me. It won't be long.'

While we waited for the coffee, he brought a carafe of wine from a side table and poured it for me and himself. I sipped it gratefully, relaxing for the first time since I had found my father's letter and my world had fallen to pieces. Lucien was standing with his back to the fireplace, glass in hand, and the likeness between him and the portrait was very striking.

I said shyly, 'Your servant called you Monsieur le Marquis. I thought I must have come to the wrong house.'

'Titles went out of fashion the day the mob broke into here and destroyed the house and almost all that was in it,' said Lucien dryly. 'But Joseph is of the old school. For him I automatically became Monsieur le Marquis after my father was murdered and I can't break him of the habit. In this last year Bonaparte has graciously permitted me to rent three rooms in what was once my father's house and I believe I still own a burned-out château on the coast of Brittany, but that is the sum total of my inheritance. Monsieur le Marquis de Rien would be a far more appropriate title.'

'I am sorry . . .'

'Don't be. I've long learned to live with it. Others have suffered far more.'

Joseph brought coffee with cheese and biscuits and a little fruit. I discovered I was starving and while we ate, Lucien said thoughtfully, 'I've had an idea. I don't know if it will work, but it might be worth trying. Do you think that you could play the part of a governess?'

'A governess? But I've never taught anyone anything.'

'That doesn't matter, at least not too much. You speak French so well, it is just possible we could pull it off.' I looked at him expectantly and he put down his coffee cup. 'Now listen. I told you I had a young brother. My mother worries that as things are now with us Louis is growing up wild and without the education she would wish for him. She tries to teach him herself, but life at Villeroy is not easy. When I came to Paris, she asked me to contact the daughter of an old friend of hers, someone who like us has had to find other means of living these last few years, but when I did, I found she could not come. Her mother is sick and she will not leave her. Now suppose you were to come in her place.'

'But I don't see how that will help.'

'Villeroy is not far from Marseilles. My stepfather has many trade connections there. There are the vineyards, the olive groves, the bulls. I am fairly certain that in a little time, a matter of weeks perhaps if we are lucky, it will be possible to obtain a passage in a ship that will take you to Spain and from there it should not be too difficult to return to England. What do you say? It is not perhaps what you had hoped, but it is the best I can suggest.'

Such an idea had never occurred to me. I said doubtfully, 'But your family? What will they say?'

'They need not be told, only my mother. She will know that you are not Mademoiselle Rainier.'

'But I am a stranger . . . it could involve them in trouble.'

'Then I will take the blame, but it will not. And even if it does, my stepfather has broad shoulders. Nothing up to now, neither the revolution nor the worst of Robespierre, nor even Bonaparte has been able to dislodge him from his native soil, and nothing will.' There was a curious emphasis in his voice. I didn't know whether it was contempt or envy.

I hesitated. If I went back to the hotel, it meant Victor; it meant confinement, restriction, everything I most hated. If I went forward, there was the risk of the unknown, but I had accepted that already by coming to Lucien and though he made no attempt to persuade me, I felt again that subtle link between us, tenuous, intangible, but unmistakeably there, urging me on. Perhaps there was more of my father in me than I had ever realized, something of the spirit with which he went into a new adventure or even to the card table, ready as he said once, 'to put his fortune to the touch, to win or lose all on a single throw.'

I said, 'I shall make mistakes. I never had a brother and I know nothing of children . . .'

'Neither, I believe, does Mademoiselle Rainier. No one will expect wonders from you and if Louis misbehaves, come to me,' he smiled, 'I will beat him for you.'

'Indeed you won't,' I exclaimed indignantly. 'A child of seven being beaten . . . it is monstrous.'

'You may change your mind when Louis puts a lizard in your bed as he did to Nicole.'

'Was she angry?'

'Furious. She complained to her father and poor Louis slept on his face for a week.'

I disliked Nicole at once. 'How barbarous and for a boyish prank . . .'

Lucien laughed. 'You see, you're on his side already. You're defending a pupil you don't even know.'

I laughed with him. The argument was over. I said, 'It is wonderfully kind of you.'

'You'll come?'

'Yes.'

'Good. Then you had better stay here tonight,' said Lucien practically. 'Joseph will make you comfortable. You can have my room. I shall be out most of the night anyway. There is a great deal to be done if we are to leave early tomorrow morning as I fear we must.'

It was an immense relief to leave everything to Lucien. I think I'd been living on a knife-edge of tension ever since that night when my father had been so brutally attacked. It seems absurd in the circumstances, but I climbed into bed between the crisp linen sheets in that small austere bedroom without a tremor of anxiety and I did not wake until Joseph knocked at the door at six o'clock to tell me that everything was ready and Lucien was waiting to breakfast with me.

I had no idea how he had contrived it, but there were papers duly made out in the name of Emma Louise Rainier. Putting in my own name was a stroke of genius. 'If there is a touch of the familiar, it is so much easier not to look surprised,' said Lucien with a smile. A cabriolet had been hired for the journey and my box was strapped to the roof.

'But how on earth did you manage to get it?' I exclaimed in astonishment.

'It was surprisingly easy. The *fille de chambre* ... what's her name? Marie, that's it ... believes that we are eloping,' said Lucien with a gleam of mischief in the dark eyes. 'She was so delighted at playing a part in such a romantic adventure that she was willing to do anything for a kiss and a little something to buy herself new ribbons.' He paused and busied himself with the last strap. 'She told me too something of what had been happening. Everyone at the hotel will probably be sent to Verdun.'

'Is that bad?'

Lucien shrugged. 'Who knows? To lose one's freedom is never pleasant.'

'Poor Victor.'

Lucien looked at me quickly. 'There has been considerable disturbance over the extraordinary disappearance of the English Milord and his daughter. Monsieur Jarrett was closely questioned by the police but could add nothing to what was already known. A search is being organized, particularly for James Tremayne who, it now seems, had a notorious reputation in more ways than one.'

I guessed that Lucien was deliberately speaking lightly and it made me afraid. I put my hand on his arm. 'They have not caught him?'

'No, not yet. Popular opinion in the hotel kitchens gives him a supernatural ability to vanish like the devil into thin air, but his daughter is another matter and that is why we must get out of Paris quickly before too many people have been alerted.'

It was not yet seven when a carriage drawn by four horses with an armed postillion and Lucien and Joseph riding at either side with pistols in their saddle holsters took the road to the south. At the barrier the guard examined our papers and then leaned forward, scrutinizing me closely. A dirty hand turned my face towards him. Now was the moment and I waited breathlessly, but presently the blunt peasant face split into a grin.

'A governess, eh?' he repeated, then looked up at Lucien

and winked. 'Well, I might have another name for her. Good luck, citizen.'

Then we were through and bowling down the road to Lyons.

Chapter 5

We travelled fast. Between posting houses Lucien pushed the horses to the limits. We set out at dawn and sometimes drove on until long past dark. For me they were strange dreamlike days jolting over abominable roads with hurried meals and often only a few hours of restless sleep in hard beds where I slept closely wrapped in my dressing-gown to protect myself from the soiled sheets ... and worse. Lucien was scrupulously courteous, looked after my comfort to the best of his ability but otherwise scarcely spoke and I began to wonder if he had already regretted the generous impulse that had me in his charge.

At one of our stopping places I heard horrific stories from other travellers of their frightening experiences. Bands of thieves infested the roads. 'It's a pity this General Bonaparte does not set about arresting these infernal bandits instead of threatening to invade Britain,' exclaimed one enraged gentleman who had been robbed of all he possessed, then put out of his carriage and obliged to trudge fifteen miles through rain and mud to the nearest village. Another had been shot at almost point-blank range, the horses had bolted and he had only been saved by the good sense and strong wrist of his coachman.

Luckily nothing like that happened to us until the evening of the last day. Lucien planned to spend the night at Avignon since it was only a short journey from there to Villeroy. As we travelled south the heat increased. During the day the sun blazed down and the carriage was stifling. We galloped through villages grey and crumbling. In the distance I caught glimpses of mountains, great splinters of rock with castles perched dizzily on the summit, so high that it seemed only birds could live there.

I felt isolated in a remote unbelievable world, stabbed

now and again with a piercing anxiety when I thought of my father. On this last evening we had been travelling along beside the Rhône. The river rushed at a tremendous pace, swirling round reedy willow-covered islands. Tall poplars grew along the banks, their strange white trunks like slender ghosts in the dusk. Weary as I was, it was an intense relief to feel the fresh evening air blow in on my face. A single mountain, the colour of a ripe plum, rose up against the fading pink of the sunset sky, but the warmth of the day had brought a light mist from the river and it floated in clouds along the road.

The track was so appalling that we could not travel as fast as Lucien wished and it was completely dark when we were still some distance from Avignon. I was leaning back in the carriage, half asleep, my back stiff and aching from the rough jolting when suddenly we pulled up with a jerk. I heard a shot, then another. Someone shouted and, peering through the window, I glimpsed the shadowy figures of horsemen surrounding the carriage. What had happened? Where was Joseph? Someone dismounted. His hand was already on the door when I saw Lucien. He seized the man by the shoulders and swung him away. There was a smothered exclamation, then laughter and after that silence.

I could still see horsemen motionless in the mist and my first thought was that Bonaparte's secret police had caught up with me and were even now questioning Lucien. I waited shivering. The silence was uncanny. At last I could stand it no longer. No one stopped me when I opened the door and stepped down from the carriage. I could see Lucien a little ahead, standing by the horses, talking to a man wrapped in a dark cloak that muffled his face. I took a step nearer and as I did so, the wind temporarily blew away the shreds of mist and the flickering light of the carriage lantern fell on the face of the stranger. He threw back his head and laughed.

'Same road, same time ... how in hell's name was I to know it was the wrong carriage?' he said.

The cloak had fallen away and I could have sworn that the wild reckless face, dark moustache and white teeth were those of the man whom I had last seen carrying my dog up the cliff at Trevira. Then Lucien moved, hiding him from view.

'Keep away, that is all I ask,' he retorted. 'Leave Villeroy alone. Hasn't my mother suffered enough?'

They were speaking in low tones so that I could not hear all that was said. Then the stranger suddenly raised his voice.

'What happened in Paris, boy? Have you forgotten what your father died for?'

'Damn you! Leave my father out of it.' Lucien's furious gesture flicked across the other's face.

'*Mon Dieu*, if anyone else had done that . . .'

'You'd cut him down, I suppose.' There was a touch of contempt in Lucien's tone. 'You know where you have to go. Are you going to stand here arguing all night?'

The stranger stared at him for a moment, then he swung himself into the saddle and galloped away, the others streaming after him into the mist.

For an instant Lucien did not move, then he turned round and his face shone white and tense in the faint light. It changed to anger when his eyes fell on me. 'What are you doing there? You should have remained in the carriage.'

'I couldn't. I was frightened. I wanted to know what was happening. What did that man want?'

'Nothing. It was a mistake. They were on the wrong road that is all.'

'The wrong road? But he knew you. I heard him say . . .'

'Never mind what was said. Get back into the carriage if you please. It is very late.'

The inn at Avignon was crammed to the doors. It was only with great difficulty that Lucien obtained a room for me. He handed me my little travelling bag and the maidservant lighted me up the two narrow flights of stairs to an attic room under the roof. It was large with an enormous bed, one chair and very little else. Thankfully I stripped off my sweat-soaked gown and standing in my petticoat dipped my face in the bowl of ice-cold water. I had just taken up the towel when the door swung open with a crash. Astonished, I saw a man standing on the threshold, a huge man with a round red face, large as a ham, a shock of yellow hair and a broad grin. He beamed at me in friendly fashion, then to my horror strode into the room and flung a bundle on the bed.

'It seems I'm to share with you, *ma petite*. Which side do you prefer to sleep, eh? Left or right?'

I recovered from my first shock and snatched up a shawl to fling round my shoulders. I said as firmly as I could, 'I am afraid there has been a mistake. This is a private room, Monsieur. Will you kindly leave at once?'

'Oh come now, Ma'mselle,' said the big man quite unperturbed. 'The inn is full. You wouldn't want me to sleep in the stables now, would you? Besides you and I might have some fun in one another's company. What do you say, eh?' He gave me a prodigious wink and sat down cheerfully on the bed.

I had been in too many strange situations with my father to scream for help. I was angry and yet amused at the same time. He so obviously mistook me for the maidservant whose room I was no doubt occupying. I said, 'Will you please go? If you do not, I will be forced to call Monsieur de Fontenay.'

'Who?' He got to his feet in consternation, his mouth dropping open. 'Not Monsieur le Marquis?'

But by this time I was exasperated by my tiresome visitor and I went to the door with the intention of calling for the landlord and having him removed. Fortunately before I did, I saw Lucien himself coming up the stairs. I went to meet him.

'Lucien, please come. There is a man in my room. I can't get rid of him.'

'A man!' he exclaimed. He went quickly past me into the room and stopped dead. 'Mouton!' he thundered. 'What in God's name are you doing up here? Get out! Get out, man, at once!'

'I'm sorry, Monsieur Lucien,' mumbled the big man, considerably crestfallen. 'The landlord said ... how could I know that Mademoiselle was a lady under your protection?'

'Well, you know now. You dunderhead! You never had any more brains than a mouse! Get down to the stables. Go on and take this with you.' As Mouton went through the door with a muttered apology, Lucien hurled his bundle after him and turned to me. 'I'm sorry about that, Emma. Mouton is an idiot, but he means no harm.'

'Do you know him?'

'Mouton works for my stepfather. He is one of the *gardiens*, the horsemen who look after the horses and bulls on the Carmargue. He must be here on some errand connected with the farm and . . .'

'And the landlord gave him to understand that he could share this room which is where the maidservants sleep . . .'

'It looks like it.'

'Oh dear, it's funny really . . .'

I giggled helplessly out of sheer weariness more than anything until I remembered how sketchily I was dressed, and blushing I pulled the shawl more closely round my bare shoulders.

I felt Lucien's eyes on me. 'I've never met a girl like you before. Days and days of travelling, now this, and you only laugh.'

I looked away. 'I suppose you think me very bold . . .'

'No, you mistake me. . . .'

'My father taught me to be self-reliant,' I went on defiantly. 'He detests women who scream or faint.'

'Does he? I wish I had known him better. We might have had much in common. I was coming to ask if you would like your supper served to you up here.'

'Oh yes please . . . and Lucien . . .'

'Yes.' He paused in the doorway.

'Lucien, would you . . . would you sup with me?'

He hesitated. 'If you wish of course, only . . .'

'Oh, for heaven's sake,' I said impatiently. 'We've been travelling together for four days, surely it is not wrong to eat our supper in one another's company.'

'Very well, if that is what you want,' he said stiffly. 'I will go and arrange it.'

When he had gone, I put on my dress again, ran a wet comb through my hair, shook some essence of lavender on to my handkerchief and felt alive for the first time since I had left Paris.

Lucien came back with two of the maidservants carrying the food and whether it was the events of the evening or because the tiring anxious journey was nearly over and we were now a long way from Paris, his mood had changed. The stiffness had vanished. We were talking freely with one another as we had at Versailles so that after a little I could ask the question that lay at the back of my mind.

'Lucien, that man tonight ... the man who stopped us on the road ... was it Pierre?'

'Pierre?'

'You remember ... the man you told me about ... your friend who sailed with you on the ship.'

Lucien kept his eyes on his plate. 'Yes, as it happens, it was.'

'What did he really want?'

'I told you. He had missed the way.'

It hadn't sounded like that to me, but I did not like to press him. Then quite deliberately he changed the subject.

'I have been thinking, Emma. As Mouton is here, I will ask him to send horses back from the farm. We will dismiss the carriage and ride from here to Villeroy. Would you like that?'

'Oh yes, above all things. I'm so tired of the jolting. It's like being on a rack. You don't know how much I have envied you and Joseph.'

He smiled. 'They will not be here until the afternoon. I will show you Avignon in the morning and we will leave later when the worst of the heat is gone.'

The coffee when it came was thick as mud and tasted uncommonly like it. Lucien pushed it aside and poured another glass of the red country wine. The room was shadowy, lit only by the pools of yellow candlelight. Fatigue together with the food and wine were having their effect. I felt happy and a little lightheaded.

I said, 'Lucien, will you tell me about your father?'

'My father?'

'Don't you think I ought to know something more about your family if I'm to play my part successfully. After all Mademoiselle Rainier would know a great deal surely.'

'I doubt if she does. I don't remember that we ever saw much of the Rainiers. What do you want to know?'

'Why did Bonaparte say what he did that night at the Tuileries ... or would you rather not talk about it?'

'No, I don't mind. It is years ago now.' Lucien leaned back in his chair, fiddling with the stem of his wine glass, not looking at me. 'My father was a patriot,' he said abruptly. 'France meant more to him than anything, more even than my mother, more than me. As a young man he was not often at Versailles. He held liberal views. He was one of those who hoped that when trouble came the king would learn wisdom; that it would be possible to find a middle path with more freedom for everyone. He knew that change had to come, but when the revolution broke, he did not run away as so many of his friends did. He stayed quietly on his estate waiting for France to regain her sanity. Fontenay is in Brittany, you know, not far from Brest. The house lies a little back from the coast but there are great cliffs there pounded by the waves. Always there is a wind, the call of the gulls and the cool salt smell of the sea . . .'

'Like Trevira.'

'Yes, like Trevira. When I met you that day, I was remembering my childhood.'

'What happened?'

'After the death of the king, my father became the leader of a royalist group in Brittany. There were many there then, fighting against the new republic, fighting for the little Dauphin imprisoned in the Temple, who had become Louis XVII. He directed their activities from the château and for a time he was very successful, but it could not last. They came by night, soldiers of the National Guard and a great crowd of others, peasants, villagers, men who looked for robbery and pillage and would murder to get what they wanted. My father had not suppressed his tenants. Though he was a stern man, he had never been unjust, but there are always those who bear a grudge. We could not fight them, there were too many. They broke down the gates and swarmed into the gardens. They smashed the windows and climbed into the château. When they had taken all they could, they threw down their flaming torches. They piled up brushwood outside and set fire to it. The house was soon ablaze. We only escaped through the loyalty of our servants. Joseph was one of them, Mouton too. He looked after the stables.' Lucien looked up and smiled. 'Mouton was our pet name for him. He is really Jean-Baptiste, but we called him "Muttonhead". He cannot read or write and he is slow in his wits, but he is a wizard with horses. I remember how he wept because he could not free the poor beasts in time from the fire. He and Joseph got us away to safety.'

'How old were you then, Lucien?'

'Fourteen. I had been at school in Paris, but it had been disbanded a year before and I had been sent home. It was a terrible journey especially for my mother. Many times we escaped capture by a hair's breadth but we got across France to Lyons and then came south. Mouton had relatives living near Arles. Poor peasants they were, but they were kind. They took us in and cared for us. My father was a hunted man by then, but he still would not leave France, though my mother begged him on her knees.'

' "Can a man take the soil of his country with him on his feet?" ' I quoted softly.

'Who said that?'

'Danton when they urged him to run away before he was arrested. My father told me. There are different ways of loving one's country.'

'Perhaps. Though he would not leave himself, my father forced me to go. A friend of his was escaping to Switzerland. Against my will I was sent with him. It was hell. For two years I lived in Geneva with émigrés perpetually moaning about their fate and doing nothing about it, while all the time I was racked with anxiety as to what was happening to my parents. At last I could not stand it any longer. I was sixteen by then and I ran away from school. Somehow I got back to France. I only found my parents with great difficulty. They were living in a tiny cottage in great poverty. My mother had to do everything; cleaning, washing, cooking, like any peasant. I remember how angry I felt because my father never seemed to notice what he was doing to her. He had become the leader of a band of terrorists fighting a hopeless battle to restore the France he loved and to prove his loyalty to a king who was dead. They called themselves the Chevaliers de Foi. The worst of the Terror was over by then. Robespierre had gone the same way as his victims. There was great hope of a restoration. The British Fleet had been in Toulon. The English were supplying gold, guns and ammunition.'

'The English?'

'Yes. One of them was a member of the band.'

There must have been more than one Englishman fight-ing with the royalists. It need not have been my father and yet I felt my heart quicken.

'Do you know who he was?'

'No. No one knew. It was safer like that. They had only code names. Not even my mother knew the members of the band and my father would not permit me to join with them however much I implored him. "It is too dangerous," he said. "When France is herself again, there must still be a Fontenay. This is what I fight for. We cannot both be killed." '

'He must have been very brave.'

'He was. He knew that for him it was only a matter of time, but it never held him back. It was Bonaparte who defeated their hopes. When the republic was crumbling, he saved it. He drove the English out of Toulon. He climbed to victory in Paris rallying them all behind him. When he came south to Nice before he led his army into Italy, the rebels planned to assassinate him.'

I had been listening breathlessly. 'So that is what he meant when he spoke to you. But your father did not succeed?'

'No. Bonaparte was cleverer than they were. He had spies too. That night his guard was doubled. They fought like demons, but it was useless. Three of them were cap-tured, the Englishman and two others. My father and the rest of the band escaped to their secret hiding place, a cave in the hills.'

'Then if he escaped, why was he shot?'

Lucien raised his head, his eyes glittered in the flicker-ing candlelight, and I knew that this was the point of the whole story. This was what tormented him then and still did.

He said slowly. 'No one knew where that cave was ex-cept the members of the band. Those who were still alive were all gathered there and yet someone betrayed them. Two days later it was stormed and they were dragged out, my father with them; they were savagely tortured and then shot.'

'Who betrayed them?'

'I don't know. No one does. It happened only a few weeks after I had come from Geneva. I never knew any of them, never saw them face to face. You see that had been their strength. The fact that no one knew who they were. They worked at ordinary occupations during the day, their guns hidden somewhere near them, and met only by night. It is long ago now, but I would give ten years of my life to know who the traitor was, to be sure . . .'

'But why? What good will it do now?'

He brought his fist down on the table with a violence that I would never have expected in him. 'It is a debt of honour, don't you see, a debt I owe my father, to find the man who sent him to his death . . .'

'And then what?'

'God knows . . . destroy him, kill him . . . how can I tell?' There was silence for a moment, then the tension went out of him. He leaned back in his chair. 'You must think me crazy to talk like this.' He smiled wryly. 'It's strange, but I don't think I have said it to anyone before, not even my mother.'

'I'm glad . . . if it helps.'

'It does if only to make me realize how foolish it sounds.'

'What happened to the three who were in prison?'

'One died of his wounds, but two escaped, the Englishman and the other, the one they called the Fox. My mother and I were arrested, but after the killings, Bonaparte decided to be merciful. Many in the Midi were on the side of the royalists and he was anxious to win their goodwill. My mother was soon released and in a few months I too was allowed to go free provided I took an oath not to fight against the republic. I found my mother sick and starving. Mouton was already employed by Henri de Labran who owned Villeroy. I went to him and begged for work. I would have done anything to get food for her. Labran had played safe for years, keeping quiet and taking no sides, but he was kind. For a time I kept his accounts for him. He was a widower with two children, Armand and Nicole. A year later he asked my mother to marry him."

I thought I understood Lucien better then. I wondered if he resented his stepfather. It must have been hard for the Marquise de Fontenay to marry a man who must have seemed like one of her husband's peasant farmers, and yet sick and starving with a young child to care for ... Lucien had not mentioned Louis, but he could only have been a baby then. What a desperate time to bear a child after so many years ... It was so strange, Lucien was French and I was English, at any moment our two countries would be at war. We should have been enemies, but I stretched my hand across the table and after an instant felt his fingers shut on mine.

'I love France, Emma,' he murmured, 'I believe in her, but where does her future lie? With a fat old man calling himself Louis XVIII and skulking in England or with Bonaparte, an upstart Corsican, who killed my father and dreams of making himself Emperor?'

I think he was speaking to himself as much as to me. The next moment he had got to his feet. 'I have worn you out with so much talking, but you did ask for it, you know. Now you must get some sleep. You will be quite safe. One of us will remain outside all night to make sure.'

'I am not afraid.'

He looked down at me, smiling. 'You have too much courage.'

'My father said that once. He said he had taught me all the wrong things.'

'If he did, then I think I like the wrong things.'

Lucien kissed my hand, holding it for an instant against his cheek in that same endearing gesture that he had used before. Then he went swiftly out of the room.

Chapter 6

I had never known such sunlight. We were bathed in it. It went to one's head like wine. We had climbed up a steep winding stair past the Cathedral and suddenly we were in an enchanted garden filled with flowers and birdsong. The view was breathtaking. The massive lines of palaces and towers were etched in gold against the dazzling blue of the sky. One magnificent peak stood out against a shadowy range of purple mountains in the misty distance. Across the madly racing Rhône stretched the crumbling half bridge of St Bénézet built six hundred years before by the shepherd boy saint who had dreamed of saving the lives swallowed every year by the torrential waters.

> 'Sur le pont
> D'Avignon
> L'on y danse, l'on y danse . . .'

I sang aloud and took a few dancing steps. The children stopped their games to stare at me. I stood still, feeling foolish, but Lucien was smiling.

'Where did you learn that?'

'At school. We used to sing it in class. Why did they dance on the bridge, do you think?'

'Perhaps in those old days the streets were so narrow, there was nowhere else to dance. Is that where you learned to speak French so well?'

'Not really, though we did have Mademoiselle Clémence from Paris. I used to speak it with my father.' It had been our secret language in dingy lodgings defeating eavesdropping landladies at keyholes. 'You see, he had spent a long time in France,' I went on quickly. 'He spoke it like a native. He had to . . .' I broke off in time. It wasn't that I did not trust Lucien, but only fools babbled on without thinking.

'When was he in France, Emma?'

'Oh years ago,' I said evasively. 'Do you think we should go back to the inn? Mouton may have come with the horses.'

'Of course, if you wish. Have we done too much exploring? Are you tired?'

'No, it is so beautiful here. I could walk about the city for ever. Why does the stone of your palaces and churches turn that lovely golden colour? In England they are always so grey and dismal.'

'It is the sun . . . and the mistral of course.'

'The mistral?'

'Our devil wind. When it blows, it drives dogs mad, women crazy and jealous husbands to murder.'

'You're laughing at me.'

'No, it is true. If you are here long enough which God forbid, you will feel it yourself. Sometimes it comes unexpectedly even in summer, tearing the young grapes from the vines. When it is hot and dry, it is terrifying. That is why most of the houses are built with their backs to it.'

'I can't imagine there being anything so savage in this beautiful countryside.'

'Every Eden has its serpent,' said Lucien quietly, and with a sudden pang at the heart I remembered the bitter story of betrayal and death that he had told me the evening before.

It was late afternoon when Mouton brought the horses. I had taken my riding habit out of my trunk wishing I had my boy's breeches with me, though they would hardly have been suitable for a prim governess. When I came down, the horses were waiting in the inn yard, five of them. They were unlike any I had ever seen, small, sturdy and white, with long sweeping tails, enormous feet and liquid dark eyes.

Mouton said proudly, 'They are Camargue horses, Mademoiselle. They are the best in the world, gentle, brave and very wise.' He fondled a velvet nose. 'But like all Provençals, they can be fierce and proud too and once in a lifetime they have their moment of madness.'

'Mouton, you are talking moonshine,' said Lucien, taking the bridle from him and leading one of the ponies to me.

'No, Monsieur Lucien, it is true as I stand here. Didn't my old grandfather have such a one? Faithful as a dog for fourteen years, then one day he caught sight of a mare he fancied and what did he do? He went crazy. He bolted into the river and nearly drowned my grandfather as well as himself. My father and I had to fish them both out and afterwards when it was all over, there he was again, docile as a lamb till the day he died.'

'Mouton, you talk too much. You will terrify Mademoiselle Rainier.'

'No, he won't. I like to hear it,' I said and put my arm round the rough white neck. The horse rubbed its face affectionately against me.

Lucien grinned. 'Wait until he bolts with you. Mouton, can't you count? Why bring five horses when there are only four of us?'

'I was wondering when you would deign to notice me, Lucien.'

The voice startled us both. I turned round quickly. A girl was standing in the shadow of the stable. She was small and very slender, her green riding dress showed off her tiny waist. She carried her hat in her hand and lustrous black hair coiled round the shapely head.

'Nicole! I had no idea!' Lucien crossed swiftly to her, taking her hand and leaning forward to kiss her cheek. 'What made you come to meet us?'

'I needed the exercise,' she said lightly. 'Besides I was anxious to meet Louis' new governess. Won't you introduce us?'

I guessed then that Lucien had sent a note by Mouton warning his mother of my arrival. Nicole stepped daintily across the rough cobbles. The cool glance from the grey eyes made me conscious at once of my unruly hair and the creases in my riding dress, what my father called my 'Scarecrow' look.

She said, 'You're much younger than I expected, Mademoiselle Rainier. I hope you won't find Louis too much of a handful. I'm afraid Lucien and his mother between them spoil him shockingly.'

'Nonsense, Nicole, to hear you talk, anyone would think that Louis was a monster.'

'So he can be, to me at any rate,' said Nicole sweetly. 'But then he doesn't like me. What is your other name, Mademoiselle Rainier?'

'Emma.'

'Em—ma? What an extraordinary name. I'm sure I have heard my stepmother speak of a Louise Rainier. Perhaps you have a sister.'

We had not been very good conspirators, Lucien and I. I glanced at him helplessly and he came to my rescue immediately.

'I don't think you ever knew the Rainiers, Nicole,' he said shortly. 'Emma Louise is named after her godmother who happened to be English. And now come along, we must be off if we are to reach Villeroy in time for supper.'

He gave her his hand to mount and then came to me. I had the impression that he was irritated by something, but what had caused it I couldn't guess, and I forgot it once I was in the saddle and following them out of the inn yard. If there was one thing on which I feared no rivalry it was my ability to ride and it was sheer heaven to be free of the stuffy bone-shaking carriage. The Camargue ponies picked their way delicately and were remarkably sensitive to the lightest touch on the bridle.

We came to Villeroy just as the sun was beginning to sink. We had been riding through the olive groves. For the first time I saw the rows and rows of low twisted trees with their silver-green foliage interspersed with cypresses, like black fingers against a sky of molten gold. We came through a wide archway in a high stone wall. Then we were in a courtyard with stables and outhouses and in front of us Villeroy itself, half farmhouse, half château, the centre of massive grey-gold stone with two fairytale turrets at either end. Great clusters of mauve-pink flowers clambered over the walls and hung in festoons above the door. As we dismounted a small boy shot out of one of the stables and raced across the yard hurling himself joyously against Lucien.

'I thought you would never come back. What were you doing so long in Paris? Did you bring me a present, you said you would? Can I ride Beauregard back to the stable?'

'What have you been doing? You look like a chimney sweep?' interrupted Nicole sharply. 'And it is not good manners to ask for presents. What would Maman say if she heard you?'

'I was speaking to Lucien, not to you.' There was something endearing about the small sturdy figure standing with legs apart, his frilled shirt ripped and a long dirty streak down one cheek. 'Does that mean that you haven't brought me anything? But you promised . . .'

'One thing at a time,' said Lucien good-humouredly. 'I just might have something tucked away in my saddlebags, but first you must greet Mademoiselle Rainier. She is going to be your governess.'

'Oh!' Louis turned to stare at me. He was a tall thin child with untidy brown hair and large hazel eyes. Lucien gave him a little push and he came towards me slowly.

'I have never had a governess before. Maman teaches me my lessons.' He gave me a stiff little bow. 'Are you very strict?'

'Not if you are a good boy,' I said, almost as nervous as my future pupil.

'Oh but I'm not,' said Louis candidly. 'No one likes me very much except Mouton,' he grinned up at the big man confidingly. 'He lets me go with him to the Camargue sometimes. Do you like horses, Mademoiselle Rainier?'

'Yes, Louis, I do . . . very much.'

'And bulls?'

'I'm afraid I don't know very much about bulls.'

'I do. I'm going to fight the bulls when I grow up. I'll take you to see them. I can, can't I, Lucien?'

'Perhaps. We shall have to see. Come along,' he lifted the child onto the back of the horse. 'Now go with Mouton to the stables and then come in. It is high time you were in bed.'

'Will you come and see me before I go to sleep, Mademoiselle?'

'Yes, of course I will.'

The boy waved his hand to me as the pony trotted away.

'I congratulate you. You appear to have made a conquest,' said Nicole coolly, going before me up the steps and in through the open door. 'I will tell Martine you are here, Lucien.'

After the light outside, the room into which he took me was cool and dim. After a moment I could see it was very large with white walls and fine old dark furniture. Here and there were gracious touches, a bowl of flowers reflected in the polished surface of the table, a fine piece of porcelain on a bracket, a wide hearth and candelabra of beaten silver.

Lucien left me for a moment and then came back with his mother. Martine de Labran who had been the Marquise de Fontenay was still remarkably beautiful despite all she had gone through. Honey-coloured hair was swept round her head and fastened with a single comb. She was dressed plainly in a flowered cotton gown. She wore a large apron of grey linen and her arms were bare to the elbow like any farmer's wife and yet she moved with the grace and dignity of a queen.

'Welcome to Villeroy, my dear Emma,' she said, 'I am so happy you can come to us.' She came towards me, taking me in her arms and kissing me on both cheeks. A faint musky perfume clung around her. 'You must be exhausted, my dear. Let me show you to your room. Then you can wash and rest before supper. Lucien, see that Mouton brings up Emma's baggage for her.'

'Yes, of course, Mother.'

He went out and I followed her up the stairs. The room to which she took me was closely shuttered but she went across and thrust them wide so that the evening light flooded in.

'We like to keep out the sun during the day,' she explained. 'Of course this is nothing to the heat in the summer months. Then you will be very glad of the coolness.' She glanced around. 'Do ask if there is anything else you need. I want you to be happy with us. We sup as soon as my husband comes in from the vineyards. I will send Lucien to fetch you.'

'Thank you, Madame.'

'Now if you will excuse me, there are still things to be done.'

As she moved to the door, I remembered the child. I

said, 'Where is Louis' room. He asked me to say goodnight to him.'

'He did?' She turned to look at me, the green eyes questioning. 'That is very unlike Louis. You must have made a great impression. He is usually shy with strangers.' She paused. She was the one person who knew the part I was playing and for a moment I thought she would speak of it, but all she said was, 'He sleeps over the other side of the house. Just follow the passage. The door is at the far end. I'm going to him now.' She smiled. 'Like all small boys, he sometimes forgets to wash.'

My room was not large, but the white walls gave a feeling of space. There were brightly coloured rugs on the tiled floor and a crucifix hung over the bed with its embroidered linen counterpane. The window looked out on a walled garden. The emerald lawn was starred with daisies and showered with golden petals from a flowering laburnum. In the centre water bubbled from a little fountain falling with a refreshing coolness into a stone pond. It reminded me of Marie Antoinette's garden at Versailles and I wondered if the Marquise de Fontenay had tried to create here a reminder of what she had lost.

After I had washed and changed out of my riding clothes, I went along the passage and found Louis' bedroom. Like mine, it was white and simple, books and toys all neatly stacked away by his mother or perhaps one of the maids. A sleepy voice said, 'I thought you had forgotten.'

I smiled down at the brown face and tousled hair and for the first time wished I had a brother. I bent down and kissed his cheek. A stout white dog wriggled up the bed and pushed his cold nose into my hand.

'Does Maman allow this?'

'She doesn't know. Pepi hides under the bed till she has gone downstairs. Do you see what Lucien brought me?'

I followed the pointing finger. A wooden figure of a black bull stood on the table, its head lowered as if about to charge. The carver had caught the look of ferocity and power. To my eye it was intensely ugly but Louis was gazing at it with ecstasy.

'He's like Bernardo. That is the most famous of all my

stepfather's bulls. Nobody yet has been able to take his cockade away from him.'

'Cockade? What are you talking about, Louis?'

'You will see. It is quite soon now and Maman has promised that this year I shall go to see it.' A small hand pulled at my sleeve. 'Mademoiselle Rainier, do you like Lucien?'

'Yes, Louis . . . very much.'

'So do I; more than anyone except Maman.'

'I must go now. Goodnight.'

He snuggled down in the bed, his eyes still fixed on his bull. 'Good-night, Mademoiselle.'

I met Henri de Labran at supper. He was a big man, not tall, Lucien easily topped him by quite a few inches, but broad-shouldered and bulky. His face reminded me of the busts of Roman Emperors I had seen once in the British Museum with my father, Nero perhaps or Titus, with a straight classical nose, well-cut full lips and determined chin. His thick grey hair curled tightly on his forehead, not unlike Louis' bull, and was still damp as if he had put it under the pump. He seemed almost to burst out of his tight blue coat and frilled shirt and I was instantly reminded of a small boy called in from the fields and compelled to wash and change before sitting down at the table. There could not have been a greater contrast to his wife, whose simple gown of lavender silk with no ornament except the cream lace at throat and wrists could not conceal her beauty and elegance.

It was strange, but when I took my place at the table that evening and shared with them the roast duck cooked in some Provençal way with herbs and pitted green olives, I felt as if I were in reality the Louise Rainier I was pretending to be. They had accepted me so simply. I looked round at them. Henri de Labran was talking to Lucien about affairs at the farm, while his wife quietly made sure that everyone had what they wanted. Armand had come in with his father. His hair like that of his sister was inky black, a stocky young man with a brown face and merry eyes. He obviously envied Lucien's visit to Paris and leaned across the table plying me with questions which were easy enough to answer. Only Nicole was silent, quietly eating and now and again glancing from me to her brother.

There was only one moment of awkwardness. Henri de Labran looked up from the fruit he was peeling with thick stubby fingers. 'Did you have a visit from the Chief of Police this afternoon, my dear?' he asked his wife.

'Police? No, why? Should we have done?'

I felt a tremor of anxiety but he went on quite cheerfully. 'It seems that the diligence coming down from Lyons was attacked last night. The driver had his throat cut and quite a considerable sum of money intended for the Marseilles garrison was stolen. The bandits all got away and when I met young Georges Montaud on his way back to Tarascon this afternoon. he told me that there was to be a house to house enquiry.'

'But why? What should we know about these robbers?'

'Not us in particular, Martine, but the whole neighbourhood.' I saw his eyes meet hers across the table and he spoke slowly almost as if he was feeling his way. 'It is just possible that they are not thieves at all. It is being suggested that the Chevaliers de Foi have taken to the roads again.'

'But that is impossible, Henri. It is all over and done with, all finished years ago.' Her voice was under control, but the hand that reached out for her wine glass was trembling.

'That's what I said to Georges, but there have been other incidents, too many these last few months, and he insisted that his Chief had certain information.'

'What information?'

'That, my dear, he would not tell me. It may be nothing more than guesswork. I shall keep double guard round the vineyards. We don't want any trouble among our own people.'

Nicole's eyes were on Lucien. She said, 'Did you see anyone? After all you must have been on the road at about the same time.'

'No, nothing,' he replied shortly.

'That's strange,' she went on in the sweet tone that already I was beginning to recognize as dangerous. 'Mouton said your postillion was boasting of his courage when the carriage was held up by armed men and he only missed being shot at by inches.'

'Mouton talks too much. The postillion was an idiot. We were stopped by a party who had lost their way in the mist, that's all; one of them was scared and fired into the air. These boys listen to so many travellers' tales, they would run a mile if a mouse squeaked.'

'It obviously scared Mademoiselle Rainier,' pursued Nicole, smiling at me, 'since you and Joseph had to take it in turns to keep watch outside her room all night.'

'My dear child,' intervened Martine, 'those inns are always crowded with the most undesirable characters. It didn't need an encounter with bandits to make Emma Louise nervous.'

Once I had asked Lucien jestingly if Nicole was in love with him. Now I wondered if I had been right, and if jealously she sensed that there was more between us than the mere casual relationship of a young man bringing home his little brother's governess. If that was so, I felt uneasily that she would not rest until she had found out exactly what it was. I began to realize that we had involved ourselves in a difficult situation without fully considering its consequences.

I excused myself and went to bed early, wearied by the fatigues of the last few days. But though I undressed and put on my dressing-gown, I still sat for a little at the open window. A scent of flowers stole in from the garden and through the evening hush came the click of the cicadas who sing all summer through and starve when winter comes according to La Fontaine's fable, something else Mademoiselle Clémence had made us learn at school.

Lucien had told me that tomorrow he was going to Marseilles. In a few days perhaps I would know my fate. Soon I would be gone from here. It was what I had wanted passionately yet now a queer pang shot through me. For the first time in my life my thoughts did not fly at once to my father. Someone had stepped between him and me; a young man alien to me in almost everything, in all probability already committed to another woman.

I was so absorbed in my thoughts that I heard the faint sound of voices below me without understanding anything that was said. Then a phrase struck me and involuntarily I listened.

'Lucien, was it Pierre you met last night?'

'Yes. I told you, Mother; he came back with me from England before I went to Paris.'

I looked cautiously from the window. Lucien and his mother were walking slowly up and down the grass below. Only a few words here and there drifted to my ear.

His mother said, 'You heard what Henri told us tonight. Has it begun again? The danger, the robberies, the murders?'

'. . . We do not know that it was Pierre . . .'

'I cannot endure it all over again, I cannot, Lucien . . .'

'Don't be afraid. I've warned him. I've told him to keep away.'

'Do you think he will care for that? He has always done exactly what he pleased . . . and Henri has been good to us. I cannot . . . I will not put him in danger.'

I should have shut the window. My hand was on the latch already when the words coming in on the breeze startled me into stillness.

'This English girl . . . you should not have brought her here. If it is discovered, it could be bad for us all . . .'

'She was so distressed . . . it was all I could think of . . .'

'Poor child. I would have felt the same but I don't trust Pierre. If he finds out, he may use her . . . just as he has used others . . .'

But now they were gone, out of sight and out of hearing, there was only the silence. It could mean only one thing. The cause for which Lucien's father had died was still a living force. It was my father's cause, England's cause, and yet I could not help a feeling of pity for Martine de Labran who had already endured so much . . . and Lucien himself . . . what would he do? Divided between his mother who longed only to live in peace and his passionate desire to avenge his murdered father? In the drowsy stillness I heard an owl hoot and a second later the small shriek as it descended on its prey, and in spite of the heat I shivered. I was glad to creep between the sheets and bury my head in the pillow.

Chapter 7

No one could have been more woefully equipped as a governess than I was and yet somehow I had to give the right impression. It was very important for Lucien's sake that I should appear to be Emma Louise Rainier, the daughter of Madame de Labran's old schoolfriend. I would have failed hopelessly if it had not been for Louis himself. Of course he was spoiled, it was only natural, the child in a grown-up household. Henri de Labran treated him with the casual kindness he gave the many dogs that wandered in and out of the house, but Armand petted him almost as if to make up for his sister's sharp dislike. The servants were obviously fond of the little boy and let him have his own way about nearly everything and though his mother tried hard to be firm, I realized very quickly that this last baby born in such unhappy circumstances was infinitely precious to her.

Of course I did not find all this out at once and since on that first morning I had not the smallest notion how to set about giving a lesson, I thought the only thing to do was to get to work on what I knew best. I would teach him English and I made a start by reading to him the old fable about the frog who longed so much to make herself as big as a bull that she puffed and puffed herself out until she burst. Louis shouted with laughter and after he had told me about the giant frogs that lived in the Camargue and done his best to imitate *Madame la Grenouille* by blowing out his cheeks and sticking out his chest, we painstakingly translated it into English.

When later in the morning Martine came in with a glass of milk for Louis and a cup of excellent coffee for me, the boy jumped up, excited and proud of the lines he had already learned.

'Maman, I can spik English ... listen! A lady frog saw a bull one day who had a very beautiful ... *taille* ... what is *taille*?'

'Figure,' I prompted.

'A very beautiful figure and she had envy ... so she ...' and he blew out his cheeks, 'and so she ... she bursted out ...'

Martine laughed, ruffling his brown curls lovingly. 'Splendid, Louis. I can see you two are going to get on famously. But now run and get ready. Joseph is waiting to take you to the village for your Latin lesson.'

'Must I, Maman? I'd much rather stay with Mademoiselle Emma.'

'Yes, I am sure you would, but Monsieur le Curé will be expecting you and you know how cross he is if you are late.' The child pouted rebelliously but she said firmly, 'Go off now. It is bad manners to keep people waiting.' After the boy had gone, she turned to me. 'When he is a little older, he will go to school of course, but he must have a good grounding first and the Curé, poor man, is only too glad of the extra money. It has been as hard for him as it has been for all of us. If there is one good thing Bonaparte has done, it is to give us back our religion after ten years in the wilderness.'

'How do you mean?'

'In England, my child, you can have had no idea of what it has been like, especially for the peasants whose life centred round the church. Etienne Michel is a good man, but he was turned out of his parish at the revolution. He lived in hiding for years, always in extreme danger, saying mass in secret when he could and carrying the sacraments to the dying. Now he has been restored, but his church was used as a barn, a stable, even worse. There is nothing left of it, but bare whitewashed walls. Nicole and I have begun to embroider an altar cloth.'

'Lucien told me something,' I said with quick sympathy. 'I don't know how you survived.'

She dismissed it with a gesture. 'It is surprising. You don't know how much you can endure until you are put to the test. You know, Emma, the nuns at the convent where I grew up taught me the finest needlework. I remember so well how we all detested the hours we had to spend learn-

ing the most elaborate stitches, but when my husband and
I fled here from Fontenay, I was glad of my skill. It saved
us from starvation. I was thankful then to be paid for the
work I used to find so tedious, little though it was. Ironic,
wasn't it?'

For a moment she was silent and I guessed at the humil-
iations she must have suffered from those the revolution
had thrust into positions of power and I admired the
courage that had kept her with the husband she loved instead of running away to the safety of England as so many
others had done.

Martine stirred herself and smiled. 'I must go back to
the kitchen. They are making the *coulis*.'

'*Coulis?*'

'A few years ago I would have been as ignorant as you.
It is a very famous Provençal sauce. Every housewife has
jars of *coulis* in her larder and it is a great favourite of
Henri's.'

In the huge stone kitchen Jeanne the cook was slicing
the tomatoes and pounding them with herbs; fennel, I
recognized, coriander and tarragon, with others I did not
know. Nicole was there too in a big apron, jealously
superintending everything they did.

Martine smiled. 'They will not let me help them.'

'You are not born to it, Madame,' said the cook stirring
vigorously. 'A foreign hand would spoil the flavour.'

'My mother made the finest *coulis* in Provence,' said Nicole. 'Everyone came to her for her recipe but she would
not part with it. It had been in the family for hundreds of
years. I am afraid that is not something learned at
Versailles, Madame la Marquise.'

For the first time I saw a flash of fire in Martine's green
eyes and I guessed that behind that calm exterior there
lived a passion and a pride that she kept hidden, but she
only said quietly, 'I thought we had agreed, Nicole, that
the past is done with. I am well aware that I can never
take your mother's place nor do I wish to do so, but all
the same I am now your father's wife and the Marquise de
Fontenay no longer exists.'

Nicole flushed at the rebuke. She said quickly, 'You are
so quick to take offence. I meant nothing.'

I saw the maidservants smile slyly at one another and

knew that, trivial though the incident was, this was one of many, a jealousy not yet resolved though Martine must have been married to Henri de Labran for more than four years.

It was several days before Lucien returned and in a strange way I did not mind. I had never lived as part of a great household before. It had always been just my father and I and there seemed to me a happiness, a feeling of content in this house that arose from the deep affection between Henri de Labran and his second wife. He was obviously a wealthy man but still liked to go out each day riding around his estates and supervising his work people personally, and sometimes Armand would accompany him and sometimes go off on expeditions with his friends, gun or fishing rod in hand. And through it all ran the child Louis, gay, mischievous, often wilful, but with a charm and sweetness that no one could resist. There was only Nicole. I would have been glad of her friendship, but she would not yield. There was something secret about her, something withdrawn and watchful. She was not openly hostile, but she held me off, cool, prickly and distrustful. I was never sure of what she thought or felt.

One day towards the end of that first week the white ponies were saddled and Louis and I set out for an afternoon ride.

'Don't go too far. Keep within the boundaries of the fields,' said Martine in the courtyard, shading her eyes against the glare of the sun.

'Don't fuss over the boy, my dear. He has got to grow up,' said her husband indulgently, his arm around her shoulders. They waved to us as we rode through the stone gateway.

We went first through the olive groves. They were so unlike our English trees, so gnarled and grey. They gave me a feeling of great antiquity. I remembered my father saying once that the olive belonged to Pallas Athene, the wise goddess of Homer's *Iliad* and this was a land where the Greeks had settled and then the Romans. On our journey from Paris Lucien had sometimes pointed out their monuments, triumphal arches and giant arenas where wild beasts fought and Christians were martyred.

Louis was pointing to a group of stone buildings ahead of us. 'That is where the olives are pressed for the oil. It is not time yet,' he said knowledgeably, 'it is almost winter before they are picked. Would you like to see them?'

Inside the stone barns it was cool and dark. One or two of the men pulled off their caps respectfully at sight of us and stood aside to let me see the purifying vats, the great presses worked by donkeys walking in a circle, the channel down which ran the golden oil. The wood was impregnated with it, the air thick and heavy with its scent.

When we came out the light seemed dazzling. We rode on through fields high with grasses. There were flowers everywhere, gold and scarlet. Beyond there was lavender, dark blue, just coming into flower, the air was perfumed with its breath. In the distance I could see the shadow of mountains.

'I said, 'We ought not to go too far, Louis,' but he dug his heels into his white pony and trotted ahead.

'I want to show you where the lizards live, Mademoiselle,' he called back over his shoulder. 'There are hundreds of them. You would like to see them, wouldn't you?'

I was not altogther enchanted at the prospect, but I spurred Beauregard to follow at the heels of the little figure ahead of me. Thyme and yellow gorse fringed the track, but soon the rich red earth gave way to grey limestone. We came upon it quite suddenly. We were out of the sunlit fields and in a wild desolate valley. Rocks lay here and there on the roadside, some like bleached skulls, others like monstrous reptiles. A ghost village clambered up steep stony slopes and above, on the ridge of the mountains, there were the ruins of a castle, its walls and towers hewn out of the living rock so that it was almost impossible to know which was natural and which built by human hands. In the blazing heat of the afternoon there were very few people about. One or two children stared at us with sullen eyes as we trotted by.

We followed a steep track above the houses. A garden had once been cultivated on these terraces, there were traces of it still, a syringa blooming unexpectedly, its sweet scent heavy in the warm air; staircases led up and vanished, great caverns opened yawningly at our feet. A tiny pavilion half destroyed was perched on a wide ledge over-shadowed by flowering arbutus. Here Louis slipped from his pony and after I had tethered them both, he seized my hand and pulled me along the path to where a limestone crag jutted out, baked white in the hot sun.

'You have to stand very still,' he said breathlessly, 'otherwise you frighten them.'

He was right. After a moment, shading my eyes against the glare, I saw them, their armour-plated bodies absolutely motionless, miniature dragons, leather eyelids unblinking in their ancient heads, long darting tongues flying out to catch their prey. I began to appreciate Nicole's anger when she had found one of these small monsters in her bed.

'Louis, what do they call this spot?'

'The place of stones. Jeanne, she's our cook, says only devils live here and if I'm not careful, they will carry me off,' he said cheerfully, 'but I like it. It is a nice place.' He pointed upwards to one of the crags, burning blue and gold in the sun. 'There are caves up there, many of them. It is too steep for me to climb but that is where my father hid before they captured him.'

'How do you know?'

'Mouton told me about it. I wasn't here then,' he said matter-of-factly. 'You see, my real Papa was shot before I was born.'

So Martine had been pregnant when her husband was murdered. How cruel life can be. No wonder she cherished this child, the last token of the father he would never know.

Louis said, 'You stay here, Mademoiselle. I'm going to climb up higher. Mouton says there are snakes up there, but I've never seen one yet.'

'No, Louis, you mustn't. It is dangerous. Come back at once.'

But he was gone already, running up the steep path, and with my heart in my mouth I watched him leaping light-footed as a goat from crag to crag. I began to climb after him. He was dancing up and down on a rocky spur, waving joyously and shouting, 'Look at me! Look at me!' He turned round and clambered higher. I heard him cry triumphantly, 'There they are. I can see them!' Then he disappeared.

Frantically I began to struggle after him, calling as I ran. It was rough going. There were clumps of gorse and broom. I tore my hands on sharp thorns and bruised myself against rocks. The path narrowed round an outcrop of stone and I dare not look down as I edged round it. Then I was safe. I took a deep breath and at the same time a man leaped down from the track above, a tall, dark-haired man dressed in brown hunting leather with an angry struggling Louis in his arms.

'You should take better care of your charge, Mademoiselle. In another second he would have thrust his hand into a nest of vipers. You are too venturesome, *mon brave*. Go back to your governess.' He set Louis down, pushing him towards me with a light slap on his bottom. I met his eyes and saw the recognition in his face. He fell back against the rock wall, staring. Then unexpectedly he began to laugh.

'*Nom de Dieu,* I seem to make a habit of coming to your rescue.'

I stood there so aghast that for an instant I could not move or speak. Louis had run to me and taken my hand. He looked from me to the stranger.

'Who is he?' he said resentfully.

'Say thank you, Louis, I said in a stifled voice. 'If it had not been for this gentleman, you might have been badly hurt.'

'No, I wouldn't,' exclaimed the boy indignantly. 'I know about snakes.'

'Excellent,' said the man, 'I'm glad to hear your education has been so thorough. Now listen. If you go to the edge there, lie down flat and look over, you will see all manner of unpleasant creatures, but don't touch. Understand?'

'No, Louis,' I interrupted quickly. 'You're not to do it. In any case it is time we went home.'

But the boy had already flung himself down on the stony plateau and the man I knew as Pierre turned to me. 'He will be safe enough,' he said in English, 'and I want to talk to you. Don't look so alarmed, Mademoiselle Tremayne. I'm not going to run to the police about you.'

'How do you know my name?'

'That would be telling, wouldn't it?' He grinned, watching me. 'You have surprised me. I thought you safely back in England by now.'

'Who are you? What do you want with me?'

'Nothing. I'm merely curious, that's all. Does Mr James Tremayne know where his daughter is hiding?'

I could not understand how he should know so much about me. 'What is my father to you?'

'I have met him . . . in the way of business, shall we say?'

'What business?'

'Oh come . . . I think that best left unanswered, don't you?' He leaned back against the crag, arms folded, perfectly at ease, chatting as if we had been in a drawing-room. 'I must admit I had not expected Lucien's little governess to turn out to be you. He is not given to deeds of gallantry. How did you persuade him to rescue you from the Bonaparte ogre?'

'What do you know about Lucien or me?'

'A great deal, more than you can guess. *C'est drôle, n'est-ce pas?* That we three should meet here in this corner of Provence. How are you getting on at Villeroy? What about Nicole, eh?'

'What is that to you?' I burst out. 'Why should I tell you anything?'

'No reason except that I am interested. When is the betrothal to be announced?'

'Betrothal?'

'Lucien and Nicole of course. Don't tell me you didn't know.'

'I have only been here a few days.'

'He'll be a fool if he lets the opportunity slip. Henri de Labran is a rich man and it will all come to Armand and Nicole one day while Lucien is a beggar.'

'I don't think you understand Lucien at all.'

'My dear young lady, do you?' He smiled provocatively. 'What in God's name brought you to this robbers' nest?'

'It was Louis who wanted to come. We were out riding,' I answered reluctantly. 'Why do you call it that?'

'Why not?' he shrugged his shoulders. 'In the Middle Ages the castle belonged to one of the most vicious, violent and bloody families in these parts and that is saying something, believe me. One of the Lords of Les Baux who suspected his wife of more than exchanging pretty verses with her favourite troubadour, had the happy idea of murdering the miserable poet, tearing out his heart and sending it to his lady served up in a gilt dish. They say Henri de Labran is descended from one of them.'

'Are you trying to frighten me?'

'God forbid.'

'Is this robbers' nest where you have made your home?' I retorted with spirit. 'What did you do with the money you stole from the Lyons diligence?'

It was a shot in the dark but I saw the quick flash in his eyes before he said quietly, 'You will not trap me so easily, but it went to a good cause, that I can promise you; your cause, Miss Emma, your father's cause.'

'Did you have to murder to get it?'

'We are not playing games. You should be thanking those who risked their lives to prevent it reaching its destination. That gold was intended to help build a fleet of ships, a fleet already being assembled for the invasion of England. Believe me, General Bonaparte is wasting no time.' He straightened himself and looked around him. 'Now I think you must go and I too, and don't imagine you can run to the Chief of Police about me.' He smiled, openly mocking me. 'We know a little too much about one another, isn't that so? I haven't seen you and neither have you seen me. Agreed?' I nodded and he pulled Louis to his feet. 'Come, boy, that's enough natural history for one afternoon.' With a gallant gesture he raised my hand to his lips and kissed it. 'You would be happy never to see my face again, I know that, but I greatly fear we shall meet again, more than once. *Au revoir*, Mademoiselle.' He waved his hand and had gone in a moment, moving swiftly out of sight.

Louis was staring after him. 'Were you talking to him in English?'

'Yes.'

'Why? What did he want?'

'Never mind about that now, Louis. We must go home.'

We clambered down the path and untethered the horses. As we trotted along the track to Villeroy, Louis chattered gaily of the afternoon's happenings in the inconsequent way of children. I scarcely listened. That Pierre was no ordinary robber was immediately obvious, nor was his manner, his voice nor his appearance that of a peasant. It was obvious too that he knew the family at Villeroy intimately. It was more and more evident that he had been one of the royalist rebels disbanded and hunted down at the death of the Marquis de Fontenay, and he had now returned from his safe retreat in England to fight Bonaparte as he had once fought the revolutionaries. And what of my father? He too must be linked with them. It seemed clear to me now that on that day at Trevira, he had been meeting Pierre in secret, giving him instructions perhaps; in Paris too . . . Paris! My heart gave a great jolt. What was it my father had said that night when he had been so brutally attacked . . .? 'Men's motives can be mixed, patriotism, loyalty, jealousy . . .' I should have had nothing to fear from Pierre, his cause was my cause, and yet there had been something in the way he spoke, something enigmatic in that faintly mocking manner that disturbed me. Could it have been he who had struck that savage blow . . . or could it have been Lucien? Lucien, whom I had met so unexpectedly in the gardens of the Palais Royal? The notion was so horrible, so preposterous, that I jerked on the reins and Beauregard stumbled, looking round at me reproachfully.

Louis said, 'Is anything the matter, Mademoiselle?'

'No, no, nothing. Go on quickly. We're late already,' but my thoughts were churning over and over. It was not Lucien, that I would never believe. Could it be Pierre? But why? Why should he have done so terrible a thing . . . unless my father was the Englishman Lucien had spoken of, the Englishman who shared the leadership with the Marquis, the leadership Pierre envied and wanted for himself? I was crazy, I told myself, I was letting my thoughts run into melodrama. It was over seven years ago. Such hatreds do not endure . . . unless it meant that my father was coming back, that something new was being planned, something only he with England's backing could set in motion. Oh, if only Lucien would return so that I could question him. There was so much I didn't know.

I looked around me and realized that we had already reached the olive groves. Soon we would be home. I must pull myself together, become again Mademoiselle Rainier, the quiet sensible governess. When we rode under the archway, we saw two strange horses tethered in the court-yard. The stable lad who came to take our bridles jerked his head towards the house.

'Madame has visitors.'

Louis slid out of the saddle and raced ahead. I followed him up the steps. He stopped short in the doorway of the living-room. Martine was there, sitting very upright in the big carved chair with Nicole beside her. There were two men facing her. One of them, short and stocky, with a broad pleasant face, was shifting uneasily from foot to foot. The other was tall and very thin; a grey man with grey hair, grey moustache, grey skin. There was nothing conspicuous about him until he turned to look at me, when I was conscious of a glance so penetrating and shrewd that a faint shiver of apprehension ran through me.

Martine said calmly, 'This is my younger son with his governess. Would you take Louis upstairs and get him ready for supper, Mademoiselle?'

'Yes, Madame.' I turned to go, but the grey man raised his hand.

'One moment. I would like a word with this young lady if you please.'

Martine hesitated. 'Very well, though I do not think she can add anything to what I have already told you. She has only been with us for a few days. Louis, go to your room.'

'But I don't want to go, Maman, I want to tell you . . . we met a man.'

The grey man was on it like a flash. 'What man?'

The boy looked at him with dislike. 'Oh just a man. He stopped me from picking up a snake . . . as if I would do a silly thing like that!'

'Louis, will you please go, at once!'

The sharpness of his mother's tone was so unexpected that the child hesitated, but I caught an imploring glance from Martine and put my hand on his shoulder.

'Go along. Do as Maman says. I will come up presently.'

When the boy had gone, Martine said evenly, 'Mademoiselle Rainier, may I present Monsieur Charles Guitry,

Chief of Police at Tarascon and his assistant, Georges Montaud.'

Both men bowed politely, then the Police Chief turned to me. 'When did you arrive, Mademoiselle?'

'It will be a week tomorrow.'

'From Paris?'

'Yes. From Passy.' I had remembered my lessons with Lucien.

'Alone?'

'No, Monsieur de Fontenay was kind enough to escort me.'

'I see.'

Martine said coldly, 'Is this interrogation necessary, Monsieur Guitry?'

I don't think she was conscious of it, but her manner had all the imperiousness of a great lady. She might have been addressing a cheating tradesman or a servant who had misbehaved and it was a mistake. I knew the grey man resented it with every fibre of his being though the only outward sign was the added edge in his quiet tone.

'News has come through to us from Paris that a certain young Englishwoman disappeared from the hotel in which she was temporarily confined by General Bonaparte's order. It is thought that she may be a spy.'

'An English spy?' replied Martine with incredulous contempt.

'Yes, Madame, an English spy. So you must understand that my orders are to enquire into the arrival of any stranger, no matter how apparently innocent.'

'What possible connection can there be between such a person and the daughter of my old friend, and what can she know of this other matter that you are investigating?'

'Maybe nothing, maybe a great deal, who can tell? I would like to remind you, Madame la Marquise, that some years ago your late husband was executed for treason against the republic and you and your son Lucien were only released from prison through the clemency of General Bonaparte.'

Martine had risen to her feet, green eyes blazing in her pale face. 'Do you need to bring that up now? Have we ever infringed our oath?'

'I hope not, Madame, I certainly hope not. Monsieur de

Labran is greatly respected round here. I would not wish to distress him. I too thought the episode was closed, but it seems that we are mistaken. Certain information has reached us.'

'What information?'

'That I am not at liberty to disclose to you, but I have been sent back here to investigate it and I do not find it easy to forget that three of my men were murdered on the night that cursed Englishman and his fellow prisoner escaped.' His glance swept round at us. 'I would be glad if you would bear that in mind, all three of you, and report to us anything, anything at all unusual that comes to your notice. And now I bid you good-day.'

He strode out of the room and Georges Montaud turned to follow him. At the door he paused, looking back awkwardly as if he would have liked to excuse his chief's brusqueness, then he shrugged his shoulders hopelessly and went through the door.

'Go after them, Nicole, see them leave. I don't want the servants upset.'

'If you wish.' Nicole crossed to the door. There was a tiny smile on her face almost as if the unpleasant little scene had amused her. Then she too went out closing the door behind her.

Martine sank down again in the chair, her face buried in her hands, but after an instant she looked up at me, trying to smile.

'Forgive me, Emma, but that man brings back memories, terrible ones.'

I moved to her quickly. 'What did he mean? What does he suspect? Is it I who have brought this trouble on you?'

'No, it isn't you, Emma. I think he used you only as an added weapon to attack me. But you heard what he said. He is like a hunter who cannot endure that his prey should escape him.'

'But it is so long past.'

'Some men have long memories. He was blamed for the escape of his prisoners. He has had years to brood over the defeat that lost him his promotion. He will not rest until he has taken his revenge. The very fact that he has been sent back here makes me afraid.'

'You mean that the whole business is starting up again.'

She gave me a quick glance. 'I don't know, Emma, I don't know. I should not say this, Lucien's father would never have forgiven me. To him, the King's cause was sacred. He died for it, but you don't know what it is like to live in fear for those you love. And not only I but the whole village here. There was not a cottage that did not tremble for a father or a brother or a son. I don't care what happens to France. I don't care what happens to the fat old Bourbon in England. I only want those who are dear to me to live out their lives in peace.'

I had never seen her so distraught and behind it I guessed that there was something more, something that I didn't yet understand. The brown mocking face of Pierre rose up in front of me like a threat and I could find no words to comfort her.

When I came down to supper that evening, the first person I saw was Lucien and I was angry with myself because just to see him again gave me such intense pleasure. I had deliberately not allowed myself to think about what Pierre had said and now to my annoyance I found I was watching Nicole's every glance and Lucien's response to it as if my life depended on it. Not that he treated her any differently than he did me or anyone. There was no opportunity to speak with him alone and the conversation round the supper table was general.

Lucien had brought important news. Marseilles was seething with excitement. War had been officially declared. British ships which had unfortunately been delayed in the harbour had been seized and their crews promptly interned.

'They say every port between here and Calais is being galvanized into action. Barges are being assembled and men gathered to man them. It appears that Bonaparte is determined to invade England before the end of summer.'

So it was really going to happen; it was true what Pierre had said. It did not seem possible and how could a few men with their puny efforts prevent that fiery little man from carrying out his threats? I was surprised at the flood of anger that swept through me. It was my country after all. How dare he believe that a single Frenchman would be allowed to land on England's shores! I opened my mouth to say so and shut it again. Mademoiselle Rainier would not have felt any such thing. I kept my eyes steadily fixed on my plate.

'There was a Sergeant of the Guards drumming up recruits already in the Place Victor,' Lucien was saying. 'He was not having much success.'

'The men of Marseilles have always thought more of their bellies than of winning military glory,' remarked Henri de Labran cynically, 'and quite right too.'

'I wish I had been there,' said Armand enviously. 'You have all the luck, Lucien. I might have been tempted to take the colours myself.'

'You will do nothing of the kind, my boy.' There was a note of sternness in his father's voice. 'Let them fight their own wars. We want none of it here. We cultivate our soil. We supply the oil, the wine and the bulls. Let Bonaparte try and make himself master of Europe if he must, we keep ourselves to ourselves.'

It was not a heroic statement but it had something to be said for it. I remembered reading somewhere that Provence had always maintained a sturdy independence of all political changes.

'What about you, Lucien?' Nicole gave him her sideways look. 'Weren't you tempted?'

Something in her tone, a slight edge of scorn, irritated me. I said quickly, 'At the Tuileries, Bonaparte offered Lucien a commission in his Guards,' and then I could have bitten out my tongue for my stupidity. They all stared at me.

'How do you know? Were you there?' asked Armand.

Louise Rainier whose grandfather and father had died under the guillotine would never have been present at any such reception. I said lamely, 'Lucien told me about it.'

'Did you, Lucien? I wonder why,' murmured Nicole sweetly.

He did not answer. What devil had tempted me to remind him of that humiliating incident?

'And you didn't accept!' exclaimed Armand disgustedly. 'You must have been out of your mind. Think of the fun you could have had. Why, in a few years, you might have become one of his Marshals, like Junot.'

'Far more likely he would have been lying in his grave like his father,' said Martine with extreme bitterness.

'Haven't we seen enough of death and glory for one lifetime?'

There was silence for a moment, then Henri de Labran began to talk about the vineyards. It seemed that a new pest had begun to attack the grapes. The best means of eradicating it were far more important to him than the war into which his country was soon to be plunged.

After we had eaten and the coffee was being served, Lucien found an opportunity to come to my side. 'Wait for me in the garden,' he whispered. 'I must speak with you.'

Outside it was still light but deliciously cool after the heat. I walked down the path to where a stone seat had been placed under a great cedar. The sweet spicy smell still lingered. White moths fluttered against my face as I leaned my head against the trunk and closed my eyes. It had been a wearying day. I had only been there for a few minutes when Lucien came to sit beside me. Under the tree it was shadowy but I could see the frown on his face.

'I thought it would be easy, but I was wrong,' he said. 'I should never have brought you here.'

'Why? What has happened?'

'There is not a chance of getting you out of France. I tried every source I could think of, indirectly of course, I could not do it openly, but regulations have been tightened. At the moment a mouse couldn't get through without an official pass signed and countersigned by Bonaparte himself.'

I should have felt dismay at his failure, but instead a little thrill ran through me because now, without any volition of my own, I should have to stay. I had no choice.

Lucien was looking at me. 'I did everything I could, I swear I did, Emma. Mother told me about Charles Guitry coming here. You mustn't be frightened. He cannot suspect you.'

'I'm not afraid.'

'I feel so guilty.'

'Why?'

'It was madness to bring you here. I might have known what would happen, but you were so desperate to get back to England and to your father. You would have done better to have remained with Victor Jarrett. He might have been more useful than I.'

'Do you want me to go so much?'

'Why do you ask that?'

'But do you?' I persisted.

'You know I don't,' he said angrily. 'All the time I was going from tavern to tavern on the waterfront, talking to this man and that, I was praying that I would fail and when I realized it was hopeless, I was glad, do you hear, glad for my sake, not for yours.'

'Then if my being here is not dangerous for your mother or for Louis, I am glad too.'

'You are?' He stretched out a hand and turned my face towards him. 'Do you mean that, Emma?'

'Yes.'

'We are crazy, both of us. You know that, don't you?'

'Yes.'

'Oh God, I'm a fool, but I don't care.' He leaned forward and kissed me gently on the lips. I had longed for it so much that I trembled at his touch. We were quite still for an instant, just staring at one another, so close there was no need for words. I had known it from the first moment I had seen him again at the Tuileries. I wondered if he had too.

I smiled before I said lightly, 'What will Nicole say?'

He jerked away. 'What has Nicole to do with this?'

'Aren't you going to marry her?'

'No.' He made a violent gesture. 'No, it is not true.'

'She loves you, doesn't she?'

'Why should she? Nicole will be rich one day. Many men have wanted to marry her.'

'But no one like you.'

'I'm no bargain for anyone, Emma, that is why I . . .' he broke off. 'Who told you about this? Was it Nicole herself?'

'No. It was Pierre.'

He swung round. 'Pierre? Where did you see him? When?'

'This afternoon when Louis took me up to that savage rocky place—Les Baux, do you call it?'

'What in God's name made him take you there?'

'He wanted to show me his lizards. I hope he doesn't put one in my bed.'

Lucien smiled reluctantly. 'Louis never plays tricks on

95

those he likes.' Then he was very serious. 'What did Pierre say to you?'

'Lucien, he knows who I am. He knows all about us. Who is he? Was he once working with your father? You must tell me.'

'Yes, he was. Afterwards he escaped to England.'

'Was it my father he had come to see in Cornwall?'

Lucien was not looking at me. He said, 'Now I believe it must have been but then he told me nothing. Pierre has never trusted me with his secrets. At that time I did not even know of your father's existence, or of you . . .'

'Except as a grubby little stable boy . . .'

He turned to look at me. 'With the most beautiful eyes in the world . . .'

'You did not think that then.'

'Yes, yes, I did, but more than ever now.'

It was sweet to hear him say it, but I had to know more. 'Why was Pierre returning to France?'

Again Lucien hesitated. 'He told me it was simply because he wanted to take advantage of Bonaparte's amnesty granted to all rebels. A great many of those who emigrated at the revolution have come back and made their peace with him.'

'But that was not Pierre's real reason, was it?'

Lucien did not answer directly. 'Emma, listen to me,' he said urgently. 'You must not be afraid. I am going to keep you out of Pierre's intrigues, do you hear? I will not let any of it touch you or my mother. I know what it is like to live in perpetual fear.'

A tiny voice inside me said warningly, 'Dear Lucien, you do not know James Tremayne. If he does come here, then he will involve you, me, all of us, if it suits his purpose, and we will obey him willingly because he is what he is.' But I would not heed it. After all I could be wrong. Would my father have been so determined to escape out of France if he intended to return? I said, 'I will do whatever you say, Lucien.'

He took my hand, holding it for a moment before he kissed it. 'We had better go in. They will wonder what has become of you.'

When we came into the living-room, Nicole and Armand were sitting together in the window playing some card game. Henri de Labran was half asleep in his big chair with one of the dogs at his feet, its head resting on his knee. Martine was working on the altar cloth. I knelt down by the tapestry frame to examine the tiny stitches. She had embroidered the figure of a girl with red-brown hair carrying a basket out of which tumbled roses, cream and crimson and gold.

'She is St Rosseline de Villeneuve,' said Martine, 'one of our local saints. She was devoted to helping the poor, but she had a tyrant of a father who detested her charity. One day when she was carrying a basket of loaves to the starving peasants, he stopped her and demanded to know what she had in her basket. "Roses," she lied desperately. He snatched the basket away from her, but when he opened it, it was indeed filled with roses.'

'What a delightful story.'

'She looks like you,' said Lucien examining it critically.

'I am afraid that I would never be so courageous.'

It was such a peaceful domestic scene, it was hard to remember that in Paris plans were going forward for a bloody war and hidden somewhere in the rocky caves of Les Baux, a few desperate men were plotting how to prevent it by robbery, violence and murder.

Chapter 8

It was not Louis but Lucien who showed me the black bulls of the Camargue. It was towards the end of June. I had been at Villeroy more than four weeks and since Guitry's visit the days had passed so quietly that sometimes I almost forgot that at any moment our peace could be shattered. That afternoon Lucien came into the room where I was sitting with Nicole and Louis and said quietly, 'I have an errand to do for my stepfather. Would you care to ride with me, Emma, and see something of the Camargue?'

Nicole looked up. For an instant I thought she was going to suggest that she came with us and my heart sank, but she contented herself with saying, 'I warn you, Emma, you won't enjoy it. It is hot as an oven and you'll be tormented by mosquitoes.'

'I don't mind. I like the sun.'

Louis had jumped up at once. 'Can I come too?'

'No,' said Lucien. 'It is lesson time. We'll take you with us as far as the village.'

'You promised that I should show Bernardo to Mademoiselle Emma.'

'Well, this time you can't.' Lucien was very firm. 'It's too far for you to ride.'

I put my arm round the boy's shoulders. 'Never mind, Louis, you shall take me another day.'

We were ready in a few minutes and we rode out towards the village leaving Louis outside the Curé's little stone house. Etienne Michel had come to the door. He said briskly, 'Run along inside, child, and wait for me.' Reluctantly the boy went into the schoolroom, his books under his arm.

The Curé was a small wiry man with a face like wrinkled brown leather and shrewd black eyes that moved from me to Lucien. I had seen him on Sundays when I accompanied Martine to mass. My father had never been a church-going man and I had felt awkward and ill at ease during the unfamiliar Catholic service. I was sure that Father Michel was aware of it, but now he looked up at me, his hand on my bridle.

'Won't you come in, Mademoiselle Rainier? I don't think you have seen our one and only treasure. The barbarians did not leave us much, but there is one thing they forgot.'

I would far rather not have done so, but it seemed churlish not to accept the little man's invitation. I glanced at Lucien and he nodded. While he tethered the horses, I followed the Curé through the narrow door of the tower. We climbed up a flight of twisting crumbling steps and then were in a round room. Light filtered through a small window where the glass had long been smashed.

The complete wall was covered by a painting. It must have been very old, the colours were fading, but the outlines were still quite clear. Pope, king, knight and lady, bishop and peasant moved together in a stately pavane, each one hand-in-hand with a spectral skeleton figure through whose garments showed clearly the bones and the grinning skull. Unaware of their doom, they were dancing a measure with death. It had a grim reality and, despite the heat, I shivered.

'It must have been painted during one of the visitations of the Black Death in the Middle Ages,' the Curé was saying. 'I have often wondered how the murderers missed it during the revolution. They destroyed everything else they found. Maybe it frightened even them. After all that was what we were all doing for a great number of years, performing a dance with death. Your father knew all about that, Lucien.'

There was a sour bitterness in the priest's voice and suddenly I did not want to stay there with the macabre picture, the savagery in the little man's voice, the look of torment on Lucien's face and the terrifying knowledge that soon it could all begin again. I mumbled something and was glad to escape out of the room into the fresh air and the strong clean sunlight.

'You mustn't mind Father Michel,' said Lucien as we

trotted down the track. 'He has an obsession about it. He can never forget what they did to his church or to him. They caught him once and tortured him. That is why he limps so badly.'

He looked disturbed and I asked no questions. I was content to ride beside him. Up until then my father had filled my life. I had never known before the enchantment of being in love, the simple joy of just being with the beloved one, hearing his voice, feeling the touch of his hand.

We took the road through Arles and out into that strange desolate beautiful delta of the Rhône which is called the Camargue. The track wound through waist-high reeds fringing the marshes. They swayed in a gentle wind rippling like the waves of an inland sea. Lucien pointed out the copses of stunted trees leaning perilously sideways tormented by the force of the winter mistral and the white-walled thatched huts where the *gardiens* live out their lonely lives, sometimes remaining for weeks without coming into the towns. Once I saw a herd of wild white horses, their flowing manes and tails blown out behind them like an antique frieze against the blue sky. Presently the great stretch of the lagoon, the Etang de Vaccarès, stretched in front of us shimmering like a mirage in the burning heat of the sun and there I saw the bulls for the first time, a huge herd of them knee-deep in the water, clouds of flies buzzing above their curved horns. There were birds too, the sunset-pink of flamingos with their slender snakelike necks and curved beaks.

While I stood entranced, we heard the trot of hooves and Henri de Labran came round the lagoon with a young man close behind him.

'Well, Mademoiselle Emma,' he said jovially, 'how do you like my bulls, eh? We have been picking out the most likely for the Courses à la Cocarde. There is not long to go now.'

'What exactly happens, Monsieur de Labran?'

'Hasn't Lucien told you? Here in the Camargue we fight our bulls with roses, not with swords.'

'With roses?'

'You think I am making fun. No, I assure you. In Carcassonne, in Madrid, the corrida brings death to the bulls, sometimes even to the matador, but here in Provence we cannot bear to kill our beautiful bulls. So we bind a rosette to his brow between the horns and it is only the bravest and the most skilful who is able to outwit him and snatch it from his forehead.'

I suppose I looked my astonishment because he laughed. 'And if you think that is easy, then believe me, you are quite wrong. Our little bulls are full of spirit and their horns are sharp as razors. Marius, show the lady what Bernardo did to you at last year's Course.'

Blushing the young man rolled up his coarse blue shirt and I shuddered at the long white scar curving just below his navel.

'Ah, Bernardo is the cunning one, but this time you will win, eh, my boy?' went on Henri de Labran.

'I shall do my best, Patron.'

'There, you see. These lads are born it it.' He turned to Lucien. 'Where are you going to take Mademoiselle Emma? Down to the sea?'

'I should like to but we ought to be going back. There is a great deal to be done. There are the monthly accounts . . .'

'Nonsense,' exclaimed his stepfather. 'Take a holiday, boy. You drive yourself too hard. I've told you more than once. There is no need.'

He waved his hand to us as we trotted round the edge of the lagoon. It was true; Lucien did drive himself hard and I thought I knew why. His proud spirit would not let him rest under an obligation to his mother's husband. He had to earn his keep in the only way he knew.

When we reached the beach, I reined in my horse exclaiming in pure delight. A deep blue sea lapped milk-soft on the white sand. A few small fishermen's huts were clustered together baking under the sun, their boats and nets drawn up outside. A little copse of tamarisks, their trunks glowing pink in the brilliant light, gave us a patch of shade.

I said, 'Oh how I wish I could strip off all my clothes and swim in that wonderful sea.'

Lucien smiled as he tethered the horses. 'You can if you wish. I promise I'll turn my back.'

I sighed. 'I haven't the courage. I did it once at Trevira

and one of our neighbours saw me. He was so shocked, it caused quite a scandal and he complained to my father.'

'And what did he say?'

'He laughed his head off, but all the same he warned me that you outrage convention at your peril,' I said ruefully. 'It was he who taught me to swim.'

'Is there anything that he did not teach you?'

There was an odd note in his voice that I had never heard before. He is jealous, I thought, jealous of my affection for my father and it gave me a queer feeling of happiness that he should care so much.

Lucien moved restlessly away, then suddenly he swung round, smashing his fist savagely against the trunk of the tree. 'Why don't you say what you are thinking? You despise me, don't you? Just as Nicole does; Father Michel too with his damned dance of death, throwing my father in my face!'

I was disturbed by the violence of his outburst. I said, 'Why should I think anything? You are yourself. You don't have to be what others want you to be.'

He was looking away from me, out towards the shining ripple of the sea. 'What should I do, Emma? Accept and play safe as my stepfather does or turn rebel and murderer, avenge my father, choose my cause, go out and fight for it?'

'And die for it,' I thought and knew why Martine felt so bitterly about men and their heroic dreams. It seemed to me then that Lucien was arguing with himself. I wondered not for the first time if he, the last of a long line of fighting ancestors, was bitterly frustrated, compelled for his mother's sake to live as he did under his stepfather's rule and I longed to give him comfort.

'I don't despise you,' I said and looked up into his stormy face. 'Lucien, would it shock you very much if I were to take off my boots and stockings and walk into the lovely cool sea?'

He stared at me for an instant as if I had gone raving mad, then he burst out laughing and dropped on his knees beside me. 'You're so good for me, Emma. You bring me down to earth, make me sound like the windbag I am. I'll take off your boots for you.'

'No,' I said. 'Shut your eyes and I'll do it myself.'

He smiled and did as he was told, but when I had stripped off my stockings, he turned to me again, taking my bare feet in both his hands, an urgent note in his voice.

'Why don't you despise me, Emma?'

'That's a silly question.'

'No, it isn't. I want to know, I must know.'

'Can't you guess?'

His grip tightened. Then he pulled me towards him. His kisses were not gentle this time. They were fierce and demanding and I wanted them passionately.

When at last I was able to draw away, I said shakily, 'I'm going down to the sea.' I got unsteadily to my feet, took a few steps and collapsed with a wail. The sand was red-hot to my bare feet.

Lucien roared with laughter at my indignation. 'You're such a child, Emma,' he said, and without more ado he picked me up bodily and carried me to the water's edge.

The absurdity had relieved the tension. We laughed like children as I splashed through the deliciously cool water, both of us far too occupied with each other to notice the black cloud that had come up from nowhere and swallowed the sun. The rain came down so suddenly, so devastatingly that it set us laughing again as we ran up the beach, snatching up my boots and stockings and taking refuge in one of the cottages where the fisherman's wife exclaimed in horror at my bare muddy feet.

The rain stopped as suddenly as it had come and the sun shone as brilliantly as before. We wandered along the dazzling white sand, so lost in one another's company that the hours flew by and it was evening before we rode back. In the west the sky was a tender flamingo pink and a hush had come over the Camargue except for the clicking of the cicadas and an occasional throaty croak from one of Louis' frogs. In the marshes the black cattle stood dreaming, chewing the cud after the heat of the day. Fantastic birds with brilliant plumage gathered at the edges of the lagoons.

'What are they?' I asked in wonder, and Lucien pointed them out to me; purple herons with long stick-like legs, bee-eaters flashing through the reeds in chestnut and iridescent green, orioles glowing like golden lamps in the dark cypresses.

It had been a magical day and I suppose our happiness showed too plainly in our faces when we came late to supper. I did not think of it then, but afterwards I wondered if it was that evening when Nicole began to suspect the truth.

The Courses à la Cocarde took place just over a week later. Louis was wild with excitement. For the first time he was to be allowed to go with us to watch his favourites in the bull ring. On the evening before he was very hard to get to bed and for once his stepfather was stern with him, threatening to forbid him the trip if he didn't obey his mother instantly. I woke up out of a deep sleep the next morning to see him perched on the end of my bed asking if it wasn't time to get up. I yawned and groped for my watch.

'Go back to bed, Louis. It is not yet five o'clock.'

'The birds are up already ... listen!'

Outside my window a lark was singing its heart out to the dawn. 'We are not birds,' I said firmly. 'Now go and lie down or you will be so tired, you will fall asleep in the middle, and think what a pity that would be.'

He went reluctantly, dragging his feet, but it was not easy to snuggle down and go back to sleep. A tiny knot of anxiety had tightened inside me. The evening before, Henri de Labran had mentioned that Charles Guitry would be posting more men than usual in the village and the fairground.

'Why?' asked Martine. 'Is he expecting trouble?'

'It's that damned recruiting sergeant Lucien saw in Marseilles. He has been going from place to place trying to drum up recruits and he is not popular.'

'He's a drunken brute,' said Lucien. 'In St Rémy he molested one of the girls and was kicked out of the town for his pains.'

There was no reason why it should worry me and yet somehow it did.

The Courses à la Cocarde were a day of holiday for everyone. I went in the carriage with Martine and Nicole, Louis squeezed between us, and when we arrived on the open space where an arena had been fenced off and I saw the crowd of happy people intent only on enjoying themselves, it was hard to believe that any violence could spoil the atmosphere of gaiety and good humour.

There were seats placed for visitors such as ourselves, but everyone else just pushed and scrambled for the best position they could find. It was then that I noticed for the first time how different Lucien and his mother were from the others gathered there. Tall, slender, bright-haired, they were like foreigners among the short dark volatile men and women of Provence. Martine was greeted with respect, but though Henri de Labran was the master, the patron, he was still one of them and they laughed and joked with him and Armand.

Louis dragged me off at once to look at Bernardo. The big bull was the star of the afternoon. He stood in his pen, his great head swaying from side to side, fierce little eyes gleaming balefully at us. His hide had been polished till it shone like black ebony; a scarlet rosette of ribbon with white tassels was fastened between the wicked-looking horns.

Here and there amongst the crowd were men in fantastic dress wearing masks that almost completely covered their faces. I saw a devil with tiny horns and grinning mouth, a pig, a wolf and a fox with pointed ears and sharp snout.

'They are the mummers,' said Louis, dragging his eyes reluctantly from his favourite bull to answer my question. 'They will be acting their play this evening, but Maman will not let me stay for it.'

When the entertainment began, I found to my surprise that it was almost unbearably exciting. My father had told me once of a bullfight he had watched in Madrid and I had felt sickened at his description of the picadors on their pitiful old horses with the blood and the killing. But this was something entirely different. Undoubtedly there was sufficient danger to provide thrills, but it was spiced with gaiety and laughter. The crowd cheered the bull almost as much as they did their own champions, expertly luring him this way and that, and as he lunged past them, snatching at the rosette on his forehead before they raced triumphantly for the barrier. When they succeeded, the applause was deafening and they tossed the scarlet rose in the air before throwing it to some blushing girl among the spectators.

By the end of the afternoon the only bull to remain undefeated was Bernardo despite repeated attempts by Marius, anxious to redeem his failure of the year before. Bernardo was led back to his pen still wearing the ribbon on his black forehead.

It was later when the ground was being cleared for the dancing that I missed Louis. He had been jumping up and down in his seat divided between disappointment and pride in his favourite's success. At first I thought he might be with his mother or Lucien, but when I went in search of him, he was nowhere to be found. Nicole was surrounded by a group of young men and shrugged her shoulders when I asked her.

'You know what he is like. He's run off somewhere just to make a nuisance of himself.'

'I thought I saw him going towards the bull pens,' suggested Georges Montaud helpfully. I had guessed already that he was one of Nicole's most fervent admirers.

I looked at Lucien. Both of us had only one thought in our minds as we pushed our way through the crowds. Martine caught us up.

She said anxiously, 'Have you found him?'

'Not yet, but don't worry, Mother, we will. You stay here.' But she came with us, heedless of her long muslin skirts dragging in the dust and dirt.

As we came up to the bull enclosures, we saw him. Louis was inside the pen with Bernardo, quite unafraid, and trying to coax the great beast to lower its head so that he might seize the rosette. The bull, already disturbed and angry, bellowed and made a lunge at the child. He dodged aside just in time and I heard Martine catch her breath.

'I'm going in,' said Lucien. 'I'll try and divert the bull's attention and you call to Louis, Emma. Don't frighten him too much, just get him out somehow.'

He tore off his coat and leaped into the pen. Dazzled by the flash of the blue coat, Bernardo hesitated and then went after it and I leaned over the fence calling to Louis. 'This way, darling. Come quickly ... this way.'

But the boy was fascinated by the challenge and ran

away from me to the other side, still trying to reach up to the rosette. The bull made another lunge. Lucien was not quite quick enough and the tip of the horn ripped the sleeve of his shirt. I stifled a scream and Martine clutched my arm. The next minute someone else had jumped into the enclosure, a tall broad-shouldered man wearing a devil's mask and carrying a length of scarlet rag. He threw it over the bull's head.

'Take the boy out quickly for God's sake,' he shouted while the big beast threshed wildly from side to side. 'I'll try to hold him.'

Lucien picked up the child swinging him over the fence and then turned back. I saw the two men poised, one each side of the bull, and I had a swift impression that Lucien welcomed the challenge. He threw back his head and laughed. The bull had tossed aside the scarlet cloth. It made a rush at the stranger driving him into a corner of the pen. In another moment the cruel horns could have ripped into him and I held my breath, but Lucien acted quicker than thought. He snatched up his coat, trailing it and drawing the bull's attention to himself. It was all so rapid that I didn't see exactly what happened. Dust flew up in clouds. Bernardo roared furiously and the masked man seemed to leap forward. 'Come on,' he yelled and ran for the fence clearing it in fine style, followed by Lucien, as Bernardo crashed after them bellowing in rage. Then the stranger was standing in front of us holding out the rosette to Louis clasped in his mother's arms.

'For you, *mon brave*,' he said.

Martine had gone chalk white. Her hand tembled so much she dropped the cockade and I stooped to pick it up.

Louis said, 'I tried and tried. How did you do it?'

'Luck of the devil,' said the stranger. The eyes behind the mask looked directly at Lucien. 'I am obliged to you, Monsieur, but for you . . .' he shrugged with a little mocking gesture, then turned on his heel and disappeared among the crowd who had come up to stare and exclaim.

There had been something oddly familiar about the tall figure, something about his voice and the way he held his head. Could it have been Pierre? But he was smaller, slighter. Then my heart gave a great lurch and for an instant I felt dizzy.

'Are you all right?' Lucien had taken hold of my arm.

'Yes, yes, perfectly all right.' It could not be my father, it could not. It was impossible. I was letting my imagination run away with me. He would never have been so foolish. I swallowed convulsively. 'What about Louis? Is he hurt?'

'Not in the slightest. He is cock-a-hoop after the dance he led us,' said Lucien dryly.

Martine was looking down at the rosette. 'There's blood on it. He must have been hurt,' she said in a queer voice. 'Who was he, Lucien?'

'One of the mummers, I suppose, but by God, he was quick.'

'He might have been killed but for you,' I said, still a little shaken.

'Oh I don't know. He seemed well able to take care of himself.' Lucien put an arm around his mother's shoulders. 'Don't look so upset. It's all right now. Louis is safe. I think we had better go back to the carriage.'

Henri de Labran was all concern for his wife who still looked white and distressed. I offered to go back to Villeroy with her, but he shook his head.

'No need, my dear. You stay with Nicole and enjoy yourself. Lucien will look after you. I'll send the carriage back later.'

I had never seen Lucien in such a reckless mood as he was that evening. His coat was filthy and he tossed it in the carriage before it drove off. In white shirt, waistcoat unbuttoned, his hair wild, he looked nothing at all like the grave young Marquis de Fontenay I had met in Paris. We joined the dancers. It was rough going over the stony ground and not like anything I had known in England. I did not know the steps but Lucien swung me into the country dances and no one seemed to mind when I stumbled and went wrong. We were stamping and rocking with all the other couples and when in the hurly-burly I was flung into his arms, he laughed as he kissed me. Armand waved to us as we whirled by. Nicole was dancing too. I wondered if she was angry that I had stolen her partner. Once when we stood together panting, I saw the men dancing together, a long swaying line, arms linked, and among the fishermen and peasants was the devil-mask and knowing how they resented foreigners, it seemed to me impossible that it could be my father hidden behind the disguise.

It was much later when I first began to realize that something was wrong. It was Bonaparte's recruiting sergeant who started it. He was a clumsy ox of a man and he was already very drunk. He lurched out of the tavern shouting at some of the young men, shaking his fist in their faces, jeering at them, calling them, 'Pigs, cowards, poltroons!'

At first they laughed at him, then they began to grow angry. Marius was there, drinking with his friends. Annoyed at the insults he gave the sergeant a push. The man stumbled and swung round, his face ugly. He hit out savagely and Marius fell backwards. He got to his feet, blood oozing from a split lip.

'Bull-fighter!' sneered the soldier and spat.

It touched Marius on the raw. He hurled himself at the sergeant. The other men closed in.

Lucien said, 'Marius is going to be in trouble and Henri won't like it. I think I had better try to stop it.'

'They won't listen to you. Much better leave it to the police.'

'They're taking good care to keep out of it. Look at them! Not stirring a finger. This is a local affair and they are from Tarascon. They don't want to be involved. Stay here, Emma.'

He plunged into the knot of men. I heard him shout something before he disappeared and suddenly I was very frightened. The dancing had stopped, but the music went on. On the fringe people gathered, staring at the heaving struggling mass where men had begun to fight in earnest, the only sound the animal grunts and the sickening thud of blows.

It was all over very quickly and it was Charles Guitry who brought it to an end. He came striding into the midst of it, his sharp voice summoning his men so that, shame-faced, they followed him as he forced his way among the fighters. As if by magic, that struggling mass opened up before him. On the ground lay the fat sergeant, ominously still, a knife half buried in his back.

The police chief looked down at him and then round at the ring of sullen faces. 'Is he dead?'

No one spoke or moved until the Curé limped forward and knelt down. After a moment he looked up. 'Quite dead,' he said and held out the knife.

Guitry took it between finger and thumb. 'Who struck the blow?' Again there was silence, then the priest stood up.

'Knives like that are used by everyone from here to Marseilles,' he said quietly.

The police chief's eyes travelled slowly from one to the other. They rested for a moment on Lucien and then moved to the man in the devil-mask.

'Take off that bauble,' he said harshly. 'I want to see every face.'

I felt stifled. I waited breathlessly while the brown hands fumbled with the fastenings, then slowly pushed up the painted mask to show not the face I dreaded to see, but Mouton's sheepish grin. I knew at once it was not what the Chief had expected.

He said angrily, 'What the devil are you doing masquerading in that nonsense?'

'It was a joke, Monsieur, just a little joke. No harm meant,' Mouton grinned stupidly.

Exasperated, Guitry snapped, 'Get out of my sight, fool. One of you is guilty.'

'It could have been an accident,' said the priest quietly.

'Do you expect me to believe that? Which one of you killed him?' His glance came back to Lucien. 'What about you, Monsieur de Fontenay? What do you know?'

'Nothing. I was simply trying to stop it before it went too far.'

'I wonder.' He clicked his fingers and two of the gendarmes came forward. He waved his hand to the body. 'Take him away.' Again his eyes went round the ring of faces. 'A man has been murdered. Don't think I shall let it remain there.' The men began to shuffle away, Lucien with them, but Guitry stopped him with a gesture. 'One moment. I would like a word with you.'

'Why with me?'

'Never mind why. Come with me, if you please.' He followed his men who were carrying the dead sergeant into the inn.

Lucien hesitated and then shrugged his shoulders. 'You had better wait here, Emma.'

'No. I'm coming with you.'

We went into the inn together. It was dark in there and stiflingly hot. Curious eyes watched as the dead man was carried into an inner room and laid on a bench. Already flies buzzed above the spreading stain of blood. Guitry kicked the door shut and looked across at Lucien broodingly.

'I am not a fool, neither am I easy to deceive, Monsieur de Fontenay. This is no accident. It is part of a plan, a plan to cause disruption by robbery and murder and it is not only here, it is spreading all through the Midi.'

'What has all this to do with me?' answered Lucien woodenly.

'That is for you to say. Sooner or later I shall lay my hands on these traitors to France.'

'Traitors to France, Monsieur Guitry, or traitors to Napoleon Bonaparte?'

'A nice distinction, Monsieur le Marquis, too nice,' said Guitry ironically. 'But General Bonaparte *is* France and the sooner that is recognized, the better for all of us. The next time this happens, I shall take hostages. You know what that means. They will pay with their lives for those who commit murder and hide behind their fellow men.'

'And you call me in here to tell me that?'

'No, there is something else, something you should know.' I think at that moment both of them had forgotten me as I stood by the door. They faced one another across the dead body on the bench. 'I have every reason to believe that the man responsible for these murderous outrages is an Englishman.'

Lucien raised his head. 'Are you certain?'

'He is clever and up to now though we know he is here somewhere, he is always gone before we can lay a finger on him.'

'Who is he?'

'He hides under more than one name but of one thing we are sure, he is the same man who operated here seven years ago.' The police chief paused and I saw his eyes glitter in the shadows. 'He is the same man who to save his own skin betrayed your father to his death, Monsieur de Fontenay, and then to our great shame, escaped back to England.'

My heart beat so thickly that I had to put a hand on the wall to steady myself. It was not my father ... it could not be ... I wouldn't believe it. And yet it was only a few hours since I had been almost sure that it had been he concealed beneath the devil-mask. I don't think I ever prayed so hard for anything as I prayed then that I was mistaken.

Lucien was silent for a moment then he said quietly, 'Is this the truth?'

Guitry was watching him intently. 'The truth as I see it.'

'Why tell me now, after all these years?'

'When it happened, you were little more than a boy. There was no point in distressing you or your mother more than necessary.'

I saw the twist of contempt on Lucien's lips. 'I have never believed compassion to be part of your policy, Monsieur Guitry. I think you tell me now in the hope that I will help you to trace this man.'

'I would prefer to regard it as a warning. The man is a double traitor, a traitor to you and your mother, a traitor to France. Surely that must mean something to you.'

'Perhaps and perhaps not. But if you think I can lead you to this man or to anyone linked with him, then you are mistaken. I took an oath when I was released from prison and I have kept it.'

'Up to now, Monsieur de Fontenay, but sometimes I wonder if you act a part and there are others, close to you, who have not been so discreet.'

Lucien's mouth tightened. 'You can make what accusations you please, but you have no proof. I work on my stepfather's estates and I know nothing of such matters.'

'I am glad to hear it, but whether we like it or not, we are all likely to be involved and sooner or later a choice will have to be made. I strongly advise you to remember that.' He looked down frowning at the dead man. 'Now I must dispose of this fool.' He waved his hand in dismissal.

Lucien stared at him for an instant as if undecided

whether to say something more, then he turned and went out. I followed after him.

I think then I understood something of Guitry's motives. Lucien might be dependent on Henri de Labran's charity, but he was still a Fontenay, one of the old aristocracy whom Bonaparte passionately wanted to win to his side. His father's name still meant a great deal to those who clung to old loyalties, particularly here in Provence where resistance to the First Consul was growing every day. Lucien's allegiance to one side or the other could carry great weight.

Outside the inn I touched him on the arm. 'How much do you think he really knows?'

He looked down at me as if he were surprised that I was still there. 'You heard what he said?'

'Yes. Was it the truth?'

'I don't know. It could be.'

It was growing dark now. They were dancing again and I could hear the music and laughter as we stood together in the shadows. Lucien put his hands on my shoulders. In the yellow light from the lantern by the door, his face looked pale and taut.

He said, 'Emma, was it your father who came here seven years ago? Has he come back again now? I have to know. You must see that. Whether I believe Guitry or not, I have to know.'

I told myself that I was not lying. After all I didn't know for certain and whatever my father had done, he would never have betrayed a friend, so I faced him steadily and said what I prayed was the truth.

'No, it was not my father. I am sure of it. He would have told me if it had been.'

He let out a great sigh of relief. 'In there for a moment it seemed to me that it must be so. Thank God, I am wrong.' His grip on my shoulders relaxed. He smiled. 'I'm afraid this wretched affair has rather spoiled our evening. Now I think we should look for Nicole. The carriage will have returned for us.'

We found Nicole with Georges Montaud. She said sweetly, 'So you have not been arrested after all, Lucien. I felt quite sure of it when he took you into the inn.'

'Why should he be arrested?' I answered indignantly.

'Oh Heaven, it was only a jest.' She gave me one of her sideways looks. 'In any case he has an unbreakable alibi. You have been with him the whole evening, haven't you, Emma?'

'What should Monsieur de Fontenay have to do with such an abominable murder?' exclaimed Georges in a shocked voice.

'What indeed? Oh go away, Georges, you think you know everything and you're just a baby. Run after your big chief. I'm tired. I want to go home.'

We said little as the carriage took us back to Villeroy, but unspoken thoughts seemed to hang heavy between all three of us. I had told Lucien no more than the truth, I said to myself, as we jolted over the rough track, but doubt persisted, nagging at me like a poisoned tooth. If that tall man in the devil-mask was indeed my father, then how would Lucien act and what should I do, torn between the two men I loved more than life itself?

Chapter 9

I did not see Martine when we got back late that night, she had already gone to bed, but the next morning she came into the schoolroom after lessons were finished and Louis had run out to play. She smiled at the books spread out on the table.

'Louis is already learning to speak a little English.'

I grimaced as I stacked them together and returned them to the shelf. 'He is beginning to pick out a few words here and there, but I am afraid I've forgotten all the history and geography I ever knew.'

'Never mind. There is plenty of time for that.'

She moved restlessly round the room pausing to pick up the wooden figure of the black bull which Louis liked to carry about with him everywhere.

'You must be thinking I behaved very stupidly yesterday, but the bulls can be savage, Bernardo in particular. The boy could have been killed or maimed for life.'

'I know. My heart was in my mouth too.'

'Louis has no sense of danger at all. It makes me afraid for him sometimes.'

'He is very different from Lucien. Does he take after his father?'

She glanced at me and then away. 'No, François had tremendous courage, but he was never reckless. He took calculated risks. It is Lucien who is most like him, and though he is so much older, he is very fond of Louis.' She put the little bull down carefully. 'It was good of him to bring this for the child. You know, Emma, sometimes I am glad you have been forced to stay here with us. You have been very good for him.'

'For Louis?'

'No, for Lucien.'

I looked at her quickly, wondering if she had guessed at what I felt for him, but she went on almost as if she were speaking to herself rather than me. 'I have never seen him look so happy or heard him laugh so much as he has done these last few weeks. Poor Lucien, he has not had it easy. He has missed out on all the things a young man of his position should have had.'

On some things perhaps, but not all, and the doubt in my mind turned itself into words before I had time to think. 'Is it true that he was once engaged to Nicole?'

She gave me a quick glance. 'Certainly not. Whatever gave you that idea?'

'I don't know. It . . . it is just a feeling I have that . . .'

'That Nicole has some claim on him, is that it?' She paused and then went on quietly. 'When Lucien first came to work for Henri, she was very young still. I suppose he was different from others she had known and as sometimes happens with a young girl, she found him attractive. Lucien had never had a sister and he was lonely and very grateful to her father. Perhaps he was more attentive than he should have been. Now they are not children any longer, but sometimes I think Nicole finds that hard to remember.'

'Are you sorry about it?'

'No,' she said decisively. 'I know that we must forget the past. I know that Lucien has nothing but his title and Nicole is an heiress, but she is not the right girl for him.'

I wondered what she would have said about me if circumstances had been different. I went on tidying away the books and after a moment she turned to me, an odd note of urgency in her voice.

'That man who rescued Louis yesterday . . . have you any idea who he was, Emma?'

'No, not at the time, but afterwards when Monsieur Guitry ordered him to take off the mask, I saw it was Mouton.'

'Mouton! But that is impossible, it could never have been he!' I don't know whether there was relief or disappointment in her tone. 'Are you sure?'

'Quite sure. I was surprised too.'

The wide green eyes scanned my face for a moment before she said slowly, 'If it really was Mouton, then I must ask Henri to speak to him. It was a very brave thing to do. They did not suspect him of this horrible murder?'

'Not any more than anyone else.'

'I wish it had not happened,' said Martine. 'I only hope that none of our people will suffer because of it. Charles Guitry is like one of your English bulldogs. When he gets his teeth into something, he will not let go until he is satisfied.' She put her hand on my arm. 'Be extra careful, my dear, never forget who you are for an instant, and don't trust anyone.'

I understood the need for caution and try as I would, I could not forget the police chief's grim warning to Lucien over the sergeant's dead body, but you cannot always live in a state of tension anticipating danger at every step. You would be a nervous wreck in a week if you did and as the days passed and nothing further happened, I forgot it all too often. A trivial incident brought it all vividly back. One evening at supper I said rashly how much I would prefer to wear breeches for riding especially in the rocky hills round Villeroy which I longed to explore. Nicole turned to look at me and I thought, 'There you go again, my girl, forgetting you are Louise Rainier and talking like Emma Tremayne!' Martine tactfully changed the subject and I thought no more of it until the next morning after breakfast when Armand came in carrying a pair of breeches and a jacket in nut-brown velvet.

'What in heaven's name are you doing with those?' said Nicole sharply.

'I thought Emma might like them.'

'Me?' I exclaimed in surprise.

'What on earth should Emma Louise want with your old clothes?' interrupted Nicole. I had already realized that she had the same possessive attitude towards her brother as she had towards Lucien and her father and I think she resented any small attention Armand paid to me.

The boy turned to me a little crestfallen. 'You did say you fancied dressing up as a boy and I have long outgrown these. I thought they might do; that is if you don't mind . . .' and he glanced from me to Nicole.

'Of course I don't mind,' I said warmly, taking them from him. 'I don't mind what I wear and it is so kind of you to think of it.' He still looked doubtful and Nicole's frown annoyed me so that I went on recklessly. 'Shall I try them on now?'

'Do,' said Lucien amused. 'I can't wait.'

'All right. Turn your backs then, both of you.'

Nicole shrugged her shoulders and began stacking the breakfast dishes while I pulled the breeches up over my muslin gown. The trouble was that Armand was longer in the leg than I as well as being a good deal broader. They nearly reached my ankles while the waistband came up to my armpits. Both young men collapsed into helpless laughter at the sorry spectacle.

'Don't,' I said indignantly. 'It's not fair. I could make them fit easily.'

'You look like a chick just popping out of its shell,' exploded Lucien, 'only with a fluffy red topknot instead of a yellow one.'

'I suppose I remind you of a certain scrubby little boy . . .'

'You do indeed, a very scrubby little boy . . . with beautiful eyes,' he said, feeling in his pocket and tossing me a coin. I caught it neatly and threw it back at him and we laughed together.

'What is all this about?' demanded Armand. 'What is going on between you two?'

'Nothing at all, just a little joke,' said Lucien lightly.

'You know,' went on Armand, sitting on the table and looking me up and down shrewdly. 'I've been thinking for some time that there's more in your coming here than meets the eye.'

'Don't be an ass, Armand.'

'No, Lucien, I am serious. I was quite sure that Mademoiselle Rainier was going to be a very sedate learned young lady and then she turns out to be someone like Emma here. Deuced peculiar.' He put his head on one side studying me gravely. 'A few tucks here and there and she'd make a very presentable boy. What do you think, Lucien?'

'Very presentable indeed. You should have been an actress, Emma. You'd have made a hit in breeches parts.'

I nearly told them that when I was sixteen and first went to the theatre in London, I would have given my soul to be a play-actor until my father laughed me out of such a ridiculous ambition.

Nicole's clear voice broke in on our jesting. She had finished stacking the plates and now rang the bell for the maidservant. 'Who on earth wants to look like a boy? You do have the most extraordinary notions, Emma.'

'It's not what I look like,' I protested. 'It's the freedom it gives you. Haven't you ever wanted to kick off your skirts, Nicole?'

'No, never,' she said with decision and it was true. Nicole had none of my harum-scarum look. Hair, face, dress, were always quite perfect. She sometimes reminded me of a small elegant cat, always exquisitely groomed, velvet paws sheathed but ready at a moment's notice to shoot out and scratch. She went on sweetly, 'I don't know what Madame la Marquise will say if you go out dressed up like a freak.'

'Martine won't mind; why should she?' said Armand gaily. 'I think Emma looks charming.' He put an arm round my shoulders and lightly kissed my cheek. 'Next time we go hunting, we'll take you with us, won't we, Lucien?'

The maid came in then and while I struggled out of my breeches, the two young men went off together. I had picked up the garments and was on my way out of the room when Nicole stopped me.

'Martine is very fond of you, isn't she, Emma?'

'What makes you think so?'

'It is so obvious.'

'Well, after all,' I said remembering caution, 'she and my mother were very old friends.'

'I wonder.'

'What in heaven's name do you mean by that?'

'What I say. I wonder sometimes if you really are Emma Louise Rainier.' She had so taken my breath away that for a moment I was speechless and she went on with her secret little smile. 'Don't worry. I'm not going to do anything about it, not yet.'

'You're being absurd, Nicole. This is absolute nonsense.'

'Is it? It's quite clear to me that you and Lucien and Martine are all busy hiding something from Papa.'

'I thought you liked Lucien.'

Her eyes narrowed. 'What is it to you whether I like him or not? In any case we are not discussing Lucien.'

I rounded on her then. 'Why do you dislike your stepmother so much?'

'Why, why?' and suddenly I saw the claws unsheathed, the long-held bitterness, the jealousy. 'Because she takes everything, everything from my father and gives him nothing.'

'That's not true. They are very happy. He loves her.'

'Oh, yes, he is bewitched. I saw that right from the start.'

'You could only have been a child.'

She gave me a scornful look. 'I was fourteen. We had always been very close, Papa, Armand and I, even more so after my mother died. Then Lucien came to work for Papa and out of pity he went to see her. Oh we all knew about her, the Marquise de Fontenay, living in a cottage, disguised as a peasant and proud as a duchess, soiling the beautiful hands that had never known before how to do a day's work. She was pregnant too.'

'Why should you hold that against her?'

'The Marquis was dead. So who was the father of her child?'

'How can you say such a terrible thing?'

'It was said by a great many people.'

'It was envy, spite . . . it must have been . . .'

'What do you know about it? She acted the grief-stricken widow, she kept him waiting for more than a year, but then she married him and goes on deceiving him.'

'You're lying . . .'

'Am I? Watch her if you don't believe me. Papa doesn't see it. She bewitches him still, but one day he will and when he does,' she paused and smiled before she said calmly, 'when he does, he will kill her and her lover.'

'You should not jest about such things.'

'I am not jesting,' she went straight past me, but at the door she stopped, looking back over her shoulder. 'We are not living at the court of Versailles, Mademoiselle Rainier. In the Midi the honour of the family is still held sacred and we know how to punish.'

The door closed and I stared after her, shocked, refusing to believe any of it. There must have been many who had resented Martine and François de Fontenay, the strangers, the aristocrats who had taken refuge in their village, bringing danger with them, like a disease, like the plague. And Nicole was only a child then, worshipping her own mother and bitterly jealous of her father's love for another woman. It was easy enough to understand, but it could be dangerous too, dangerous for Martine and for all of us. I had been happy at Villeroy, but now the room seemed filled with Nicole's malice and I felt stifled by it. I longed to get out into the air where I could breathe, where I could feel free. I would ask for a horse to be saddled and ride away from the house up into the hills.

But that was easier said than done. There was luncheon to be eaten, a strained meal at which Nicole said nothing. I had never known anyone who could be so silent and yet make her presence felt so strongly. Martine was preoccupied, answering Louis' incessant questions absent-mindedly. I was glad to escape. I rode down to the village with the boy, leaving him with the Curé, and then turned my horse towards the olive groves.

It was some time later when I looked around me and realized that without thinking I must have taken the path I had followed with Louis weeks before. Above me towered the rocky ruins of the castle of Les Baux, the place of stones. The sure-footed little horse picked his way delicately up the path and I let him have his head. It was hot and very still. Here and there lizards basked on the rocks, vanishing instantly at the crunch of Beauregard's hooves. Louis had spoken of the caves where his father had lain hidden and though it was absurd to imagine that Pierre and his band would be rash enough to choose the same place, I had a restless desire to explore further.

I climbed up to where we had left the horses before and to my astonishment found a pony already there tethered in the shade of a little copse of stunted pines. Beauregard whinneyed in greeting as I dismounted and led him to the same spot. I regretted not wearing Armand's breeches but I hitched up my riding skirt and began to climb.

I could see above me a dark hollow that could only be a cave and I made it my target. It was a hot difficult climb, but I had not scrambled up and down the cliffs at Trevira for nothing and I was curious about the horse waiting below. I lost sight of the cave as I went up a steep slope almost on hands and knees, but then as my head came over the ridge, I nearly let go my hold. On the ledge only a short distance away from me stood Martine beside a man whose arm lay familiarly around her shoulders. Everything Nicole had said rushed back into my mind. Even while I watched, I saw him lead her towards the dark narrow opening of the cave.

I should have gone away at once. It was no business of mine what she did. Her life was her own, but she was Lucien's mother and I wanted to know, I had to know. I pulled myself up on to the path and as quietly as I could crept along the ridge. I paused at the edge of the opening. At first the sudden change from light to dark prevented me from seeing anything, but then slowly I began to make things out. Instead of lovers clasped in each other's arms as I had half expected, I saw someone lying on a blanket with Martine kneeling beside him and the man who leaned back against the rocky wall looking down at them was Pierre.

In my surprise I must have made an unwary movement. A piece of rock dislodged itself and fell with a clatter. Pierre whipped round. I saw the gleam of a gun in his hand, then he was beside me, his hand gripping my arm, his surprise as great as my own, until his face broke into the familiar grin.

'*Mon Dieu*, it is lucky for you that I did not fire first. You're alone, I hope. You've not brought the boy with you hunting snakes again.'

'No.'

'Good.' He pulled me inside. 'We have a visitor, Martine.'

She looked up, pale but quite calm. 'How did you find us?'

'I didn't ... I mean I was not looking for you. I was climbing up to explore and I saw the pony ...' then I gasped as the man on the blanket stirred and I saw his face. It was Marius and he had been badly hurt. Blood soaked his shirt and the rough bandage Martine had removed. 'What is it? What has happened?'

'The police came to arrest him last night for the murder

of the sergeant. He resisted and managed to get away but not before he had been wounded.'

'But why Marius? Why he more than the others?'

Pierre shrugged his shoulders. 'It's a damnably clever move on Guitry's part. He has no shadow of proof but the boy is popular and by arresting him he is bound to provoke anger from which he could learn a great deal. Marius should have gone with them. Nothing would have happened to him and what are a few days in prison? But the boy panicked and now it will go against him.'

'He is very bad,' said Martine. 'He needs a doctor.'

'There is no doctor nearer than Tarascon, you know that, and even if he would come, how could we trust him?'

'I will do what I can and I will send word to the Curé. He is skilful with wounds.'

The boy groaned and tried to sit up. Martine gently pushed him back. 'Don't move, Marius. You will only start the bleeding again.'

I was touched with pity for the brown-faced merry young man who had shown off his scar so proudly on the shores of the lagoon. I said impulsively, 'Let me help you. I don't know much about such things, but I am not afraid.'

There was a bowl of water and Martine had brought linen and healing salves. Between us we cleaned and bandaged the wound and then washed the young man's face and hands with the cool water.

When we had made him as comfortable as we could, Martine said, 'I must not stay longer. Etienne Michel will bring some light food this evening. You will take care of him, Pierre?'

'Trust me,' he said lightly. At the entrance when he gave her the basket, he leaned forward and kissed her. 'I know it is damnably selfish of me coming to you for help, but bless you all the same.'

She touched his cheek for a moment, then followed me down the path. We said nothing as we helped each other down the steep track, but when we had freed the horses and were jogging along side by side Martine said quietly, 'Ask your questions, Emma.'

'I don't know that I have any. You see I already know about Pierre. It was he whom Lucien and I met when we came from Paris. I saw him again in these hills when I came up here with Louis. He was your husband's right-hand man, wasn't he, and now he has come back again, only this time he is fighting Bonaparte.'

'Did Lucien tell you all this?'

'Some of it.' I stared straight ahead. 'There is something else which maybe you don't know. I think Nicole believes him to be your lover.'

Martine laughed, a bitter little sound. 'Nicole dislikes me so much, she has to invent crimes to justify her hatred. Do you believe it too, Emma?'

'I don't know. I don't want to believe it.'

'As it happens she is wrong. Pierre is my brother.'

'I don't know why such a simple explanation had never occurred to me. I said, 'But why didn't Lucien tell me?'

'Perhaps he did not want to involve you too much in our family problems. Pierre has always been what you would call the black sheep. Even in the old days when we were all young together, he was the wild one. When he was a Guards officer, he killed a man in a duel and offended the king so deeply, he had to escape out of France to avoid being sent to prison. When the revolution was at its height, he did not stay away as any sensible person would have done. He came back and joined François here in the Midi.'

'He must have had courage.'

'Yes, but he enjoys it too,' said Martine with bitterness. 'The danger, the intrigue, for him it is the breath of life. He would have liked to be the leader, but the men didn't trust him, he was too reckless, too ready to take risks. It has always seemed to me a cruel irony that it was François who was captured and executed while Pierre went free'.

'What will happen to Marius?'

'I don't know. Even if he recovers, he dare not return to the village. Guitry will regard his running away as an admission of guilt, and I dare not tell Henri. He has known the boy since babyhood, but he has always kept himself free of political involvement. Oh dear God, Emma,' she said with a kind of quiet desperation, 'Nicole is right. I should never have married him. I can only bring him harm.'

'I am sure that is not true. He loves you very much.'

'That is the worst part of it. He loves and trusts me and every day I betray his faith in me.'

It was all very well Martine saying she would keep it hidden from her husband, but when we got back to Villeroy we found Henri de Labran there before us and in a towering rage. Martine tried to calm him, but it was useless. I realized then that inside this seemingly placid even-tempered man there existed a passionate pride of possession. For centuries Labrans had lived and cultivated their soil, ruling as ruthlessly as their feudal ancestors with absolute authority over their family and dependants, and now a jumped-up bastard of a policeman from Paris, he almost spat out the words, had dared to lift his hand against a young man born and bred on his lands.

'Why Marius?' he raged. 'All right, there was a fight and a man was killed. It is regrettable but the sergeant was a drunken bully and these things happen. I would have dealt with it in my own good time. What right had he to interfere? I shall send out a search party, bring the boy here and then we shall see what Monsieur Charles Guitry finds to say to me.'

'I should not do that, Henri, if I were you. It will only make matters worse.'

Martine's calm voice stopped him in full flood. He said, 'Why do you say that? What do you know?'

'Marius is safe. Let it slide for the time being. Times are different now. Guitry has the weight of Bonaparte's authority behind him.'

He looked at her frowning, chin thrust forward. 'Martine, are you telling me that Marius has fled to the hills, that he is hiding with this band of robbers who like to call themselves the Chevaliers de Foi?'

'Yes, I believe so,' she answered evasively.

'My God! And you have known about them all these weeks. Who else is involved? Is Lucien one of them?'

'No, Henri, you must believe me. I have kept my promise to you. I will not do anything that can injure you or Armand and Nicole, but some of these men ...' she made a little helpless gesture, 'a great number of them are still loyal to François and everything he stood for ...'

'And to you too and to Lucien, isn't that so? Mouton

for instance and Joseph and how many others? Half my household. I should have sent them packing years ago only you pleaded for them. What a blind fool I have been. What the devil does it matter who rules in Paris so long as we are left untouched? I thought all this was behind you, that you were happy with me, and now ... What more do you want from me? What else can I do?' his voice roughened with feeling. 'Martine, don't go away from me. Don't desert me for them.'

'Never, Henri, never,' she moved towards him and he stretched out a hand to pull her close.

I went quietly out of the room feeling an intruder into something that did not concern me.

We supped early that night and afterwards Martine asked me if I would carry a basket down to the Curé for her. 'It is bed linen and baby clothes,' she said. 'It is for one of the villagers who is soon to be brought to bed. She has many children and they are destitute.'

Her husband said impatiently, 'Can't it wait until morning?'

'I did promise and in the kitchen where they always know everything, they say the midwife has been called already. I should have sent them before but other things put it out of my mind. If Emma would be so kind ...'

Her eyes pleaded with me and I knew that under the linen and blankets there was a note for Etienne Michel and food suitable for a sick man. She would not want to trust it to one of the servants.

It was not a great distance, hardly more than a mile, and I decided to walk. The Curé was not in and the old woman who cooked and cleaned for him told me that he had gone to the village.

'The baby has come, Mademoiselle, but it is sickly. It must be christened, you understand, to save its little soul.' She crossed herself. 'Shall I take the basket?'

'No, there are things here that may be needed. Which is the house?'

'House? Hovel more likely,' she grumbled. 'It's not fit for the likes of you, Mademoiselle, but if you must, then you must, I suppose. It is down there,' she pointed, 'just beyond the crossroads.'

I found it easily. The door was wide open and women

crowded in the porch. They parted to let me through. The heat inside was intense. There was a sickly smell of poverty and childbirth, but the woman propped up in the bed in the corner was smiling down at the baby in her arms. A white cloth had been laid over the stool beside her and on it as well as the water for the baptism, there had been placed a bowl of salt, a loaf of bread, a large brown egg and a long stick.

The Curé touched the baby's downy head. 'Don't fear, he will do well enough now.' He smiled as his hand hovered over each gift in turn. 'May he be as wise as salt, as true as bread, as full as an egg and as straight as this stick.' The women behind me were murmuring a prayer. I felt awkward and out of place. It was no more than a hovel yet there was happiness there and the wonder of a child coming into the world. Then the Curé looked up and saw me.

I held out the basket. 'Madame de Labran sent these.'

'It is good of her.' Some of the women were already exclaiming at the fine quality of the linen. The priest caught my eye. 'Tell her I will see that all is done as she would wish,' and I guessed that he knew already about Marius and would find an opportunity to reach the sick boy.

I had never had anything to do with babies, but something about the symbolic gifts and the traditional words moved me. Deep inside me something stirred ... supposing it was I holding Lucien's son in my arms? My cheeks burned. I hurried down the rutted path and reached the crossroads. It was a lovely evening and I did not want to go back yet. I took another path which I thought might take me home a different way. The fields were sweet with the scent of newly cut grass, but it was farther than I expected and it was already almost dark when I reached the stone barns where the olive presses were housed.

A tree had been cut down and I sat on the fallen trunk thinking of the afternoon, of poor Marius, of the new-born baby and the strange restless desire inside me that I had never felt before. Presently the gentle calm of the evening soaked into me. I leaned back dreamily, looking up towards the hills shrouded in a blue haze, and it was then that I saw the tall figure come swinging down the path between the olive groves and knew with absolute certainty that it was my father. This time it was no dream, no trick of my imagination, everything about him was familiar.

I started to my feet, my heart beating so fast I could scarcely breathe. He knows I am here, I thought to myself, he is coming for me. I began to run towards him, but it was not me for whom he was looking. His eyes were searching beyond and when I turned, I saw why. Martine was moving swiftly through the trees, pale as a moth in her muslin dress, her face alight with joy, her arms outstretched.

'Jacques,' she said with a little sob, 'Jacques, it has been so long,' and went into his arms as if she belonged there.

Chapter 10

I ran away from them through the trees, stumbling over the hard earth, fighting the stupid tears. I was so shocked and upset that if I had stayed, I would have screamed at them, horrible vile things. Martine had lied to me, telling me about Pierre, arousing my sympathy, playing the loyal and devoted wife, only to fling herself into another man's arms a few hours later ... and that man was my father. That was the worst of all. It was not I whom he had come back to find, not the daughter he had callously abandoned to her fate in Paris, but Martine, his mistress, Lucien's mother ... a vulgar sordid intrigue.

All this raced through my mind and it was not until I reached the safety of my bedroom that I faced up to it. I think I grew up that night once and for all. The little girl devoted to her god-like father was left behind for ever, but it was a painful process. Reason and good sense battled with a fierce jealousy and lying on my bed, alternately sweating and shivering, I at last conquered my first bitter sense of betrayal. He was a man like other men and who was I to judge? It was absurd to feel so hurt, yet again and again I wondered about the past. He must have known her when he was here before, when Lucien's father had been alive. Had she played a part in the betrayal of her husband? Had they been lovers then?

'I believed that your love had deserted me, Now I know I am wrong, that you will love me always ...'

It must have been Martine who gave him that book. Was that when he had left her and returned to England? Did Lucien know? Lucien! Realization swept over me in a flood so frightening that I sat up in the bed. I had been right after all. The man Guitry was hunting, the man who had sent the Marquis de Fontenay to his death, was my father! I could not rest. I got out of bed. I walked round and round the room. I flung open the casement glad of the cool night air on my fevered face.

Never, never, would I believe that my father had betrayed his friend . . . and yet . . . oh God, what was I to do if Lucien believed it? I lay down on my bed again but I couldn't sleep. My pillow was a hard hot lump under my aching head. When Louis put his head around the door as he did almost every morning, eager to perch on my bed and amuse me with boyish chatter, I felt I could not endure it.

'Go to breakfast, Louis. I have a headache. I'll be down later.'

'Poor Mademoiselle Emma,' he said looking at me gravely, his head on one side. 'Does it hurt very much? I'll tell Maman. She will make it better.'

'No, Louis, please . . .' but he had run off, quietly closing the door after him. I lay still, trying to brace myself to get up and face the day as if nothing had happened. It was some minutes later when a knock startled me and Martine came into the room.

An unreasoning anger seized me because she looked no different. She was beautiful and calm as usual. 'Louis tells me you are not feeling well. Is it a migraine?' she came to the bed. I would have shrunk away from her, but her hand was cool on my forehead. 'You feel a little feverish. Perhaps it is a touch of the sun. Stay in bed and I will make you a tisane. It is an old herbal remedy. My grandmother used to dose us with it when we were children and it is wonderfully soothing.' She moved to the window, closing the shutters so that only a thin streak of light came into the shaded room. 'That is better. You will rest more easily now. Don't hurry, my dear. Get up when you wish.'

I watched her go through the door with her graceful step, wondering how she had contrived to escape from her husband last night and if she and my father had made love in the cool dark of the stone barns . . . but I must not think of that any longer. Somehow I must remain calm. When after a little, one of the maids came in with the tisane, I drank it gratefully. It was slightly bitter and

tasted of mint. Afterwards I slept and when I woke, it was
nearly noon. I felt refreshed and better able to face things
more practically. While I washed and dressed, I realized
that I must meet my father somehow, find out how he had
come and why, warn him about Lucien. He must know already that I was at Villeroy. Pierre would have told him.
Had he spoken of it to Martine last night? How much did
Monsieur Guitry really know of the Englishman hiding in
the hills? One of these questions at least was to be answered only too soon. I was brushing my hair when Nicole
came in abruptly without knocking, closing the door behind her and leaning back against it.

'I see you are up already. The Chief of Police is here.
He is asking to speak with you.'

I dropped the brush and bent to pick it up with trembling fingers. 'With me? Why?'

'How should I know? Perhaps he has found out something.'

'Found out what?'

She shrugged her shoulders. 'That's for you to discover,
isn't it?' she came up beside me, looking over my shoulder.
There was a curious look of triumph in the black eyes reflected in the mirror. She ran her fingers through the hair
that curled on my forehead and round my ears. 'Why did
you cut it short like this?'

'It was the fashion in ... in Paris.' London had so
nearly slipped out that I bit my tongue to hold it back. I
was going to need all my wits about me in the next few
minutes. 'Where is Monsieur Guitry?'

'He is waiting for you in Papa's room.'

'I'll go down to him now.'

Nicole watched me go down the stairs.

The room where Henri de Labran conducted the
business of the estate was a small one. There were cabinets
for papers, a desk, a couple of chairs and little else. Light
flooded in from the one window. Guitry was only a tall
dark shadow against its dazzle. The sharp voice hit me immediately I was inside the door and he spoke in English.

'Where did you meet your father last night, Mademoiselle?'

It was obvious that he believed in shock tactics. If I had
not been prepared, I could so easily have blurted out the

truth. My mind raced. I must remember to spice my English with a French accent. Thank God for school plays and my skill as an amateur actress. I took my time.

'That is a strange question, Monsieur. It is true I have seen him often in dreams since he died. If you wish to know when I last saw him alive, then it was ten years ago almost to the day when they came to arrest him.'

'Are you sure?'

'I was twelve, only a child, but I am not likely to forget that he died under the guillotine.'

I could see him clearly now. He had moved to behind the desk and something about the grim set of his mouth frightened me.

'Suppose I were to tell you that I do not believe that you are Emma Louise Rainier, that enquiries have been made at Passy and your lies have been discovered?'

My heart was beating thickly now, but I must not give way. He could be bluffing and I must not let him see my fear. I tried to counter his attack with sarcasm. 'Well, suppose you did. What did you find at Passy? That Emma Louise was still living there and that I was an impostor?'

'No,' he tapped his finger on the desk irritably, but his eyes were still watchful. 'No, the house is empty and neighbours say that Mademoiselle Rainier is not there and her mother is staying with friends.'

So Lucien had covered my tracks. Perhaps my relief showed in my face too openly, for my persecutor gave me no time before he attacked again.

'You speak English remarkably well for a Frenchwoman, Mademoiselle Rainier.'

'Thank you.'

'Where did you learn it? Not at a French convent surely?'

Again I had to make a quick decision. I plunged in recklessly. 'My godmother was English, a Lady Emma Ross.' (She had been my grandmother and she was dead so that was safe!) 'I was named for her and as a child I stayed with her in England.'

'Where in England?'

'At her house in Cornwall.' In a difficult situation tell as much of the truth as you can, had been something my father once said to me.

132

'*Vraiment?* You are a very remarkable young lady to be wasting your time as governess to a little boy,' he said dryly.

That was easy to answer. 'You of all people, Monsieur Guitry,' I said reproachfully, 'should know that a great many of us have been reduced to occupations far worse than that. Besides Madame de Labran was my mother's friend.'

'So I understand, yet there are certain facts . . .' but I was spared further interrogation because at that moment the door flew open and Lucien appeared on the threshold. My heart nearly stopped at the look of anger on his face. 'He knows,' I thought, 'he knows!' But his anger was not for me. He came at once to my side.

'May I ask by what right you subject my fiancée to this brutal questioning?' he asked furiously.

It was so utterly unexpected that it took my breath away and even surprised the Chief of Police but Guitry recovered all too quickly.

'Your fiancée?' he repeated with a sneer. 'A very sudden engagement, is it not?'

'Not sudden at all, and if at present it is known only to Emma Louise and myself, that surely is no concern of yours.'

'Maybe not, but I think others may be surprised, your mother for instance, or Mademoiselle Nicole . . .'

A dull flush ran up into Lucien's face. 'I see no reason why we should be subjected to this persecution or to your cheap insults. I should be obliged if you would leave the house before I have you thrown out.'

He spoke with the same unconscious pride of birth and position that still clung to Martine and I saw again the angry resentment on Guitry's face.

'May I remind you that it is your stepfather's house, Monsieur de Fontenay, not yours, and I go when my business is finished and not before.' With a deliberate slowness he picked up gloves and papers from the table, nodded curtly to us both and strolled out of the room.

'Damned insolent devil!' exclaimed Lucien. 'How I wish I could make him feel the toe of my boot!'

The reaction after the strain was too much. I collapsed

into a chair and began to laugh weakly. Lucien turned to me at once.

'What has he been saying to you? I would have got back before but I only heard by chance that he was here.'

'I think I managed to answer his questions without giving myself away.'

'Are you all right? Mother said you were not well this morning.'

'It was nothing, only a headache. I'm better now. Lucien, why did you tell him we were engaged?'

'It gave me the right to interfere. I thought it would stop his questioning quicker than anything else. Do you mind, Emma? We need only pretend for a little while, only until you are safely out of France.'

Of course it could only be pretence; what else was possible for us in the circumstances in which we were placed? I was not even sure that Lucien felt as I did. A few kisses on a sunlit beach are one thing, love and marriage are another. I wanted to tell him about my father but I didn't dare. I must see him first. I must find out the truth.

I tried to smile. 'I have never been engaged before.'

'Neither have I.' He took my hand. 'You are not angry with me? I did it on the spur of the moment.'

'Of course I am not angry. I'm grateful.' How does one behave when one is engaged and yet not engaged.

'I think I should tell my mother. We will try to keep it secret, but she should be warned.' He leaned forward and kissed my cheek. 'You still look pale. You should go and lie down.'

'Perhaps I will.'

I spent the afternoon quietly, altering Armand's breeches to fit me. I had a feeling that a time could come when I might need some kind of disguise. The ordeal of the morning had somehow diminished the shock of the night before. I found I could face it more calmly, but Guitry's suspicions worried me. How much did he really know? Something surely or he would not have tried to trick me. How could I warn my father and how could I go on keeping it from Lucien?

I don't know whether the police chief deliberately mentioned Lucien's rash announcement of our pretended engagement or whether the rumour had spread in the strange way things are always known to servants before anyone else, but when we were all gathered at the supper table that evening, it had already come to Henri de Labran's ears.

'Well, well,' he boomed, 'it seems that I must congratulate you, Lucien, and Emma Louise too. Slyboots, the pair of you, not saying a word.'

'Henri please,' intervened Martine. 'Lucien has only just confided in me. They neither of them want anything to be said about it yet.'

'Why not?' objected Armand. 'I should be proud if Emma had agreed to marry me.'

'It is far too early. I have already told them. They have not known one another long enough. There are so many problems and Emma has not even had time to write to her mother and ask her consent.'

'We can still drink their health, I suppose, even if we keep our mouths shut,' said Henri cheerfully. 'Fill up your glasses. You know,' and he bestowed a large wink on his daughter, 'just a little while ago, I could have sworn my little Nicole was hoping to see herself as the Marquise de Fontenay.'

'Don't be silly, Papa,' interrupted Nicole quickly.

'Silly old Papa I may be, but I have eyes in my head,' said her father jestingly. 'Then Emma Louise comes along and in next to no time you let her snatch him away from you. Shame on you, girl, where is your pride?'

'Must you go on and on with this nonsense?' Nicole stood up so abruptly that her glass toppled over and the wine ran across the white linen cloth. Angry spots of colour flamed in her cheeks. 'When I marry, I want a real man, not one like Lucien who hangs on to my father's coat-tails. Mademoiselle Rainier can have him with pleasure.'

She went out of the room slamming the door so that Henri looked after her frowning.

'Now what have I said? It was only a joke . . . unless . . .'

He turned to Lucien, his voice suddenly stern. 'Have you been playing fast and loose with her, Lucien, is that it?'

'No, never,' Lucien's hand clenched on the table and I

guessed at the effort he was making to control his anger at Nicole's insult. Then Armand came to his rescue.

'Of course he hasn't,' he said with brotherly scorn. 'You ought to know Nicole by now, Father. She has always believed she had Lucien at her beck and call like a little dog on a string, and now she finds she hasn't she doesn't like it, that's all.'

It sounded so simple and it agreed with what Martine had told me, but for the first time that day I wondered if it was Nicole who had brought Guitry to the house. A hint dropped to Georges Montaud who sought so many opportunities to call would be all that was needed and it could have been successful. If I had blundered, it would have meant internment, even prison. She would have been rid of me once and for all. I knew she did not like me, but it was horribly disturbing to feel that I had made an enemy who would not scruple to do me harm.

For more than a week nothing happened. It fretted me to know that my father was there somewhere hidden in the hills and out of my reach. News came to Martine by way of the Curé that Marius was recovering but the quiet routine of life went on as usual at Villeroy so that once or twice when the heat grew more intense, the olives ripened and the fields turned to gold, I felt as if I were living in a dream, that I really was Emma Louise Rainier teaching Louis, going for walks, helping with household duties and happily dreaming of her marriage. Lucien was properly attentive as befitted a newly engaged young man so that sometimes, madly, I thought it is not pretence, one day it will all really happen and we shall be married. I even began on a piece of fine needlework, not that I ever had the skill or patience of Martine, but it occupied my hands to work on a set of chair backs for our future home ... how foolish even to think of such a thing! Our future home ... a crumbling ruin on the coast of Brittany or Trevira ... Trevira which had receded so far, it seemed that I must have lived there in some other existence.

Then one day I went back to my bedroom before luncheon and there on my dressing-table under my hand mirror there was a tiny scrap of paper. I picked it up with a queer jolt. There were only a few words: 'The place of stones. This afternoon. Come alone.' Nothing else, but my father's hand had written it, that I knew for certain. How had it got there? Was it Joseph? How many others in the house led a double life? Louis, who was with me, pulled at my sleeve.

'What's that you are looking at?'

'Nothing. Go and wash your hands, Louis, there's ink on them,' and while he obediently poured water into the bowl, I tore the note into tiny fragments.

It was not difficult to escape in the afternoon. Now in July the sun burned down at noon so that the whole household settled into a sleepy siesta after luncheon. When I went into the courtyard, even the stable boys were drowsing in the heat. I saddled Beauregard myself and took the familiar path through the olive groves and up the track to the place of stones. When I reached the tiny pavilion, I saw a man waiting in the shadow of the doorway and my heart thudded uncomfortably, but it was not my father. It was Mouton grinning at me in his friendly fashion.

'We leave the horse here, Mademoiselle. I am to take you the rest of the way.' He tethered Beauregard and then pulled a white silk scarf from his pocket.

'You must forgive me, Mademoiselle . . .'

'Do you mean you're going to blindfold me?'

'You need not be afraid. I will take great care of you. You will not fall.'

'But why me?' I was indignant. 'Do you think I would betray your hiding place?'

'It is not that,' he said apologetically. 'It is orders, you see . . .'

'Orders from whom? I won't do it.'

'I am afraid you must, Mademoiselle Emma, if you want to see Monsieur Jacques.'

Jacques? That of course must be the name they knew him by. I hesitated, angry at what seemed to me play-acting. What was my father thinking of? We were not engaged in a game of blindman's buff. Mouton shuffled his feet, looking sheepish.

'Oh very well,' I said at last. 'Do what you please.'

He tied the scarf gently but firmly round my eyes and we set off. A time was to come when I would know this path intimately and though it twisted and turned, it was not so precipitous as it seemed that first afternoon. Mouton guided my every step, his hand always firm on my arm, encouraging me, never letting me slip, showing me where to place my feet. I had no idea of where we were going or how long it took, but it must have been half an hour or longer when I felt a breath of cooler air and knew we had moved out of the sun.

'Steps to climb now,' said Mouton. 'Go up slowly,' and I felt him close behind me, steady and reassuring as I groped my way upward. Then we halted. He unbound my eyes. I was not in a cave as I had half expected. I was in the small round room of a crumbling turret built into the rocks. There were stone walls, narrow arrow slits for windows, a stool, a table, a straw mattress with blankets, but all these things I noticed afterwards. Then I had eyes only for my father standing in a streak of sunlight, elegant still even in rough leather breeches and coarse linen shirt.

'Well, Emma,' he said and smiled. 'Here I am, you see. I've come back for you.'

I forgot everything except that he was there. I went stumbling across the stone floor into his arms and idiotically burst into tears.

'Now, now, what is all this? I thought you'd be glad to see me.'

'I am, I am, only . . .' I groped for my handkerchief and he gave me his. Then I was sitting on the stool, he was bending over me and Mouton had disappeared. 'I'm sorry to be so stupid. It's just that it has been so long . . . so much has happened . . . how did you know I was here?'

'I didn't, not until I had arrived and Pierre told me. I had been worried sick about you, particularly when Victor told me how you had disappeared from the hotel.'

I stared at him. 'Victor told you.'

'Yes. You always underrated him, my dear. Dull stick though he is, he's no fool. He pleaded such a tragic tale of a dying father and coupled it with a look of such crass stupidity that he actually convinced them that he was harmless and he was allowed to return home.'

How extraordinary, I thought; if I had stayed with Victor, I might have gone quietly back to Trevira and none of this would have happened . . . only then I would never have known Lucien, never known about Martine, never have been here sharing my father's danger . . .

'Are you listening to me, Emma?'

'Yes, yes, of course. How did you get here?'

He sat on the table close beside me. 'In actual fact, it was Victor's *Sea Witch* that brought me.'

'What! You can't mean . . . does he know everything?'

'Some, not all, but Victor is a true-blue patriot, my dear. He doesn't altogether approve of me, but he would willingly lay down his life for his country; so against his will and seasick all the way, he took the risk and landed me at Quiberon Bay. Incidentally, my pet, he is greatly distressed about you. I had tremendous difficulty in preventing him from coming with me and rushing to your rescue. I pointed out that his schoolboy French would hardly provide a passport in the Midi just now.'

'Is Quiberon Bay far? How did you make your way here?'

'Far enough. It is in Brittany. It was a fiendish journey, but I have an excellent set of forged papers.' He waved his arms with a flourish. 'Behold Jacques Dupont, traveller in fine wines, with a pass signed by Paul de Barras, retired revolutionary, bloodthirsty ruffian, former lover of Madame Bonaparte, but worshipper of good wines. The pass won't stand up to close scrutiny, but it has proved very useful with republican soldiers who read with difficulty and are dazzled by official stamps.'

'It won't deceive Charles Guitry,' I said quietly. 'You do know that he is here, don't you?'

'Yes, I know,' he dropped his bantering tone. 'It's damned bad luck that of all people the one man who knows me by sight should be posted in Tarascon.'

'He guesses something already. He questioned me.'

'Did he, by Jove? When? What did he say?'

'It was a week or so ago.' Quickly I told him about the interrogation and he nodded approvingly.

'Good girl. I knew I could rely on you.' He grinned. 'So my little Emma is engaging herself to be married. That was quick thinking on Lucien's part. Tell me, how did you persuade him to act the gallant cavalier and carry you off from Paris to Villeroy?'

'You misjudge him,' I said stiffly. 'He has been wonderfully kind.'

'Has he indeed? If I may say so, my love, a life of adventure suits you. I've never seen you look prettier . . .'

'Don't, Papa.' I got up and moved away from him. 'Don't make fun.'

'But, my dear, you can't be seriously thinking that Lucien . . .'

'Please, I would prefer not to talk about it.'

'As you wish, but I meant what I said.' His hand on my shoulder turned me to face him. 'You've grown in looks . . . I thought so on the night of the bull fighting.'

'Then it *was* you who . . .'

'Yes, it was I. That mask was devilishly useful. Luckily I passed it on to Mouton otherwise . . .' he shrugged his shoulders. 'Your Lucien has his wits about him. I'd not have cared to risk my skin with that evil-tempered bull.'

'But you did. You took a terrible chance.'

'Only afterwards. Snatching the rosette was easy. If it had not been for your young man, it might have been all up with me before I began.' He paused before he said casually, 'I didn't know about the child. Is he Henri de Labran's son?'

'No. He was born after the Marquis was killed.'

'I see. I had no idea . . . poor Martine.'

There was tenderness even in the way he spoke her name. I didn't want to hear it. I said abruptly, 'Papa, why did you bring me here today?'

'To see you of course. Isn't it natural? Shouldn't a father want to see his daughter?'

'But that's not all, is it? What are you doing here? What are your orders?'

'Now that I can't tell you, not yet at any rate. It is like having you brought here blindfolded. What you don't know, you cannot give away.'

'Do you think I would?'

'Not intentionally, but no one knows better than I what pressures can be brought to bear, and make no mistake about it, Emma, Guitry can be ruthless. Much more than my life depends on this, but you're quite right. I wanted to see you, but I want you to do something for me too.'

'What is it?'

'Come back here to me and listen carefully. I want to explain something to you. Do you know how information is gathered in times like these? It is not just one person passing on bare facts. It is a great number of tiny details coming from many different sources which when put together form a pattern and you can begin to see your way, and that brings me to what I want you to do. You are living at Villeroy as a member of the family. You hear them talk, Henri de Labran, Armand, Lucien. There are visitors to the house, you go out and meet neighbours, you hear things spoken of in the village. I want to know everything, about troops, about recruiting, about Bonaparte's movements, about what people feel and think. I will arrange for you to pass it on through Mouton or Joseph or others, sometimes even direct to myself. I will find a way.'

'But why? For what purpose?'

'You will know that all in good time. Will you do it?'

I hesitated. The idea revolted me. I said unwillingly, 'But they like me, they trust me. It would be playing the traitor.'

'It will not harm them and they will never know.'

'That only makes it worse.' A sudden hot flood of anger boiled up in me. I said, 'Why don't you ask Martine?'

'Martine?'

'Oh don't pretend. I saw you with her in the olive groves. Why don't you ask your mistress to spy for you?'

I saw by his face that it had come as a shock and perversely I wanted to hurt. 'It's true, isn't it? You were lovers years ago when Lucien's father was alive. She betrayed him then, why shouldn't she do the same to Henri de Labran now?'

'Be quiet, Emma. You don't know what you're talking about.'

'Oh yes I do, and I think it is vile, hateful.' I thought of what Lucien had told me that night at Avignon, of what Guitry had said when the sergeant was murdered, and I let my anger sweep me into wild accusation. 'Was it you who betrayed the Marquis de Fontenay so that he would never find out about you and her, so that you could go on sleeping together?'

'Stop it, do you hear, you're out of your mind!' He slapped my cheek hard.

I gasped, my hand flew to my face. 'You've never done that before.'

He stared at me for an instant, fighting for self control, then he turned away. 'I'm sorry, but never repeat that abominable lie to me again.' He walked across to one of the window slits and the bar of light showed me the torment on his face. In the silence a drowsy bee hummed across the room searching for escape. Then my father said quietly, 'Since you know so much, you had better know a little more. You're quite right. Martine and I fell in love when I came to France before. After her husband was killed, I would have done anything to get her out of the country. I wanted her for my wife more than I had ever wanted anything, but I was on the run myself. It was impossible.' His hand struck against the wall in a futile gesture, then he turned round with a wry smile. 'She might have been your stepmother.'

'And now?'

'Now,' he made a helpless movement. 'I have seen her once ten days ago for a few minutes, that is all. She is utterly loyal to Henri de Labran, God damn him! You're only a child,' he went on wearily, 'how can you possibly understand?'

'That is where you're wrong. I'm not a child, not any longer ...'

He looked at me for a moment before he said slowly, 'It's true. It's only a few months and yet you have changed. Is it possible? You and Lucien ...' I looked away, confused, unwilling to answer and he put out a hand and drew me towards him. 'What an ironical twist of fate if it should be he ... Martine's son ...'

'Please, Papa, I'd rather not talk about it. I'm sorry I said what I did.'

'And you will do as I ask?'

'I will try, but I don't think I shall be able to find out very much.'

'Every little helps. You can be sure of one thing, Emma, nothing is going to stop Bonaparte trying to make himself master of Europe. I told them that in London but they're only just beginning to believe it. If I succeed in what I plan to do, we may be preventing five, perhaps ten years of war, and what are our lives, yours or mine, to the slaughter of thousands? I know it is asking a great deal from you, but it will be worth it in the end.'

'Will it?' Does the end ever justify the means? But I knew I would do what he asked however much I hated it.

'And you will speak of it to no one, not even Lucien?'

'Papa, there is something I must tell you.'

He watched me for a moment. 'Is it about Lucien?'

'Yes. You see he believes that you are the man who betrayed his father.'

'Lucien does?' There was genuine surprise in his voice. 'But why? He was a boy then. We never even met. His father kept him out of it.'

'He didn't know then, not for certain, but he has never forgotten it . . . and now he is sure. Guitry told him.'

'Guitry?' he repeated incredulously. 'But he of all men knows the truth.'

'I think he has done it deliberately . . . to set him against you.'

'You could be right.' He was silent for a moment, then he said thoughtfully, 'It is something I never anticipated. Does he know who I am?'

'Not yet . . . Oh Papa, I am so afraid for you.'

He drew me against him, stroking my hair. 'Don't fret too much, my pet. I'm not easy to kill, you know, and now I know how things stand, it will not be difficult to take extra precautions. But it's a damnable situation for you.'

I longed to tell him how much I loved Lucien, how I hated to deceive him, but I didn't and I don't know how much he guessed. He said gently, 'One of the worst parts of this kind of work is that you can never completely trust anyone. Now you must go. Mouton will take you back.'

He came with me down the steps and I saw that we were in a corner of what had once been a mighty castle literally hewn out of the mountain, so steep and so precipitous that it must have been entirely impregnable from every attack.

'Queer old place, isn't it?' he said as I looked around me in wonder. 'A robbers' nest if ever there was one.'

'That was what Pierre called it.'

'There are so many nooks and crannies, so many hiding places, that it is child's play to deceive anyone foolhardy enough to pursue us here.' He held my hand for a moment. 'Have you forgiven me?'

I reached to kiss him. 'How can I help it?'

'Take care of her, Mouton.'

'I will, Monsieur Jacques. Don't you worry.'

Mouton took out the white scarf but my father stopped him with a gesture. 'No need for that. She is my daughter.'

I saw by the flash in Mouton's eyes that it had surprised and pleased him. I wondered if he had thought me something not so respectable.

The climb down was in some ways worse than when we went up. I could see the narrowness of the path, the steep slopes where a fall could mean an unpleasant unjury or death, and even without the blindfold I doubted if I could ever find my way back up again. When we reached the ledge, Beauregard whinneyed with pleasure at seeing me, rubbing his nose against me. Mouton helped me into the saddle.

'Go carefully, Mademoiselle. I will come down by a different path. It is better if we are not seen together.'

I was coming up the track to the house when Lucien came to meet me. He stopped me with a hand on my bridle. 'Where have you been? It is very late. We were getting anxious about you.'

'Just riding.' I said. 'Up in the hills.'

'You should not go alone. It could be dangerous.'

'I have done it before several times.' I would have gone on but he still held me back.

'Did you go to meet Pierre?'

'Pierre? No, of course not.'

His hand slid along the rein and closed over mine. 'Emma, what are you hiding from me?'

'Nothing. Why should I hide anything?'

'I don't know, but there is something, you and Mother too. What is it?'

'There is nothing. You're imagining it.'

I jerked away from him urging Beauregard into a trot because more than anything I hated lying to him. He followed slowly and though he said nothing more and was as courteous as always all that evening, I was very conscious of the tension. It was the beginning of the rift between us.

Chapter 11

We led a quiet life at Villeroy with few visitors so that I learned nothing that was worth passing on until the unexpected arrival of Jean de Rennes. It was about a week after I had seen my father. I had just finished giving Louis his English lesson when we heard the clatter of horse's hooves in the courtyard. Louis raced to the window.

'It's Jean,' he cried pushing open the casement and leaning out to wave a greeting.

'Who is Jean?' I asked, but the boy was already half through the door. I called to him to come back but he was running down the stairs. I put the books away and followed after him more leisurely.

A young man in a showy green and gold uniform had just dismounted in front of the steps. Armand came hurrying from the stables and called one of the boys to take the horse. The newcomer slapped him on the back cheerfully.

'*Voilà, mon vieux,* how goes it?' Nicole went past me down the steps, stretching out her hand in welcome and the young officer bowed over it and then drew her towards him and kissed her cheek. 'It's good to see you, Nicole, you're ten times prettier than when I was here last.'

She laughed and blushed. 'You look very mignificent, Jean. Have you been promoted to Captain?'

'Yes and more than that. When we returned from the Austrian campaign, he appointed me one of his aides-de-camp no less.'

'Bonaparte did?'

'Who else?'

Louis was gazing rapturously at the gold-tasselled sash and the sabre that hung from his hip. The young man smiled down at him ruffling the brown curls. '*Mon Dieu,* but you've grown in the last year. Still going to fight the

145

bulls, eh?' He swung the child up in his arms and then his glance fell on me, still standing in the shadow of the doorway. 'Who is this? I don't think I have had the pleasure . . .'

'That's Emma Louise. She's my governess,' explained Louis.

'Your governess, eh?' The bold brown eyes in the good-looking face took me in at one sweeping glance. He set the boy gently on his feet, and came up the steps to kiss my hand. '*Enchanté*, Mademoiselle. Jean de Rennes, at your service.' He looked up at me, laughing. 'Louis is fortunate. I remember my governess, a dragon, with a face fit to frighten the devil himself.'

Nicole took his arm. 'You will lunch with us, Jean?'

'Thank you. I'd be delighted.' They went before me into the house.

I thought that Martine greeted him with a certain reserve, but it was only afterwards that I realized why. Jean's father, the Comte de Rennes, had prudently taken himself into exile at the first hint of revolution, but his son had felt differently. As soon as he came of age, he had quarrelled with his father and returned to France to enlist under the rising star of General Bonaparte. Now his father had accepted the new order, returning with a free pardon and his lands restored. It was natural perhaps that Martine should feel a certain bitterness when she remembered François de Fontenay and his lonely battle for his exiled king.

But all this I learned later. Lucien came late to the meal and sensitive to all his moods I knew at once that he disliked the handsome newcomer. Jean de Rennes greeted him boisterously.

'Glad to see you, Lucien. Still working harder than anybody else I see. Don't you ever grow tired of making out bills for barrels of oil and casks of wine? Better you than me. I could never add two and two and get the right answer.'

I saw Lucien's mouth tighten. He said coolly, 'You surprise me, Jean. I was under the impression that General Bonaparte did not suffer fools gladly.'

There was an angry gleam in Jean's hard brown eyes. 'I am not a clerk or one of his secretaries.'

'No indeed,' Lucien let his eyes travel over the gold braid and fringed sash. 'No doubt you find the sword easier to handle than the pen.'

Nicole was looking from one to the other, her eyes sparkling with malicious amusement. Then the servants brought back the hot dishes for Lucien and while he ate Jean leaned back in his chair, keeping us amused with army gossip and scandalous titbits about Bonaparte's quarrels with his wife. Coffee was being served when he sat up, slapping his hand to his forehead.

'It has been so pleasant seeing you all again, I nearly forgot my mission. Father is opening up the house again at St. Rémy and he is giving a ball in the gardens. He would be delighted if you could all come.' He glanced at me, smiling. 'Louis' charming governess too of course.'

'I think you ought to know, Jean,' said Nicole sweetly, 'that Emma Louise is Lucien's secret fiancée.'

'The devil! I had no idea.'

'Nicole please,' interrupted Martine. 'You know that neither Emma Louise nor Lucien want it to be made public yet.'

'Why not?' said Lucien suddenly. 'I'm not ashamed of it.'

'I should think not,' said Jean heartily. 'Congratulations, my dear fellow. You have won a prize.'

'I know I have.'

Lucien's eyes met mine across the table. There had been a coolness between us for the past week and I couldn't imagine what had induced him to speak out as he did. The knowledge of how much I was hiding from him made me feel uncomfortable. I blushed and looked away.

Martine came to my rescue. She said quietly, 'What is the date of your father's ball, Jean?'

'Very soon ... 14th July, in fact.' There was a momentary silence. 14th July ... the day the mob stormed the Bastille, the day of liberation that had also rung the funeral knell of the royal family and the thousands who had followed them to the guillotine. It was hardly tactful in present company and Jean was obviously conscious of it. He went on hurriedly, 'There is a chance, a very good chance that the First Consul will honour us with a visit during the evening.'

147

'Bonaparte coming here?' said Lucien. 'Is that wise?'

'What do you mean?'

'Surely he must be aware that he will not be exactly welcome in the Midi. There has been trouble already, even here in our village.'

Jean shrugged his shoulders. 'A few peasants looking sideways at him won't worry General Bonaparte. In any case his visit is being kept secret. He is on his way to Toulon and he doesn't want the workers in the dockyard to be forewarned. He is making a lightning tour of all the ports where ships are being built. They are too slow for him.' Jean laughed. 'You should have heard his language a few days ago when a hundred invasion barges ordered to be ready at Boulogne turned out to be only twenty. A few heads rolled, I can tell you. But nothing is going to stand in his way. He intends to celebrate Christmas in St James's Palace if it kills him.'

'He will never succeed,' the words burst out of me before I could stop them. 'He will never defeat the British Navy, never, not while there is a ship still afloat and an Englishman left alive to man her.'

Jean turned to look at me with a little smile. 'You sound very sure, Mademoiselle. Is it possible you know something that we do not?'

Lucien answered for me. 'Emma Louise was in Paris in the spring and so was I. There were still a great number of English visitors. They spoke with great confidence.'

'Oh they are loud-mouthed enough when no one stands up to them, but Bonaparte has their measure,' said Jean easily. 'Look at their ministers! Why even their own gutter press laughs at their antics. When some dirty-mouthed writing fellow tried the same thing in Paris, Napoleon had him hanged for it with his newspaper stuffed into his mouth.'

'The revolution spilled enough blood to fill an ocean in the cause of liberty,' said Lucien dryly. 'It seems a pity that a man still cannot speak his mind.'

Jean flared up and I think this time there might have been open quarrel between them, but fortunately they were interrupted by Louis whose eyes had been going from one to the other.

'I don't think I want to fight the bulls, after all,' he announced suddenly. 'I shall be a soldier like Jean and kill the English.'

Armand laughed and clapped the boy on the back. 'Spoken like a true hero.'

'Louis, you had better go up to your room and get ready,' said Martine. 'It is time to go to the Curé for your lessons.'

'Oh no, Maman, please . . .'

Jean suddenly slapped his hand on the table. 'What a fool I am not to have thought of it before. Some actors from the Opéra-comique are to perform a burlesque during the evening and afterwards there will be a presentation to our guest of honour. They asked if we could supply a small page since their own child actor has gone sick. Madame, will you be very kind and lend us Louis? I am sure he would fit the part to perfection.'

'No,' Martine's reply was quick and emphatic. 'No, I could not allow it. He is far too young.'

'Oh Maman, please please let me go,' the boy's large hazel eyes were pleading.

'No, Louis, it is not at all suitable.'

'I agree with Martine,' Nicole was equally firm. 'He will be a great nuisance and ruin everything.'

'Don't be such a spoilsport,' said her brother. 'Why shouldn't he come with us and enjoy the fun?'

'Yes, why shouldn't he?' It surprised me to realize how fond I had grown of the little boy. 'I will look after him, Madame. It will be no trouble.'

'I don't know,' Martine hesitated and looked at Lucien.

He frowned but said nothing and she went on quickly. 'I will ask my husband. If he agrees that we shall attend the ball, then I will think again about Louis.'

'*Bon*, then that's as good as settled,' said Jean confidently.

The child gave me a beaming smile and soon after Jean rode away leaving me with a problem I was not sure how to solve. Bonaparte was coming here to Provence on or before 14th July. Was this the information my father was looking for? Part of me still found the thought of spying distasteful though this had been spoken of so openly that anyone around that luncheon table could have repeated it.

That evening when Martine mentioned the ball to Henri de Labran Lucien was vehemently against it.

'The Comte de Rennes ran away at the first smell of danger, lived ten years in comfortable exile and now comes back to grab what he can. I despise men like that.'

'Oh, I don't know,' said his stepfather tolerantly. 'After all Gilles de Rennes was a neighbour of mine. I knew him well in the old days. We used to hunt wild boar together. He doesn't lack courage. If he knows which side his bread is buttered these days, who is to blame him? One has to be a realist in these matters.'

Lucien looked disgusted. 'You must do as you wish, Mother. I shall not go.'

'I think you should,' said Martine decisively. 'The past is done with. We must learn to forget it. Besides you are not being fair to Emma Louise. She cannot go without you especially as you spoke so openly of your engagement. It would look very strange.'

Lucien frowned. 'I had not thought of that. Do you want to go, Emma?'

'I don't know. It is for you to say.'

'Of course she wants to go,' said Henri de Labran comfortably. 'All pretty girls like balls and we have few enough of them. Don't be a dog in the manger, Lucien.'

He gave me a reluctant smile. 'I'm sorry. I'm out of temper this evening. All right, we will go. I only hope we won't regret it.'

All night I pondered my problem and the next afternoon came to a decision. I would ride out to the Camargue, find Mouton and tell him what I knew. After that it would be up to him to carry it to my father.

It was blisteringly hot along the track and when I reached the reed-thatched cabin where Mouton lived, it was shut and locked. It was another hour before I found him thigh deep in the marshy waters, guiding a herd of black bulls with the long three-pronged trident that all the *gardiens* use. He shouted to me to remain where I was and after a few moments came splashing through the mud towards me.

'It's dangerous to venture too near,' he explained. 'There are quicksands that can swallow you up before you've time to shout for help.'

'Mouton listen. Will you take a message to my father? It could be important.' I repeated all I knew and he listened carefully.

'I'll tell him, but he knows something of it already.'

'How?'

He shrugged. 'There are those amongst us who hear things, Mademoiselle.'

I wondered wryly if my father had really needed my help or whether he had simply wanted to please me by making me feel important to him. I said, 'Mouton, what is he going to do?'

He shook his head. 'He's close. He gives nothing away, not to any of us, until it is decided. I'll tell you something though.' He leaned closer, whispering. 'If Monsieur Pierre had his way, it would be . . .' and he slid his hand across his throat with a significant gesture and grinned. 'That would be the end of the Corsican.'

'Murder him, do you mean?' I exclaimed in horror.

'That's right, but Monsieur Jacques says no, he has other plans, and he is the clever one, make no mistake about that. You will see, Mademoiselle.'

He waved his hand to me and plunged back into the water, bellowing to the bulls, while I stared after him, comforted somehow that, enemy or not, it was my father who was reluctant to kill in cold blood.

We set out early for St Rémy on the day of the ball. I was wearing the white and gold dress my father had chosen for me in Paris and I felt happy in it until Nicole came down. The burnt orange of her gown set off her black hair to perfection making me feel colourless and uninteresting. We were waiting in the hall for Martine before getting into the carriage when Lucien came down the stairs with something in his hand.

'It is for you,' he said and gave me the velvet case, 'an engagement gift.'

It was a necklace of rubies in an exquisite gold filigree setting. I had never possessed anything so lovely. I knew Nicole's eyes were on us, but Lucien ignored her. He took the jewels out of their case and fastened them around my throat. I shivered as I felt the feather-light touch of his lips on my neck and I wondered if he too was thinking of the ball at the Tuileries.

The track past Les Baux and the place of stones was too narrow and rutted for the large coach so we went by way of Tarascon. For the first time I saw the castle high on its rock with a steep drop to the swift-flowing waters of the Rhône. The round towers at each corner, the crenellated walls, the golden stone were like some quaint medieval painting and yet this lovely place where troubadours had once sung of love was now a grim gaol where the men Charles Guitry hunted down were shut in cells behind grilled windows, where my father had been imprisoned, where the Marquis de Fontenay had been tortured and shot.

Martine stared straight in front of her as the carriage lumbered by. Sitting opposite I saw Henri de Labran's hand steal out, closing over hers, and I saw the grateful look she gave him.

The road wound through vineyards and olive groves, protected against the mistral by tall screens of dark green cypresses. Beyond I could see the lilac-grey slopes of the mountains and could just make out the steep bare crags of Les Baux. I wondered where my father was and whether, somewhere on the high road, an ambush waited for the First Consul and his escort.

The house of the Comte de Rennes was a large white villa set in a magnificent park and an army of gardeners must have prepared it for this day. Elsewhere in Provence the sun was already burning up the flowers and turning the grass golden brown, but here the lawns were like green velvet, white scented geraniums tumbled out of pots and clambered up stone pillars. Velvety roses in deep crimson and pink still bloomed, ivies clustered round the tamarisks and tangled with periwinkle among the mossy roots. It was already dusk but coloured lamps glowed in the trees and the evening air was warm and sweetly scented.

The Comte de Rennes was on the lawn to greet us, a plump grey-haired man with charming manners and keen light eyes that seemed to me to miss nothing. He and Henri de Labran immediately fell into conversation about old times and Martine stayed beside her husband while we moved across the grass to the house. On the terrace an orchestra was playing. They were dancing in the drawing-room and on the lawn outside. Armand and Nicole were soon surrounded by friends and acquaintances. Jean came to welcome us, kissing my hand and murmuring compliments.

'Can I tempt you to join the dancing, Mademoiselle Emma?'

'Later perhaps,' Lucien's manner was cool.

Jean moved away to greet other guests and Lucien looked down at me. 'Do you wish to dance?'

'Not unless you do. I would rather see more of the gardens.'

We took a path that led through the trees, but although he kept hold of my arm, Lucien did not speak immediately.

At last I said awkwardly, 'I did not thank you as I should have done for the necklace. You ought not to have given me anything so vulnerable. I shall think of it as a loan, to be handed back when all this is over.'

'That was not my intention.'

We had come out from the trees and into a wide green stretch ringed with lamps that a gardener was lighting one by one. Lucien stopped and stared down at me.

'You're looking very lovely tonight, Emma.'

'You don't have to make pretty speeches. We are not in public now.'

'My God, must you say things like that to me? I suppose you would rather Jean de Rennes paid you compliments.'

'What makes you say that? I care nothing for him.'

'Heavens knows, I don't like this farcical situation any more than you do.'

'It's not that ... you mistake me ...' he made an impatient movement and then swung round to face me. 'Emma, will you marry me?' he said abruptly.

He had so taken me by surprise that it was an instant before I could find an answer. 'Marry you? But you can't mean it. It is impossible. How can I?'

But now he had seized my hands. The reserve was all broken down, the words came out in a rush. 'I know what you would say. I am French and you are English. Our two countries are at war. You are masquerading here as someone else whereas I ... I have nothing to offer you, nothing but an empty title and the miserable salary of a clerk on my stepfather's estates. There is everything against it, but I love you, Emma ... I've fought against it ... I've tried not to say it ... but now I must. I love you, I want you ... you don't know how much ...'

It was everything that I had dreamed of, everything that I had longed to hear. I wanted to throw myself into his arms, but my father stood between us. If I were to tell him what I knew, would he believe in my father's innocence as I did or would I see his face darken with anger as it had done at Avignon, would he turn away from me to join the hunters who sought to destroy him? All these things went through my mind and I knew I dare not risk it and so I hesitated.

'I did not know you felt like this ... how could I?' I said lamely at last. 'You must give me time, just a little time ...' and he mistook me. He thought I didn't care. The light died out of his face. He dropped my hands.

'I understand. You need not say any more. God knows I'm a bad bargain, I know that only too well. I was a fool even to think of such a thing.'

'Lucien, listen to me ...'

'No, forget it. You will go back to England, to your father. It is better like that, far better.' He moved away from me and after a moment he went on in a changed tone as if I were no more than some casual acquaintance. 'Since we are here, we might as well make the best of it. Do you know what this place is?'

'No.' Bewildered by his manner I swallowed down the catch in my throat, trying to match his coolness. I looked around me. We were in a shallow green bowl, the turf shaped in a semi-circle and cut into rows of seats, looking down towards a raised platform. Here and there were remnants of ancient stonework, half columns, part of a colonnade. 'What is it? It looks like a theatre.'

'It is. This is where the actors will perform their operetta. St Rémy was once a Roman city and they say that some retired proconsul built himself a sumptuous villa here and installed a theatre for his private amusement. It is magnificent for sound. Sit here and I will go down to the stage and speak a few lines.'

I could not understand him. It was as if for a few moments he had been crazy and now was sane again, but I fell in with his whim, climbing to the top ring of seats and sitting down wretchedly on the turf. I could see Lucien far below me, the lamps round the stage lighting his face into dramatic hollows, but before he could speak a group of men and women fantastically dressed had come climbing up on to the stage. They must have been the actors making sure that everything was ready for their performance. One of them had a lute. He plucked the strings and the sweet poignant notes floated up absolutely clear. It was stupid but I knew that the tears were running down my face.

'What is wrong, my pet? What has Lucien been saying to you?' murmured a voice close beside me.

I turned round quickly. The man who leaned over my shoulder wore the same brilliantly coloured costume as the actors with powdered wig and black silk mask, but the voice was that of my father.

'You must be mad,' I whispered. 'What in heaven's name are you doing here?'

'Masks are like ghosts, my dear. One can lose one's identity behind them. Who would know me here?'

'Lucien will, for one.'

'Perhaps.' He smiled. 'Don't look so worried. It's bound to happen sooner or later.'

His indifference to danger exasperated me. 'How did you get in?'

'I knew Gilles de Rennes in London. He likes to keep a foot in both camps, but he'll not betray a friend. Where did you get those rubies?'

'Lucien gave them to me.'

'Did he, by God! They are about all that is left of the Fontenay jewels.'

My heart seemed to miss a beat. So that was why Lucien had given them to me and I had not realized their significance. 'How do you know?'

'Martine once asked me if they could be pawned.'

'Was it she you came here to meet?'

'One of the reasons, but not the only one by a long chalk, my dear. Quiet now. They are coming.'

If he had thought to escape, it was too late. Some of the guests were strolling towards the theatre. I saw Martine with Henri de Labran. They began to climb up through the tiered seats. Louis was with them. He scrambled ahead, calling out to me excitedly.

'Emma Louise, listen. I have to speak a line. I've been practising it.'

'What is it?'

He was already dressed in the blue satin page's suit, his red brown curls brushed till they shone. He drew himself up importantly. 'I have to say, "I present this gold cup to the victor of Austria and Egypt, to the saviour of the Republic." '

'Splendid,' said my father. 'Spoken like a true patriot.'

Louis eyed him curiously. 'Didn't I do it well? Who are you?'

'An actor like yourself.'

'You were not with the others.'

'I play the villain,' said my father in mock heroic tones. 'I come by night and stab the hero to death like this.' Dramatically he drew a dagger from his belt and buried it up to the hilt in the boy's chest. The child squealed and then began to giggle as it was drawn out again leaving him unharmed.

Let me see. Do please let me see,' he exclaimed. My father wiped the blade clean with a flourish and handed it over. Louis was enchanted with it. 'It's a trick, Emma. Look! The blade goes into the hilt. I've never seen one like this before. Will you give it to me?'

'With pleasure when the play is over.'

It was at that moment when the two heads were bent together over the toy dagger that I guessed the truth and at the same insant wondered if Martine had told him. Did he know that the bright-eyed child looking up into his face with such eagerness was the son he would have liked to have, the son whose substitute I had been?

The others had reached us by now and Louis ran to meet his mother, waving the trick dagger. 'Look, Maman. Isn't it clever? The gentleman says he will give it to me afterwards.'

I saw my father look swiftly from Martine to Henri de Labran. 'I hope you do not mind the liberty, Madame,' he said quietly. 'It was just a joke to amuse the little one.'

'It is very kind of you, Monsieur. Say thank you, Louis. Are you one of the players?'

'An actor certainly as you can see, Madame. Jacques Dupont, at your service.'

I was sure that Martine had recognized him by the way she studiously avoided meeting his eyes. She said, 'I'm rather tired, Henri, and the play doesn't begin for another hour. Perhaps we could go back to the villa for a short while.'

'Yes, of course, my dear.' He offered his arm and they walked away together, taking a reluctant Louis with them.

My father was looking after them, an odd smile on his face. Then he touched my cheek lightly before moving away in the direction of the steps. My mind was in turmoil. I still could not imagine why he had come. Was something being planned? Murder perhaps, here in this beautiful garden, in front of so many guests? It could not be possible. It seems strange to say it but for these few minutes I had forgotten Lucien and his hand on my arm startled me.

'So that's it,' he said in a furious whisper. 'I might have guessed. What a fool you have made of me between you, you and your precious father!'

'I don't know what you mean.'

'Of course you do. Do you imagine I didn't recognize him even in that ridiculous fancy dress? He must be insane to take such risks. There must be others here who would know him.'

'Why should there be? You know nothing about him. If he is here, it is for a very good reason.'

Other people were drifting along the paths, staring at us curiously, thinking it some foolish lovers' tiff. Lucien took my arm, pulling me away out of earshot. He stopped under the trees that bordered the green amphitheatre.

'God Almighty, what a prize ass you have made of me! This was arranged, wasn't it? That night when you came running to me in Paris with a sorry tale of being abandoned, all those tears, it was all part of the plan, wasn't it? To get yourself here. You had it all worked out between you and I was an easy victim. I let myself be taken in. I believed every damned word . . .'

'But it was true, I swear it was. I knew nothing then.'

'Do you expect me to believe that? I'm not to be deceived twice.'

'Lucien, will you listen to me? I did not know then that my father had been here in Provence before. He told me so little. I never expected him to come back again ... I wanted only to escape to England.'

'Don't go on lying, it only makes it worse.'

'I'm not lying ...'

But he swept on, anger roughening his voice. 'Why weren't you honest with me? I might have understood, but instead you used me ... you made me believe ... Oh God, what does it matter what you made me believe?'

'What are you going to do?'

'What do you expect me to do? You let me tell you everything and all the time you knew ... That night the sergeant was killed, you heard what Guitry said and then you lied to me ... Oh Christ, that of all men, it had to be your father!'

'But it was not he who betrayed the Marquis. It was not, I swear it, Lucien. You don't know him as I do. You must believe me.'

'Why should I believe you? You would defend him whatever crime he had committed. Do you think I don't realize that? Why couldn't you have told me at first?'

'I didn't know, not for certain ...' I said desperately.

But he was not listening to me. 'That day I met you coming down from the hills, you had been up there with him, hadn't you? I knew there was something but you went on lying.' He seized me by the shoulders, holding me in a painful grip. 'And my mother? Does she know? Is she part of it too?'

But nothing would make me tell him what I knew about Martine and my father. 'Let me go. You are hurting me.'

His hands fell to his sides. He said flatly, 'I realize now that I meant nothing to you; a means to an end, that is all I have ever been. How you must have laughed at the fool who tried to keep you out of trouble when you were in it up to the neck. Well, you're on your own now. My responsibility is finished. You can do what you please.'

'Lucien, I have never laughed, never. You must believe me,' but he was already walking away from me, refusing to listen, and I couldn't blame him. I realized how it must appear to him. He had poured out his heart to me and I had thrown it back in his face. I stood there for a long time trying to regain self control, fighting the foolish tears. But the evening had to be got through somehow and presently I took the path back to the house. At the door of the villa Jean met me.

'You look exhausted,' he said, 'Has Lucien tired you out? Let me fetch you some refreshment.'

I answered him mechanically. 'Thank you. That would be delightful.'

I sat on a sofa in the drawing-room while I waited for him, my eyes on the dancers, my thoughts far away. Then I started. My father had not yet left. He was dancing with Martine. His audacity took my breath away. Perhaps it was simply my knowledge of what lay between them, but it seemed to me that in that whole ballroom these two had eyes only for each other. I saw Henri de Labran watching them and wondered if it was obvious to him too. Then Jean was back with glasses of iced wine.

I took one gratefully and he sat beside me. 'My father is beginning to grow worried,' he said cheerfully. 'Our guest of honour has not turned up yet and the performance can't be delayed much longer.'

'Is Bonaparte coming far?'

'No, but there have been several unpleasant incidents on the mountain roads lately if all Lucien says is true.'

I studied the wine in my glass. 'Surely the bandits would not dare to attack the First Consul.'

He gave me a quick glance. 'If they are bandits. Bonaparte is a very impatient man. He has the habit of riding ahead of his escort though this time he should be safe enough. He is bringing Fouché with him.'

Fouché, the Chief of Police in Paris, the most feared man in all France.

'I thought he had been banished.'

'He has had to be recalled. No one can keep order as Fouché can. They are carrying plans for the dockyards as well as money chests so they will be well guarded.' He smiled at me. 'I don't know why I am boring you with all this when I should be paying you pretty compliments. Lucien is a lucky fellow.' He got to his feet. 'Will you forgive me if I leave you, Mademoiselle? I see my father looking for me. The entertainment must go on, I fear, Bonaparte or no Bonaparte.'

Too much had happened to me that evening. I felt too weary and sick at heart to move. I must have sat there quietly for more than half an hour before I realized that everyone was moving out of the ballroom and streaming across the lawns. The performance was about to begin at last. I saw Martine with her husband coming towards me. My father had vanished and I could not see Lucien anywhere.

'Come with us,' said Martine. 'The actors have taken charge of Louis.'

'The evening seems likely to end in a sorry fiasco without the man it was intended for,' said Henri de Labran ironically. 'Still I suppose poor Gilles de Rennes must go through with it.'

I remember almost nothing about the little burlesque operetta, only that it was superbly sung and the music was gay. What happened afterwards drove it out of my mind. I suppose it must have been nearly over when there was a sudden disturbance. The Comte de Rennes in the front row got to his feet. The singers paused and then went on again until he raised his hand for them to stop.

A bedraggled little group of men had appeared through the trees. It was quite dark by now but the lamps showed them clearly. Bonaparte was at their head. The audience half rose to its feet as he strode down the steps, followed by a thin-faced man whom I guessed to be Fouché. Dust and dirt smeared the General's face and there was a slit in the back of his uniform coat. He skidded on one of the grassy steps, stumbled and recovered himself. His ferocious glance effectively quenched the nervous titter that ran round the spectators.

He had reached the Comte de Rennes. 'Is this the way you receive your guests in Provence?' he thundered. 'With an armed ambush only a few leagues from your gates? Did you plan to have me murdered?'

'You wrong me, *mon général*. I deeply resent such an accusation,' was the Comte's dignified reply. 'I am grieved and shocked that you should have been attacked. It is our shame that bandits still infest our roads.'

'Bandits be damned! These were no bandits. They were

traitors, do you hear, terrorists who call themselves the Chevaliers de Foi and spill the blood of the country they profess to love.'

'What happened? Have you been robbed? Are any of your men killed?'

'What happened?' roared Bonaparte. 'We were following the mountain road and we found the track blocked—a landslide, fallen trees, peasants trying to get them moved, peasants who apologized respectfully and offered to lead us by another route, one that would be both quicker and safer . . .' he spat disgustedly. 'I ought to have smelled a trap. They led us up into those damned hills till we were hopelessly lost and then they fell upon us.'

'Many of them?'

'How the devil do I know how many! They sprang out of the rocks. They seized on the coach. They dragged out poor Fouché here. One of them was an Englishman . . .'

'An Englishman?' exclaimed the Comte. 'It is not possible.'

'Do you call me a liar? He laid hands on me. He laughed in my face but I got away from him.' His voice rose to a scream. 'I, Napoleon Bonaparte, was forced to run like a scared rabbit or God knows what he would have done with me.' He made a furious gesture and the torn coat split from top to bottom. It was too much. A ripple of laughter ran through the guests, suddenly silenced when he swung round scowling. His pale face framed by the lank dark hair was contorted with rage. He glared from one to the other.

'I'll not rest until I have this Englishman in my hands. Fouché! Where the devil are you?' The thin bedraggled man took a step forward. 'Fouché, arrange for hostages to be taken. Six young men. Pick them from around here. Their lives shall pay for that of the Englishman.'

'You cannot do that,' the bold voice startled everyone. Heads were turned.

'Who dares to tell me what I can or cannot do?'

Lucien leaped over the last row of seats. 'You cannot demand six innocent lives for one Englishman. It is unjust, it is inhuman.'

It was fully dark now but the lamps cast long shadows about the two men who faced one another. I stood up in my seat, clasping my hands over my heart to still its wild beating. Now, I thought, he will tell them everything about me, about my father. They will search the grounds. They will find and seize him.

Bonaparte threw up his head with an arrogant gesture. 'Those who fight against me, fight against France. They have their remedy. Let them root out this nest of traitors and their cursed leader and the hostages will go free.'

I waited breathlessly. There was something formidable about the small implacable figure in the torn coat.

'These men have done nothing,' said Lucien loudly. 'Take me instead. You were not afraid to murder my father. Let me take their place.'

'Oh no, Monsieur de Fontenay,' Bonaparte said contemptuously, 'I want no heroes, no martyrs.'

'Why? Are you afraid?' went on Lucien, tauntingly. 'Do you think if you kill me the people of France will begin to recognize you for what you are?'

Bonaparte made a threatening gesture and the Comte de Rennes intervened quickly between them.

'I beg of you, *mon général* . . .'

'Well, Monsieur le Comte, what is it now?'

'If you carry out this threat, you will put the whole of Provence against you. You cannot wish for that. It would not be wise. Believe me . . .'

'I do not choose to believe you. I know how to deal with traitors and it would seem that Provence is full of them. Where is your Chief of Police? Where is Charles Guitry?'

'I do not invite such persons to my house,' said the Comte stiffly.

'So much the worse for you. Have him brought here?'

'But it is past midnight. He will be in bed.'

'Then wake him. *Mon Dieu*, are you all determined to thwart me?'

'He shall be sent for at once, and while we wait, may I suggest that you come to the house?' said the Comte tactfully. 'You must be in need of rest and refreshment.'

Bonaparte was staring at Lucien with narrowed eyes. Then he turned abruptly away. 'Very well, let us go.'

He strode off, the others following hurriedly, joined by the guards who had waited at the edge of the trees. The guests looked at one another in dismay. The evening was irretrievably ruined and they wanted only to get away as quickly as possible.

Martine was very pale. She said, 'Will he carry out his threat?'

'Why not?' replied her husband dryly. 'It could be a bluff, but his vanity has been pricked. Nothing galls a man like that more. Whoever planned this has made the First Consul look ridiculous and nobody has done that up to now. Whatever possessed Lucien to act so foolishly? He could have got himself arrested.'

I wondered too with a sickening feeling of dread, but there was relief and gratitude too because he had not done what I feared. Instead he had offered himself as victim, he had tried to deflect Bonaparte's anger away from my father to himself and I loved him for it.

Louis came running up to us, looking disappointed. 'They would not let me make my speech. They said he was too angry to listen.'

'I'm afraid he was. Never mind,' I said consolingly. 'You had a lovely evening, didn't you?'

We had begun to move away when one of the actors jumped down from the stage and came after us. 'I was asked to give you this, little one,' and he held out the toy dagger.

'I thought he'd forgotten,' said the boy delightedly.

'Wasn't he one of your troop?' asked Henri de Labran.

'No, Monsieur, he was not one of us. He borrowed one of our costumes, for a private jest, he said. He left the villa some time before we started the play.'

'I see. Well, it must be a disappointment to you all, but no doubt you will be well paid.'

"N'importe," said the man with a laugh. 'It is all in a day's work.' He saluted Martine and went back to his companions.

Henri took his wife's arm. 'I think the sooner we leave the better, my dear.'

I followed after them across the grass, holding Louis by the hand. I would have liked to speak to Lucien but I could not see him anywhere. A cool wind had sprung up and I shivered in my thin dress. That night the icy breath of danger seemed to have come very close.

Chapter 12

It was the next day when we knew that it was no bluff, that Bonaparte had meant what he said. Two young men had been taken at random from Villeroy, one of them the father of the baby I had seen christened. The poor woman came herself to the château with the child in her arms, weeping and distraught. I saw Martine trying to comfort her. But worse was to follow.

It had been a disturbing morning. We were sitting down to a late luncheon when Nicole came hurrying into the room. She slammed the door and leaned back against it panting.

'They have arrested Armand.'

'What!' exclaimed her father getting to his feet. 'Arrested my son! Why in God's name?'

Martine put a restraining hand on his arm. 'Are you sure?' she asked quietly. 'There could be some mistake.'

Nicole rounded on her furiously. 'There's is no mistake. I saw it with my own eyes. He was riding back with Lucien from the vineyards. They were stopped by Guitry with his men. They would not even let him come back to the house.'

'Where is Lucien now?'

'He stayed to argue with them, but he won't be able to do any good, not after what he did last night,' said Nicole impatiently. 'Father, you must go now, at once. You must bring Armand back. Why should they take him? He has never done any harm to anyone. He is innocent.'

'They are all innocent,' said Martine.

'I don't care about the others. It is Armand who matters, and it's not true that they are innocent. You know that. We all do. Why should Armand suffer for them?' She pointed a finger at Martine, her voice rising. 'You know why they have taken him. It is because of you. It is you who have been in league with them all along, helping them, giving them food and money . . .'

'Be quiet, Nicole,' interrupted her father sternly.

'I won't be quiet. It is time someone said it. If you weren't blind, you would have seen it for yourself months ago. She swears she will do nothing to hurt you, but she lies. She takes all you can give her and cares nothing for you, nothing at all . . .'

'Stop it, Nicole, do you hear? I will not listen to this raving.' Henri had seized his daughter by the shoulders. 'You must be out of your mind to say such things. Have you forgotten that Martine is my wife?' She began to cry helplessly, leaning against him, and he held her close for a moment, awkwardly stroking her hair. 'There, there, child, I understand. You are upset about your brother. Hush now, it will be all right.'

It was then that I saw Lucien standing in the doorway. He must have followed Nicole into the room and heard her wild accusations. Henri turned to him at once.

'Is it true what she says?'

'Yes. I tried to reason with them, but Guitry was adamant. It is just possible that they may have taken Armand for questioning.'

Henri de Labran released his daughter. 'By what right does this policeman take my son? Are they all mad in France? I don't know which are worse, the fools hiding in the hills with their murderous plotting or this damned Corsican who wants to throw our country into war for the sake of his own glory.' I had never seen him so angry. He did not raise his voice and yet you could feel it like a pent-up flood that could burst its banks at any moment and sweep all to disaster.

Martine took a step forward. 'Let me come with you, Henri.'

'No, my dear, it will not help. It is best that you stay here. Put some things together, fresh linen, a change of clothes, the boy may need them. Lucien, come with me. There are one or two things that must be done if I should be detained.'

The two men went out together. Nicole raised a tear-stained face glaring from me to Martine. 'Why does Papa always believe you and not me? Why? Why?' She pressed a hand to her mouth and ran out of the room.

'Poor child. She and Armand tease one another but they have always been very close.' Martine crossed to the door shutting it quietly, then she came swiftly to me. 'Emma,' she whispered, 'you know where he is, don't you? You can reach Jacques quickly.'

'Perhaps.' I drew away from her, all the old hostility surging back, feeling, unjustly maybe, that it was for her sake that my father took so many risks and put himself into so much danger. It was obvious to me why Guitry had picked on Armand. All along he had had his suspicions and now he saw a chance of getting at the truth. Henri de Labran worshipped his only son. He would sacrifice anyone and anything to ensure his safety.

Martine put her hand on my arm. 'Go to him. Tell him he must get away, no matter what his plans are. He must leave France now. I know these people. They are independent. They care nothing for kings or governments, they act only to suit themselves, but they are fiercely loyal to their own. Attack one of them and they will fight back ruthlessly, and your father is a foreigner.. While he is successful, while he puts money in their pockets, they will follow him gladly, but let him put them in danger and they will hunt him as they would a wild animal.'

'That's not true of all of them.'

'No, not of all, but there are some ... I know, believe me,' she paused and then went on quickly. 'If Guitry does not release Armand and I don't think he will for one moment, then I am terribly afraid of what Henri may do.'

'Has he guessed that Jacques Dupont is your lover?' It was a cheap jibe and I was ashamed the instant I said it. Martine looked at me and then sighed.

'I know you resent me. It is natural, I suppose, but there is no need. There have been times when I've wanted to tell you about it.'

'I don't want to hear.'

'You are very fond of him, Emma, aren't you?'

'What does that mean to you?'

'A great deal, and since we both love him, my dear, can't you see how desperately important it is that we save him from himself? He cares nothing for danger. He will risk anything just as he did before but this time he mustn't. He will not escape again. I tried to tell him that last night, but he only laughed at my anxiety. Perhaps he will listen to you.'

'I doubt it . . . but I will go.'

She caught at my hand. 'Emma, don't hate me,' but I pulled myself away unwilling to yield anything. It did not take me long to change into my riding dress and when I came down I found Beauregard already saddled. Louis came running from his playroom wanting to come with me, but I sent him back.

'You know what Maman said. You were out very late last night. You must rest today.'

'I am not tired.'

'Louis, this time I cannot take you.'

The boy pulled a long face, but he let me go. It was a still afternoon with no sun but a heavy overpowering heat that brought a prickle of sweat at the least movement. When I reached the little pavilion, I slipped from the saddle, tethering Beauregard in the old place. It was a hard climb. I had only done it once before and then it was with Mouton, so that this time I went wrong frequently and had to retrace my steps. At some of the worst places I was forced to scramble along the rocks on hands and knees, pulling myself up by the scrubby thorn that tore at my hands. It seemed a long time before thankfully I saw the crumbling turret and made my way to the stone steps. My path was immediately barred, but the young man with the rifle and the threatening gesture was Marius. He stared at me for a moment and then lowered his gun.

I said urgently, 'Marius, I must speak with Jacques. Is he up there?'

'Yes, Mademoiselle,' he grinned at me and I guessed that already Mouton must have told him who I was.

'Is your wound healed, Marius?'

'Oh yes, a little stiff that is all, thanks to Madame la Marquise. If it had not been for her, I should have been gone . . . *pouf!* Like that. It was worse than when the bull got me last year.' He stood aside to let me pass.

My father was in the little turret room with Pierre, bending over a plan spread out on the rickety table. He looked up as I came in.

'Emma, for God's sake, what are you doing here?'

'I had to come . . . to warn you . . .'

'I think I know what you're going to say. Bonaparte doesn't care to be made ridiculous so he's taken six hostages and it is their lives or mine. Don't be afraid, my dear, it is no more than a threat. He will never dare to carry it out.'

'You don't know everything. There is more than that, much more. This morning they arrested Armand.'

'Armand!' exclaimed Pierre. *'Mon Dieu,* that's a devilishly clever move on Guitry's part. Don't you see what it means? The peasants . . . well, that could be bad enough, but Henri de Labran will move heaven and earth to save his son.'

'Perhaps.' My father shrugged his shoulders. 'We have to take the risk. I still do not think I am in any immediate danger and nor are they. There is time yet.'

'Time for what?'

'Many things. You look exhausted, my pet, and I don't wonder, climbing up here in this heat. In the passage along there, you will find some coffee and a disgusting little stove. Brew some for us, there's a good girl.'

I had known it was useless before I set out. He would never run away from danger. It was the kind of challenge he could never resist, but despite his casual manner, I sensed he was on edge and glad to be rid of me so I did as he asked. I went into the side passage and found mugs and a pan of black coffee still warm on the charcoal brazier. I had to blow on it to revive the heat. And while I was kneeling by the embers, I heard a sudden clatter below, the sound of booted feet running up the stone steps and with a sickening fear, I thought, 'I am too late. They have come for him and this is the end.' I got to my feet though God knows there was little I could have done, but it was not Guitry in the doorway with his policemen crowding behind him, it was Lucien standing there, but a Lucien who looked somehow different, no longer hesitant, no longer diffident, but taut and resolute.

My father showed no surprise. 'Come in, my dear boy,' he said, 'we have been expecting you for quite some time.' He moved towards him, smiling, holding out his hand, but Lucien ignored it. He strode into the room, frowning, looking from Pierre to my father.

'What the devil happened last night? What went wrong?'

'Nothing went wrong,' replied my father calmly. 'We did just as you had planned. We got the money chests, the papers, the plans for the dockyards. They are all here, waiting to be shipped to England. What surprised us was the presence of Bonaparte himself.'

'I understood that he was travelling separately.'

'So did we. That was our information,' said my father wryly. 'When I tumbled that insignificant little green-coated rat off his horse and seized him by the throat, I got the greatest shock of my life. We were not ready for it. You know that well enough.' My father grinned at the memory. 'I never saw anyone look so surprised, but by God, he fought back, agile as a cat, and never did I see anyone run so fast when I let him go.'

'And missed the best opportunity ever likely to come our way,' said Pierre. 'A knife in his belly and we'd have been rid of Napoleon Bonaparte once and for all.'

'No, my friend, you're wrong,' said my father. 'Assassination turns a man into a martyr and martyrs can be the very devil to destroy. Capture him alive and he becomes merely absurd. There is nothing like laughter for cutting a man down to size and the Bonapartes of this world cannot afford to be laughed at, neither can they afford to be defeated. That is left to us British. Isn't that so, Lucien?'

For a moment there was silence. I leaned against the wall, utterly bewildered. It seemed impossible and yet it had to be true. Lucien had deceived me. He had deceived us all. He had pretended to know nothing. He had accused me of lying and it was he who had lied to me. I still did not completely understand and I stayed where I was, half hidden, listening, trying to grasp the meaning of what they said.

Lucien looked directly at my father. 'You know about the arrests?'

'Yes, I know.'

'You realize what it can mean. Have you guards posted? Guitry is out already scouring the hills and there will be others with him. There are plenty only too anxious to curry favour with General Bonaparte. Captain Jean de Rennes for one. He will enjoy hunting men, it is more exciting than wild beasts.'

My father nodded to Pierre. 'Go the rounds. Make sure they are on the alert.'

I thought Pierre went reluctantly as if he disliked the peremptory order. Lucien watched him go and then turned to face my father. He said crisply, 'You must have wondered why I have not come up to meet you before. Since the murder of the sergeant I have been almost sure that Guitry has had me watched. I had to go carefully if I was not to involve my mother and my stepfather ... your daughter too.'

'You have played the simpleton damned well if I may say so,' said my father dryly. 'It seems that up to now no one has guessed your part in what has been happening here during the last few months ... not even Emma. I congratulate you. You have your father's genius for organization.'

'Perhaps. I don't know.' They faced one another across the table and something I saw in Lucien's face made my heart beat faster, but he only said quietly, 'Until last night I did not know your identity.'

'Didn't Pierre tell you?'

'Pierre sometimes likes to keep things to himself. It makes him feel important. Even when the ship picked him up at Trevira last spring, he told me nothing of you. It was safer, he said. I had no idea it was you who were to replace the English agent we had expected.'

'Neither had I. Until orders came from London a few weeks ago, I had never thought to return to Provence and I certainly never expected to find my daughter here. I have you to thank for that.'

But Lucien did not seem to be listening. He said angrily, 'What the devil took you to St Rémy last night? You could have ruined everything.'

'I had my reasons.'

'I hope they were good ones.'

'They appeared so to me. If you will pardon my saying so, you took a considerable risk yourself. Bonaparte could have had you arrested.'

'He made me angry.'

'As he did in Paris,' said my father ironically. 'One cannot afford personal feelings at times like these.'

'Sometimes they cannot be ignored.' Lucien paused and

then went on. 'As it happens, there is something personal that must be settled between us, Monsieur Tremayne, before we go any further.'

'Indeed.' My father smiled a little. 'You are not by any chance asking me for my daughter's hand, are you?'

For an instant Lucien looked taken aback, then the colour surged up into his face. He still had his riding crop in his hand and he raised it threateningly. 'If I thought you were laughing at me ...'

'You would no doubt thrash me within an inch of my life,' said my father lightly. 'Believe me, I am very far from laughing. I am deadly serious. Emma is very dear to me. If it is not that then what is it?'

Lucien drew a deep breath. 'When you were here before, someone betrayed my father to his death. Was it you?'

'No.'

'Charles Guitry was very definite.'

'He was deliberately twisting the truth.'

'Am I to believe that?'

'You must please yourself. I am not in the habit of lying.'

'Do you know who it was?'

'Yes.'

I think the answer startled Lucien as much as it did me. He leaned forward. 'Who?'

My father did not move. He spoke almost lazily, but his eyes never left Lucien's face. 'It is better that you do not know. Guitry has many unpleasant methods of extracting information. Some men cannot endure pain as easily as others.'

'That still doesn't excuse betrayal,' said Lucien fiercely.

'Doesn't it? The soldiers of the Republic, I remember, had a particularly charming habit of roasting the soles of one's feet over a slow fire. Ask the Curé if you don't believe me. He still limps, poor man. Or would you rather I took off my boots?'

I shuddered, realizing how little my father had told me. The coffee began to bubble. I poured in a little more water from the jug and as I did so, I saw that Pierre had come back and was leaning up against the wall within the shadow of the doorway as if he did not wish to be seen.

Lucien had his back to him. He was still watching my father. 'This man you speak of . . . is he still alive?'

'That is neither here nor there. It is not relevant to our present problems. It is over and done with long ago.'

'I demand to know. It is my right.'

'No, it is not your right, Lucien. It is no one's right. Whatever he did is now between his conscience and his God. Revenge is useless. Your father would not have asked it from you.'

Lucien was silent for a long moment, then he said slowly, 'Very well, I accept that.'

'Good, then that's settled.' My father relaxed. He let himself drop on one of the wooden boxes that served for chairs. 'There is one thing I would like to say before we get down to business. Your father was one of the bravest men I have known, Lucien, and one of the most far-seeing. He realized at once that after revolution there must come tyranny. It is inevitable. He recognized it in Bonaparte before any of us and he gave his life to try and prevent it.'

'Do you think I don't know that?' Lucien had moved away. He was staring through one of the window openings. 'Ever since his death I have had it in my mind, but for years I could do nothing. There was my mother, there was my brother Louis. We had to live. Now it is different and yet sometimes I wonder what it is we are fighting for.'

'Isn't it what the first revolutionaries fought for and then lost sight of so completely—liberty, equality and fraternity?'

'Do you have that in England?'

My father laughed. 'Good God, I wish we had. Men being what they are, England is far from being free, but I think we have glimmerings of it. We keep individual freedom before us as a great ideal and if sometimes it is only a mirage and sometimes we forget it, still it is there and we grope our way towards it.'

Lucien said broodingly, 'At first I thought we had it too. I wanted to believe because France had suffered so much; now I know it is impossible and all because of one man. When I was in Paris, I saw how much had been lost already. Liberty is engraved above the doors of the

Tuileries, but armed sentries halt you at every step. One word of criticism and you are clapped in gaol, two words and it is the guillotine.'

'Make no mistake, Lucien,' said my father gravely. 'Bonaparte is an able administrator and a soldier of genius, but he has a ravening ambition. If he is given his head, he will turn France into an armed camp and that is what we in Britain intend to prevent if we can.'

'I too, and those who think like me, but to others he is a hero. That is why we must act soon before all power is in his hands.' Lucien was resolute and determined again, all doubts vanished. 'What is our next step? How far have we got with the plan?'

'Quite a long way, but let us have some coffee first.' My father glanced towards me. 'Is it ready, Emma?'

'More or less, but there is no milk, only sugar.'

'Good enough. There is a bottle of brandy there some-where. Bring it with the coffee.'

Lucien looked at me as I brought the steaming mugs to the table. Obviously he had not known I was there, but he said nothing. While my father poured a generous measure of brandy into the mugs, Pierre came forward into the room.

'All is quiet. Not a mouse stirring.'

'Splendid. Come and sit down. Emma, have we some coffee for Pierre?'

I went to fetch it and when I came back, they had all three pulled up the wooden boxes and were sitting round the table. My father leaned forward, the mug in his two hands, sipping it before he spoke.

'Bonaparte is still at St Rémy with the Comte de Rennes, but we know that he intends to visit Marseilles be-fore he goes to Toulon.'

'Isn't it possible that after last night he may change his plans?'

'It is possible, but I do not think so. It would be admit-ting to fear of what might happen to him on the road and his pride will prevent that.'

'This time he may be heavily guarded.'

'Perhaps, but we are prepared for that too, and we have someone very close to him who will keep us informed. It all depends on how long he stays at St Rémy. This may be the very opportunity we have been waiting for and if so we must be prepared to seize it when it comes. It is a heaven-sent chance that we cannot afford to miss. Time with us is the all-important factor.'

'I realize that.' There was silence for a moment, then Lucien said quietly, 'Do we kill him?'

'No. I discussed this very question at great length with certain persons before I left London. Assassination had to be considered of course. Some of your exiled fellow countrymen are hot for it, but in England we have a distaste for murder until every other method has failed. No, we take him prisoner and this is where I come in. Now, on the coast this side of Les Saintes Maries de-la-Mer, there is a tiny harbour, isn't that so, Lucien?'

'Yes, I know it well. It is a good spot. There is only one narrow opening into the lagoon.'

'Thank God for the Camargue. It is impossible for Guitry to patrol everywhere along those deserted shores. He would need a legion. An English ship is cruising just outside. As soon as the Captain receives the signal, he will sail in as near as he can to the shore and send in a boat while we carry our prisoners across the marshes. Then hey-presto, we sail for England. Weather permitting he'll not be feasting at St James's as he boasts, but eating humble pie in the Tower of London before the end of the summer.'

'And then what?'

'Then it will be out of my hands. I will have done my part. Then it will be up to you, Lucien, and those like you.'

'I still think you are wrong,' argued Pierre, for the first time breaking into the conversation. ' "Stone-dead hath no fellow", isn't that one of your English sayings?'

'The man who first made that remark was something of a traitor to liberty himself,' remarked my father dryly.

'It is a good plan,' said Lucien. 'I like it. I have been thinking over our plan of campaign. We should divide our forces. I will command one and Jacques the other. Then we can take him in a pincer movement. If he does take the mountain road from St Rémy and pray God he does, then there is an excellent place ... look here ... on the map. There are woods spreading high into the hills on either side. It is an ideal spot for an ambush ...'

The two heads bent over the table, but Pierre drew back. He was watching them with a curious expression of anger and jealousy. The absurd thought struck me that it was almost like that of a child who has been denied his part in the game, only this was no game. It was a matter of life and death. Then my father drew his attention to something and he too bent over the map.

I stood in the passage, my untouched coffee in my hand. It seemed impossible to believe that the night before in the gardens at St Rémy Lucien had asked me to marry him. Why had he done it knowing what he did? He had attacked me for deceiving him, while ever since I had met him first in Paris it was he who had been living a lie. How could I trust any longer in anything he said? I collected the mugs from the table, but he did not look up. I watched him mark the place on the map while he listened to my father, his face intent. Then I carried the mugs back into the passage and stacked them by the charcoal stove. When I returned, they were on their feet.

My father was saying, 'You must go, Lucien. Will you be kind enough to take Emma down with you?' He put out a hand and drew me to him. 'This daughter of mine takes too many risks. I'm half afraid of her falling down the rocks and breaking her neck.'

'I am ready when she is,' said Lucien. 'I will wait below.' He went out with Pierre.

'Emma,' said my father quietly when they had gone, 'find a way to reassure Martine without giving too much away.'

'She begged me to warn you of treachery.'

'I know what she fears, but I am prepared for it. Take care of her, Emma, for my sake ... and tell her if she needs me for any reason whatsoever, she has only to send me a message.'

He thought only of her. A bitterness caught at my throat. Then my father put his arm round my shoulders and pulled me close to him. 'My brave girl, I'm proud of you. It will not be long now and when we go, then you will come with me.'

'Papa, why didn't you tell me about Lucien and what he was doing? Why did you let me go on thinking of him as I did?'

'My dear, it was his own decision. It had to come from him and not from me. Lucien has his own life and it is not an easy one. He must make his own choice. Remember that.'

Did he understand how I felt? I think he did and wanted to prepare me for what might happen. I put my arms round his neck, clinging to him, suddenly very afraid.

'Papa, take care of yourself please.'

'When have I ever done anything else? I'm a selfish devil, Emma, always have been.' He smiled down at me touching my cheek with one long finger. 'But we've had some good times together and we'll have some more. Now go quickly.'

Lucien was waiting for me. At the bottom of the steps I looked back at my father standing in the ragged stone arch and knew that here in this wild haunted spot he was completely at home as he had never been in the drawing-rooms of fashionable society. This was the life he loved. I felt again that shiver of danger that had always clung to him and realized suddenly and overwhelmingly that this was what I loved in him, just as I loved it in Lucien. I had thought it was the difference between them, that it was Lucien's gentleness, his quietness that I loved, but it was not. It was the hidden violence, the unpredictability that he shared with my father and it frightened me as nothing else had done.

We scrambled down the steep path together and he gave me his hand at the rough places. His own pony was tethered close to Beauregard. He helped me into the saddle. We had almost reached Villeroy before he spoke.

'I would be grateful, Emma, if you would say nothing of this afternoon to my mother.'

'If you wish.' Then my anger at his deception got the better of me. I said, 'Lucien, why did you bring me here from Paris?'

'You know why. I wanted to help you.'

'And lied to me about everything from the very first moment we met.'

'Not about everything.'

'I wish I could believe that.'

'I had no choice, Emma, surely you must realize that by now.'

But I was still sore at heart. I said bitterly, 'Thank God, I shall soon be out of this country.'

'You will go with your father. That is what you've always wanted, isn't it, Emma?'

'Is there anything wrong in that?'

'No, nothing wrong, only . . .'

'Only what?'

'Nothing. It doesn't matter.'

An enormous weariness swept over me. So much worry, anxiety and turmoil and all for what? What fools we were, my father, Lucien, Pierre, all of us, committed to what my practical mind told me was a desperate and foolhardy enterprise. Martine was right. What did I care who sat on France's throne, or England's either come to that, provided those I loved were safe and unharmed.

Chapter 13

It is not easy to behave just as usual when every day, almost every hour, you live in fear for those you love. There was in any case a brooding tension throughout the whole household. Armand was a favourite with everyone at Villeroy and he was still in prison.

'They're treating him decently enough,' said Henri de Labran when he returned from Tarascon that evening. 'I saw to that, but the Chief of Police is under strict orders to produce the head of the Englishman before Bonaparte leaves Provence.'

'And when will that be?' asked Martine, her face bent over her embroidery so that no one could read her expression.

'Within the next week if not before. The man's restless as a flea. He stays nowhere long. My guess is that Guitry's future depends on it and Fouché is driving at him to produce results. He has begun a systematic search of the caves and hills and they are questioning rigorously all suspects. Sooner or later someone will crack and then there will be an end of it.'

I was never quite sure of Henri de Labran or of how much he guessed of his wife's involvement with the rebels. Despite his open manner he was a man who kept his own counsel and he had balanced on a political tightrope for a long time.

The hours seemed endless. I could concentrate on nothing. Louis' lessons suffered badly and I lay awake at night seeing the dark figures of men that combed the honeycomb of caves at Les Baux. Once I dreamed I was back in the turret room. My father was there, sitting at the table, and it was dark except for the feeble gleam of a lantern. I saw the shadowy figure in the doorway and knew he was in danger. I tried desperately to warn him, but as always in a nightmare, no sound came out of my throat and I watched paralysed as the figure crept up behind him. I saw the lifted knife. The light fell on the face of the murderer and it was not Guitry, but Lucien. I woke up, terrified and sweating. It was a long time before I could stop trembling. It was only a dream, I told myself. Lucien had accepted my father's denial, but doubt nagged at me. Did the fact that he did not know the name of his father's betrayer still burn inside him? We had not spoken of it and I saw scarcely anything of him. He went out early and came back late.

It was two days after we had come down from the hills and I had gone up to my room early pleading a headache because I could not endure to sit downstairs and listen to Georges Montaud who had brought a message and stayed to give an account of how the search was proceeding. Nicole had questioned him eagerly. I suspected that there was nothing she would not have done to save her brother. I had not seen Lucien all day. He had gone to Arles on an errand for his stepfather and had not returned to supper. I was in my dressing-gown but had not gone to bed when there was a tap at my door. I thought it was Martine, but when I opened it cautiously, Lucien was standing there, his coat and boots white with dust as if he had been riding hard.

'What has happened?' I whispered. 'They have not taken my father?'

'No, but I must speak with you for a moment.'

The house was quiet, but Nicole's room was only down the passage and she might still be awake. I said, 'You had better come in.'

He slipped into the room while I shut the door as quietly as I could. He said quickly, 'I have been with them tonight. They have moved from the old castle, much further into the hills. It was a long ride.' The candle lit his face. He looked resolute and determined. 'It is all fixed.'

'When is it to be?'

'Four days from now. We have all the details. Bonaparte will set out in the early evening by the mountain road. There we shall wait for him.'

'Suppose it is only a trick . . . intended to deceive you.'

'Why should it be? Our informant has always been reliable. He has never failed before. In any case it is worth the risk.'

'Lucien, if you succeed, if you do capture him, what will you do?'

'That is what I wanted to tell you. Your father must go back to England with him and Mouton will take you across the marshes to the ship. It is all planned down to the last detail.' He smiled grimly. 'Do you know who is waiting in the *Sea Witch*? It is Victor, the worthy Victor, who would so much like to marry you.'

I turned away so that he should not see my face. He doesn't care I thought. I have been an amusement for a little while but now it is all over. He has used me as he believes that I have used him.

I heard him say, 'As for me, I must stay in France. It is what my father would have wished.'

I felt as if I were being torn in two. One part of me wanted to say, 'Let me stay with you. I don't care what happens if only I can share your life.' One word from him and I might have thrown myself into his arms, but he said nothing, and then there was my father. How could I let him go from me when I had only just found him again?

I said, 'Lucien, you should not stay any longer. Please go. Someone might hear us talking. They will wonder.'

'Yes, of course, but I wanted you to know at once.'

I felt his eyes on me, but I could not endure any more. I pushed him towards the door. 'You must go quickly.'

As I watched him slip soft-footed down the passage, I was almost sure that I heard another door open and shut very gently, but though I looked up and down, I saw and heard nothing more and I thought that perhaps in my anxiety I had only imagined it.

Another day dragged by and it was almost a relief when very early the following morning Jean de Rennes drove a light carriage into the courtyard. I saw him from the window as he swung himself to the ground throwing the reins to one of the stable boys.

'I have come to say goodbye,' he said when he was shown into the sitting-room. 'General Bonaparte is leaving soon and I shall be going with him, but I thought we might have a farewell picnic.' His eyes went from me to Nicole. 'What do you say?'

'I don't know. I'm not in the mood for picnics,' said Nicole, but now Martine had come into the room.

'Nonsense, Nicole. It will do you good.'

'I was sure you would agree with me, Madame,' said the young man, smiling at her. 'I thought we might go to the fountain of Vaucluse. We will take Louis if we may and Louis' governess too of course. Have you visited Petrarch's fountain yet, Mademoiselle Emma?'

'No, never.'

'Excellent. You will enjoy it, and Lucien too. Where is Lucien?'

Nicole still refused but Martine persuaded her. 'I know you are worried about Armand,' she said, 'but it won't help him to make yourself ill and you will not bring him back any sooner by staying in the house. You have scarcely stirred out since he was arrested.'

Lucien was at home that morning and when he came in, Martine urged him to go with us.

'I have other things to do,' he said curtly.

'Nothing important and I am sure Emma will be glad of your company.'

Louis was clinging to his hand, begging him to come, and to my surprise he gave in to the boy's pleading. It seems strange that in the midst of so much stress and anxiety we should go off on a light-hearted picnic but I think that all three of us, Lucien, Nicole and I, in our different ways welcomed it as a relief and were glad to be out of the oppressive atmosphere of the house.

We set off within the hour packed into the light carriage, an excited Louis squeezed between Nicole and myself. Peppi the dog was perched on top of the picnic basket at our feet while Jean and Lucien took turns at driving the two sturdy horses. At first the road took us through the olive groves and vineyards and I felt myself relax for the first time for days. It was hot but I was wearing a thin green muslin dress and at the last moment I had pinned a little cluster of dark purple lavender at my breast. Louis had picked it for me. It was something he often did, running into my room in the early morning with a few wild flowers and they would stand on my dressing table in a glass of water till they withered.

I leaned back with eyes half-closed listening dreamily to the boy's chatter, the light hood of the carriage protecting us from the worst of the sun's glare. Presently we came to a village where the River Sorgues divided into several small channels running in and out of the houses and where little water mills splashed and murmured. The road followed the river until we saw the high limestone ridge and came to Vaucluse itself.

We left the carriage and walked along the mossy banks to where the spring gushes out from a deep cavern, dark and haunted, into a fathomless pool, cool, mysterious and shadowy. We sat on the bank under the shade of trees to eat our luncheon. The wine we drank was no clearer than the translucent water. Louis lay on his stomach dropping white pebbles among the water weeds floating like strands of emerald-green hair. Peppi plunged in to bring out the dripping stones, barking joyously and shaking the water from his coat in diamond-sparkling spray.

'For heaven's sake, Louis, keep that wretched animal away,' exclaimed Nicole pettishly. 'He is soaking me.'

Jean laughed, giving her his hand and helping her to sit beside him further up the bank. We had been talking about the Italian poet Petrarch who had lived out his life close to this lovely place writing passionate verses to his beloved Laura.

'He saw her first when he was twenty-three,' murmured Lucien dreamily, 'in a green dress with violets at her breast and he loved her for the rest of her life and his.'

I met his eyes across the child's head. Something inside me leaped with hope and then died down again.

'What a stupid waste,' said Nicole. 'To spend a whole life loving someone whom you can never have. That would not do for me.'

'Nor me,' said Jean lazily, taking Nicole's hand and playing idly with her fingers. 'I could not live on dreams and neither could our poet. Lucien has forgotten to tell you that with all his fine ideals Petrarch still contrived to leave two bastards behind him in Avignon.'

'What is a bastard?' asked Louis suddenly sitting up and forgetting his game with the pebbles.

'Ah, that would be telling,' said Jean with a grin. 'A bastard, Louis, is a little boy who doesn't know his own father.'

'That's me,' said the child. 'I never knew my Papa.'

'Well now, that's a very ticklish question,' went on Jean with a touch of malice, looking from the boy to Lucien. 'Come to think of it, you know, there is not much likeness between you and your brother.'

Lucien who had not appeared to be listening sat bolt upright. 'What the devil do you mean by that?'

'Nothing at all, my dear fellow. How touchy you are. Can't I make a little joke?'

'It's hardly a matter for jesting.'

'I'm a bastard, I'm a bastard!' chanted Louis, jumping up and down on the bank, enchanted with his new word.

Lucien caught at the boy's arm and shook him hard. 'Be quiet, Louis. Don't ever let me hear you use that word again, do you understand? As for you, Jean, you ought to have more sense.'

'What a fuss over nothing,' said Nicole coolly. 'The child has to grow up some time. You can't keep him a baby for ever, Lucien.' She got to her feet putting up her parasol. 'I'm walking back. It's too hot here and far too many flies for my liking. Are you coming, Emma?'

The trivial incident was over but was not quite forgotten. When we drove back I sat beside Lucien with a tired Louis on my lap and a soaking-wet Peppi pressed against my skirts. Behind me I heard Nicole and Jean whispering and laughing together and for some reason it made me uneasy.

That night the mistral began to blow. I woke up and heard it, a thin whining blast that tore at the nerves. It was my first experience of the wind that everyone spoke of as if it were a living monster. The next morning it had become almost unbearable. It had risen now to its full ferocity and none of us could leave the house. Even Henri de Labran who had known it all his life was driven back by it.

'Till it breaks in a storm, it will just have to be endured,' he said irritably as he came in, slamming the heavy oak door. He was a man who spent most of his time in the open air. It did not improve his temper to be shut in the house.

It was still intensely hot and the gale was a scorching blast hurling itself against the walls. Even with doors and windows firmly closed, dust whirled in the corners of the rooms. It choked the throat until it was an effort to breathe and my thin cotton dress stuck to me at the slightest exertion.

'Our devil wind,' Lucien had called it on that first day at Avignon, 'it drives dogs mad, women crazy and jealous husbands to murder.' In the golden sunlight I had laughed and thought he exaggerated. Now I knew it was true. While the mistral blew, I don't think any of us was quite normal.

That morning a hammer of pain beat incessantly in my head until I did not know how to bear it. Louis, as much on edge as any of us, was unusually tiresome. He would not settle to anything. Jean had given him a toy drum. He marched about the room beating a deafening tattoo on it until I lost my temper and slapped him hard. I had never done such a thing before. He screamed in outrage and ran out of the room and down the stairs, banging the drum harder than ever. Peppi barking furiously raced after him. In the hall they crashed into Nicole who was carrying a tray into her father's study. Glass, wine, coffee, china flew everywhere. Exasperated Nicole grabbed the child and boxed his ears. Peppi who did not like her leaped at her growling. In the midst of the confusion the study door opened and Henri de Labran stood on the threshold.

'What in God's name is going on?' he thundered. 'Stop that child screaming.'

'She hit me,' sobbed Louis, lost to all reason. 'She hit me because she hates me. She calls me a bastard.'

There was silence for a moment broken only by the boy's noisy crying, then Henri said quietly, 'Where did you hear that word, Louis?'

Frightened, the boy looked up into his stepfather's stern face. 'I don't remember . . . it was Nicole and Jean . . .'

'Is this true, Nicole?'

'No, of course it isn't. He's picked it up from the stable boys. You know he's always out there with them. The little beast is lying.'

I had reached the bottom of the stairs by now and the boy ran to me burying his head against me. I put my arm round him. 'Louis does not tell lies,' I said indignantly.

'Oh of course not, Louis is a little angel; he can do no wrong,' said Nicole spitefully. 'Don't listen to her, Papa. You're all so fond of singing her praises, but you're wrong. You don't know her as I do. I saw Lucien coming out of her room the night before last.· Under your roof, Papa!' She swung round on me. 'Find an answer to that if you can.'

Henri de Labran frowned. I was taken aback by her attack but before I could stammer a reply, Martine had appeared at the door of the sitting-room. She said, 'Control yourself, Nicole, please. You are making a mistake. You don't understand what you are saying.'

'Oh yes I do.' Nicole whirled round on her, her face contorted with hate and jealousy. Outside the wind rose to an unbearable scream and her voice rose with it. 'You would defend her and Lucien too. Like mother, like son. Look at her standing there, Papa! Madame la Marquise, whom you love, the saint who has suffered so much! Ask her who Louis' father was? Ask her whom she goes out to meet night after night?'

'Nicole, stop it, stop it, do you hear?' Henri de Labran was only rarely moved to anger, but now he slapped his daughter's face. She glared back at him, the marks of his fingers scarlet on her pale cheek.

'You think I'm lying, don't you, yet you believe every word she says to you. Well, It's the truth. Go to Jean de Rennes, go to Charles Guitry, ask them, they will tell you. She slept with the English spy before she married you. No doubt she is sleeping with him now.'

There was an appalled silence. Then Martine said quietly, 'Emma, will you call one of the servants and have this mess cleared up. Nicole, I think you had better go to your room.'

Henri de Labran was staring at her as she stood there, proud and dignified as if nothing had happened, as if her stepdaughter had not just all but screamed 'Whore!' in her face. Then startled I saw Lucien at the back of the hall. He must have come in through the kitchens. I had no idea of how much he had heard, but now he came towards his stepfather.

'May I speak with you for a moment?'

'Later, boy, later,' said Henri abruptly. He went into his room and slammed the door against us all.

Nicole went past me up the stairs, her head held high. Lucien stood uncertainly for an instant and Martine put a hand on his arm. He patted it.

'It's all right, Mother. It will blow over. The mistral has upset her, that's all.' He freed himself gently and went to the front door. The wind blew in as he opened it, a long shuddering blast scattering dust and leaves before it closed behind him.

I called one of the servants and then took Louis upstairs. He was still upset and it took time to calm him down. At last I settled him into the armchair and began to read him one of his favourite stories. As the day wore on, the feeling of tension grew. Lucien did not return and Nicole stayed in her room. The thought of eating supper with Martine and her husband after the scene of the morning appalled me. I asked for food to be brought upstairs and ate it with Louis on the plea that he was still very disturbed and restless.

After I had got him to bed, I went to my own room but it was impossible to sleep. The mistral was blowing harder than ever, a fierce relentless gale that whined and shrieked. It tore my casement open though I had latched it and sent it crashing back against the wall. I had to get out of bed to shut it. It took all my strength to pull it in and bolt the shutters and it made the room unbearably close and hot. Sleep was miles away. I kept seeing Lucien's face when he stood in the hall. He loved his mother, I knew. Had he guessed about her and my father or had it come as a terrible shock? I had no clue to his reaction or even whether he believed it. I walked up and down the room until my throat felt dry as dust and I could stand it no longer. I put on my dressing gown and went to find a drink. As I came down the stairs, I saw a light in the sitting-room and found Martine there before me.

'I came to make sure that the shutters were fast,' she said. 'If the wind gets worse, it will find out all the weak spots.'

'Does it last long?'

She shrugged her shoulders. 'It could be a day, it could be a week. When it comes like this, in the summer, it is very unpredictable. Are you all right, Emma? When you are not used to it, the mistral can be very unnerving.'

'It is so hot. I'm thirsty.'

'I will get you something to drink.'

I followed her into the kitchen. Though the wind rattled the shuttered windows, it was cooler there surrounded by the thick stone walls. Martine brought two glasses of water from the pitcher that was kept standing on the damp flags of the scullery. She squeezed a lemon into it and we sat at the table sipping it, the candle flickering between us.

The big clock ticked and one of the cats asleep on the hearth stretched herself lazily at full length making a little murmuring sound of contentment. In the dim light, her long honey-coloured hair loose on her shoulders, Martine seemed no more than a girl and I stiffened myself against her. She seemed so calm, so untouched, that anger boiled up in me.

I said, 'Are you going to tell Lucien how you betrayed your husband for love of my father or does he know already?'

She turned to look at me. 'You must think so badly of me, Emma. I would like to try and make you understand. Things are so rarely what they seem.'

I wanted to get up and go away from her, but I couldn't and presently she went on.

'I remember so well the first time I saw him. I had never known any of the others. François was careful to keep them away from me. He thought it was safer for them and for me. Then one day Jacques came down to the cottage where I lived with an urgent message. I've forgotten what it was now, but I know I must have looked terrible.' She smiled a little. She was looking away from me into the shadows and she spoke in a whisper as if she were reliving the time that was past.

'I had been doing the washing down at the stream with the other women. They resented my being there with them and I was so bad at it. He came to look for me. He took the heavy basket from me as I struggled up the path with it. He wrung out the sheets and linen in his strong hands and we pegged them out together. It was so absurd, so totally unexpected, but he made me feel alive for the first time for many many months ... he made me feel a woman again ... and beautiful ... at such a time it shouldn't have mattered of course, but it did. I think I fell in love with him that first afternoon.'

'What about your husband? Didn't you care for him?'

Her eyes came round to me almost as if she were surprised to see me sitting there. 'François? I had been married to him when I was fifteen and he was twenty. We had only met once or twice before. That kind of arranged marriage was the custom in families like ours. I liked and respected him. He was a kind man and our marriage like many others seemed good enough, but I knew nothing about love until I met Jacques. Can you understand that, Emma, or are you too young? It took me by surprise. It was like a revelation. I became a different person.'

'Did you see him often?'

'No, not often, but he and François were close friends and sometimes he came home with him and all three of us would talk far into the night. He made us laugh again, but he could be serious too, and he was clever, full of ingenious ideas. Just to see him and be near him was joy enough.' She raised her eyes, looking at me almost pleadingly.

'Go on.'

'After that everything seemed to happen at once. Lucien found his way back to us from Geneva. François was angry with him and determined that he should not be involved in any of their plotting. Jacques did not come any more. There was the attempt on Bonaparte's life when Jacques was captured with Pierre and another of the men.'

'Pierre was captured?'

'Yes, his code name was the Fox, but I knew he had been there with them. He had come to see me more than once. It made François angry. He warned him to keep away, but you know what Pierre is like. He always went his own way and he was jealous of François and his influence on the others.'

'Was that when your husband was caught and shot?'

'Yes. Lucien and I were arrested too but I was released within a few days. I went back to the cottage. I found

Jacques there hiding in the loft. I knew that he and Pierre had escaped, but it had been a desperate affair. They had fought their way out and he had been wounded ... badly, in the leg. He could not walk more than a few steps. Pierre had gone without him.'

'Did you hide him?'

'For a month. At first he was very sick, but afterwards ... how strange it is that so much happiness can come out of so much wretchedness. When my husband was shot so brutally, I felt my life was ended. I was worried about Lucien, I could see no end to our misery, yet we lived those few weeks, Jacques and I, in a trance of joy, so fragile the least thing could have destroyed it. We knew it must finish soon, we knew he had to go. Again and again he begged me to leave France with him, but how could I? There was Lucien, but even more than that. To have taken a woman with him would inevitably have led to his capture and death. For a day ... two days ... he was angry with me. He walked out of the cottage and I was so unhappy I thought I would die, but then he came back ...'

'I believed that your love had deserted me, Now I know I am wrong ...'

I whispered.

'How did you know that?'

'I saw the book you gave him. He has it still.'

'He never told me.'

'He did not want me to know either. He despises what he calls sentimentality.'

'But he has not forgotten,' she said softly and I saw the light in her eyes.

'Does he know that Louis is his son?'

'How did you guess?'

'It was when I saw them together at St Rémy.'

'I could not tell him. He would want to take the boy and I could not bear to let him go. He is all I have.'

'Has my father asked you to go with him?'

'You need not be jealous, Emma. I shall not go. Seven years ago ... yes ... if there had been the ghost of a chance I would have gone anywhere with him, but not now. He has changed and so have I. I am the wife of

Henri de Labran to whom I owe a great deal. I will not let him down.' She smiled. 'You know Jacques, Emma. He won't take no for an answer. "Send me one line and I will come to fetch you," he said, but I shall not. All I want, all I pray for, is to know him safely out of France.'

'Does Monsieur de Labran know about my father?'

'I am not sure how much he guesses about the past. He has never spoken of it. It was over and done with before I knew him. But now today, after what Nicole said, I don't know . . . he has shut himself away from me. I think if he believed that Jacques was my lover, he would kill him, but why should he believe what is not true?'

'Isn't it?'

She was very still, looking down at her clasped hands. 'Once only. I should have denied him, but I could not. You will understand that one day, Emma.'

Perhaps I would, but I could not help remembering how Henri had watched their unguarded looks in the garden of the Comte de Rennes and I was afraid, desperately afraid.

Martine turned to me. 'I know that you have not succeeded in persuading him to go.'

'No. He will not leave until his mission is completed.'

'Don't tell me about it. It is better that I do not know. But will it be soon?'

'Very soon.'

'Thank God.' She got to her feet. 'Now I think we had better go back to bed.' Her hand rested on my shoulder. 'Thank you for listening to me.' Then she was gone softly up the staircase and I followed after her.

I lay on my bed empty of hate and jealousy, empty of everything but weariness. Her love had brought her grief but it had given her joy too while I was tossed between Lucien and my father and whichever way I turned could find no peace.

Chapter 14

Lying wakeful hour after hour that night I began to think that sleep had deserted me for ever and when at last I did doze off, I woke in a fright certain that somewhere I had heard a door slam. The wind seemed to have abated a little and the room was stiflingly hot. I got up and opened one of the shutters cautiously. Outside the darkness was beginning to recede, but the sky was still leaden. Someone had come out of the house and was crossing the grass towards the olive groves. I could not see who it was, the long dark cloak and wide-brimmed hat concealed him completely.

I don't know what drove me to follow. I think I had some confused notion that I must reach my father, I must tell him what had happened and warn him about Lucien, though at any other time I would have realized the absurdity of such an idea. I dressed myself quickly, putting on my riding skirt and tying a scarf tightly over my head. I went down the stairs and let myself out by the garden door, pulling back the bolts carefully so as not to wake the servants. Outside the wind hit me at once throwing me back against the wall, but I put my head down and battled on, finding its buffets easier to endure than the tension and friction within the house. Whoever had gone out before me had already vanished, but I crossed the garden and took the path through the olive trees, almost enjoying the fierce struggle with the mistral. When I reached the stone sheds where the olive presses were kept, I had to stop to get my breath.

I leaned against the corner of the wall panting and in a lull of the wind I thought I heard movement inside. A voice cried out something, there was a scuffle, then silence. For some reason it terrified me. Trembling I put a hand

against the stone wall to steady myself. It was then I heard
a door creak. Someone must have come out of the sheds,
but I was on the far side and could see nothing. There was
the sound of footsteps. I flattened myself against the
buttress in case whoever it was should come my way, but
they didn't. I waited for a long time before I edged carefully along the wall and then I heard it, a queer shuffling
sound as if something were being dragged across the floor
followed by a gasping moan like an animal in terrible
pain. I stiffened against it, then tried hard to get a grip on
myself. Perhaps it was Peppi or one of the other dogs.
Whatever it was, I could not just leave it. I took a deep
breath and pushed open the door. It was very dark and it
was an instant before I could distinguish the figure of a
man lying just inside. He was trying to drag himself up by
the wooden bars of the press, but while I watched, his
hands slipped and he fell heavily. It was so horrible, I
wanted to run away and yet knew I couldn't. Whoever it
was needed help badly. I pushed the door wide. A grey
morning light flooded in. The man groaned again and
turned on his side. I saw his face quite clearly. It was my
father.

For a moment my head swam, then I was kneeling
beside him, trying desperately to raise him. 'Papa, what is
it? What has happened?'

'Martine . . .' he muttered thickly. 'Is it Martine?' His
eyes opened. They stared blankly, then very slowly there
came a flicker of recognition. 'Tell Martine . . . I did come
. . . tell her, Emma . . .'

'Are you hurt? Has someone attacked you?'

'Always knew I'd come to a bad end . . .' there was a
faint glimmer of the old familiar grin and it tore at my
heart.

'Who was it, Papa? Who has done this to you?'

'Lucien . . . it is Lucien who . . .' his body jerked and his
head fell back. A little trickle of blood ran down from the
corner of his mouth.

I could see no wound. Frantically I tore his shirt open
at the throat. I stroked his cheek, calling to him, begging
him to speak to me. I could think of nothing else so that I
didn't notice anyone come in until Lucien spoke to me.

'I saw you leave the house. What are you doing out here, Emma?'

I looked up into his face and it was like my dream all over again. I knew what had happened as certainly as if he had been standing there with the bloody knife in his hand. 'You killed him,' I spat at him. 'You murdered him.'

'No, I did not.' Lucien came closer. 'Let me see. It may not be as bad as you think.'

'Keep away. Don't touch him. It was you . . . he said so . . . he spoke your name,' I could not help myself. I could hear my voice rising into hysteria and Lucien gripped my shoulder, shaking me roughly.

'Stop it, do you hear, stop it!'

It shocked me into silence and he knelt down beside my father slipping his hand inside his shirt. After a moment he looked up. 'I think he is dead.'

The wound was so small, there was so little blood, it did not seem possible that it could have killed him, but it had been struck by someone who knew exactly the right spot. If there had been anything within reach, I think I would have hurled it at Lucien then. But I had nothing, only empty words.

'How could you do it? He trusted you and you killed him.'

Lucien ignored me. He got to his feet. 'Can you stay with him? I am going for help.'

The door opened and closed again. I knelt there in the half light, my father's head on my lap, too stunned to move. I could see it all so clearly and my heart contracted. Something must have happened between Henri and Martine. She must have sent him a message, by Joseph perhaps, I didn't know. I only knew that I hated her because she had lied to me, trading on my sympathy. He had come as he had promised and Lucien had killed him. I could not think beyond that. It went round and round in my head with a dreadful monotony till I felt I was going mad.

I was so numbed that the next few hours became mercifully blurred. Lucien came back with his stepfather. Joseph was there with some of the other servants. Henri de Labran looked down at my father.

He said, 'I know this man. He called himself Jacques Dupont.'

'Yes, but that was not his real name. He is the Englishman,' said Lucien. No point in hiding it any longer, I thought dully.

Henri gave him a sharp glance. 'How do you know?'

'Does it matter now?'

'Perhaps not.' He showed no surprise. It was as if he had long expected it. 'So ... then it is finished. We had better send for the Chief of Police.' He gestured to the servants. They took up my father's body and began to carry him down the path.

No one had asked why I was there and I followed blindly. They had what they wanted. He was dead and Armand with the other men shut up in Tarascon Castle would be released. Once when I stumbled, Lucien put out a hand to take my arm, but I thrust him away.

'Don't come near me. Don't touch me.'

A shattering blow that comes unexpectedly can have the effect of making everything seem unreal. It is too unbelievable to be accepted. At any moment you expect to awake from it. I went through the next few hours as if in an evil dream, some remnant of sanity keeping me aware that I must still play a part. I was still Emma Louise Rainier to whom the murder of an English spy would mean nothing more than relief from danger. Charles Guitry arrived with Georges Montaud at his heels. The questions went on and on relentlessly.

'For what reason did you leave the house at such an early hour, Mademoiselle?'

'I couldn't sleep and it was very hot. I needed some air.'

'In spite of the wind?'

'It was because of the wind.'

'Ah yes, our mistral. You are not accustomed to it yet you went out in it just the same and you walked towards the olive sheds.'

'Yes.'

'And there you found the Englishman. Dying or already dead?'

'Dying. He spoke to me.'

'Did he? What did he say?'

I saw the trap into which I had nearly fallen. I said quickly, 'I can't remember. I was frightened.'

'How did you know who he was?'

'I didn't, but I had heard talk of the Englishman and he was a stranger . . .'

'A stranger you had never seen before?'

'No.'

'And yet you went out to meet him.'

'No, no, I didn't. Why do you say that?'

'He was expecting to meet somebody, isn't that so? Who was it?'

'How should I know?'

'Are you quite sure? Was it Monsieur de Fontenay?'

'No.'

'Or Madame de Labran?'

'No.'

But here Henri intervened. 'I resent such a question. You have no right to insinuate anything against my wife.'

'My apologies, Monsieur, but I am trying hard to discover the truth.'

On and on went the questions till my head was spinning and my anger and wretchedness got the better of me. 'The man you were hunting is dead,' I burst out bitterly. 'Isn't that enough for you?'

'No, Mademoiselle, it is not nearly enough. I would far rather he had been taken alive. This could be an act of private vengeance, but there are still those who worked with him. We need them too.'

'Do you think he would have betrayed them?'

'Why not? He did before.'

'That is a lie and you know it.' I think then that I would have screamed out the whole truth but Lucien stepped in front of me.

'You seem to forget, Monsieur Guitry, that my fiancée is suffering from a great shock.'

'I have no doubt of that.' The police chief's half smile as he looked at me made me shiver. I wondered how much he guessed.

He questioned all the servants, but no one can be more dumb than a Provençal peasant if he does not choose to open his mouth and they were fiercely loyal to their master. He got nowhere.

Martine was deadly pale, but he could not break through the steel of her pride and Henri de Labran supported her unfalteringly. No one could have guessed that the man lying dead in the next room had been her lover, the father of her child. I only saw her tremble once and that was at the end when Guitry was preparing to leave.

'I will send the police cart,' he said. 'My men will take the body away.'

'No,' said Henri de Labran unexpectedly. 'No, whatever the Englishman did, he was acting for his country and he is a man, not an animal. He died on my land and he will remain here until the Curé is fetched and he can be buried decently.'

I saw Martine look gratefully at her husband. A sob caught in her throat. She murmured something and hurried from the room.

'It seems that Madame is distressed,' said Guitry with his bitter smile, 'and yet after all the man is a heretic and the enemy.'

'Enemy or not, a murder almost on your doorstep is not a pleasant experience,' was Henri's cold reply. 'Is there anything further you wish to know, Monsieur?'

Guitry was obviously not satisfied, but for the moment he could do no more. He left reluctantly.

It was over for the time being at least and I was free to escape for a little, but the four walls of my room closed in on me like a prison. The mistral still blew. There was a heavy thunderous feeling in the air that weighed on me like a stifling blanket. My thoughts were going round and round like a rat in a trap. My father was dead and Lucien had killed him. The only two people I had ever loved and both were lost to me. There was nothing left. I cared no longer for plots or Bonaparte or England. Everything that mattered had crumbled around me. I think that in those hours I was a little mad. Villeroy had become hateful to me. I wanted only to get out of it.

'You must try to eat something,' Martine had said gently to me when Guitry had gone, but I had shaken my head. The thought of food turned me sick. Now when I crept down the stairs, I knew they were all in the dining-room. The stables were empty. The servants, disturbed and upset, had gathered in the kitchen to eat and gossip. I saddled Beauregard myself with no notion of where I was going, only that I had to get away. I think the pony took the old path almost by instinct. I woke up suddenly to the realization that we were following the track to the hills and I let him have his head. When we reached the place of stones, the threatened storm broke. A streak of jagged lightning split the dark sky and the thunder rolled. Beauregard halted, trembling all over. I slipped out of the saddle, gentling him. By the little pavilion it was sheltered. I tethered him there and went on alone.

It was madness to climb up the crags in such weather, but something urged me on and in a way the storm was part of my mood. If the lightning struck at me or I slipped on the rocks to my death, I no longer cared and strangely enough my very despair seemed to give me strength. By some miracle I never went wrong or made a false step. I climbed and climbed until I came out on the level place and went on up the broken stone staircase. The room where I had first met my father was empty. They had gone as Lucien had said; all that was left were the boxes on which they had sat, an empty bottle on the table and the straw palliasse burst and rotting in its corner.

I did not stay. There were more steps and I climbed higher. The storm was still raging. I came out on to the battlement of a half-ruined turret with a low parapet. I could see across the hills to the great open plain of the Camargue. I watched lightning tear across the sky and come down like a ball of fire. Somewhere on those wastes the trees dry as tinder burst into flame. The rage in the sky unsoftened by rain had a savagery and a magnificence that terrified and yet exalted me. I wanted to disappear into it. My resolution hardened. I began to look for a foothold. The wind tore at my hair. If I climbed up on to the parapet, I could let it take me where it wished. I took the first dizzying step. I caught a lightning glimpse of a jagged black precipice far below me, then two arms seized me round the waist and lifted me to the ground. I fought back savagely, but Lucien was stronger than I.

'Murderer!' I screamed at him, struggling to free myself. 'Do you want to kill me as you did him?'

The thunder drowned his reply, but he had swung me over his shoulder. Kicking and clawing at him, I was carried down the steps and into the stone room. He flung me none too gently on the straw palliasse and glared down at me.

'Now,' he said, 'now perhaps you will listen to reason.'

'Leave me alone. Why did you follow me?' I tried to struggle up. 'You cannot stop me. My life is my own affair.'

'No, it is not. He left you in my charge, God help me. So you will do as I say.'

'When did he do that?' I spat at him. 'Before you murdered him?'

'Once and for all, I did not murder him and I don't know who did. I am sorry for it, more sorry than you realize. But now it is done, we have to go on living.'

'You may but I can do what I like.' I sprang to my feet and made for the archway at the head of the steps. The rain had come at last. It was tearing down in a blinding sheet. He caught hold of me and flung me back. I collapsed on the mattress again. 'You don't understand,' I cried out at him in bitter resentment. 'How could you? What do you care how I feel?'

'Christ Almighty! You dare to ask me that. Are you blind to everyone but your father? Don't you realize what you have done to me?'

I stared at him and after a moment, he let himself drop on the straw beside me. 'Listen to me, Emma,' he said more gently. 'I fell in love with you in Paris. God knows why. I never wanted to. You were English, you were different from any girl I had known and I had nothing to offer any woman. I hadn't a hope in hell of making a life for myself or for anyone and I knew then that you were obsessed with your father.'

'You make it sound like a disease,' I said sullenly.

'No, not a disease. I was sorry for it, but I understood it and so, like a fool, between love and pity I brought you here.'

'Why are you telling me this?'

'Because I want to make you realize. I thought you cared about me too, sometimes we seemed so close, but always he was between us like a wall of glass. The moment he reappeared, he was all-important. When I was crazy enough to ask you to marry me, you looked at me as if I

198

didn't really exist, and now he is dead, you want to die too.'

'You speak so callously. He loved me. All my life he has meant everything to me and now he has died so uselessly, so cruelly.' At last the numbness was fading and the pain became unbearable. My throat ached with the tears I had not shed.

'Do you still believe I killed him?'

'I don't know,' I said waveringly, 'I don't know.'

'Life is for the living, that is what he would have said. I love you, Emma, so much. Why won't you believe that?'

'I did once,' I said dully, 'but it was lies, all lies, and now it doesn't matter any longer. Nothing matters.'

He looked at me for a moment and there was anger in the dark eyes, then he pulled me towards him. He began to kiss me, gently at first and then more and more deeply. I fought him wildly, trying to turn away my face, beating at him with my fists, but it was my body that played the traitor. Against my will it was responding to him, it was clamouring for his kisses. He forced me back against the straw and my senses began to whirl. After a little he drew back and it was the Lucien whom I had glimpsed first in the turret room with my father, strong and confident.

'I'm done with acting the fool,' he said, 'I've held back too long.' He pressed his lips against the hollow of my throat.

'No,' I murmured, 'no, Lucien please.'

He raised his head. 'Yes, Emma, yes. You love me, you know you do. Don't be afraid of it. Put your arms round my neck. Kiss me.'

An extraordinary weakness had taken possession of me. Fleetingly before I drowned in his kisses, I remembered what Martine had said about joy that springs out of wretchedness. She had known it with my father as I knew it now with Lucien. Perhaps this was the only way I could be released into freedom though it had to come through loss and pain.

What seemed a long time afterwards Lucien stirred and sat up. He touched my cheek gently. 'Why are you crying, Emma?'

I turned my face away, the tears running down my face. I couldn't stop them and I didn't want to. There was relief and healing in them. Wisely he said nothing, then after a little he got up and moved to one of the window openings.

'Listen,' he said. 'The wind has dropped and it's not raining any longer.' He held out his hand. 'Come and see.'

When I joined him, he put his arm round me. The sky was a tender blue. We could see every rock, every tree right across to the Camargue and as we watched the flamingos rose, long necks stretched out, legs dangling, their rosy plumage making a skein of colour across the horizon.

'Do you know what they call them here?' he said. '*Les fleurs qui volent,* the flowers that fly.' He smiled down at me. 'I had to do it. I had to make you know about yourself. Have you forgiven me?'

'There is nothing to forgive.' I looked down the sheer rock face, shuddering. How could I have ever wanted to throw myself into that dark abyss? 'But for you, I might be lying down there.'

'No, I don't think so. Your father's spirit would have triumphed in the end. He loved life too much to throw it away.'

'Lucien, who did kill him?'

His face was sombre. 'I'm not sure. I can only guess. Someone sent him a message knowing he would come and then waited for him.'

'He thought it was Martine.'

'I guessed that.'

'Did you know about her and him?'

'I realized something a long time ago, but it was not my mother who sent the message.'

'Was it your stepfather?'

'I hope not. I pray not, for her sake.'

'I thought it was because of what Nicole said about your mother and because you still believed that he had betrayed your father . . .'

'And so I murdered him. Emma, my love, you have a very poor opinion of my judgment. Do you think that I cannot tell when a man deliberately lies? If your father had acted the traitor, if he had cracked under torture, he would have admitted it and defied me to do my worst. It was the kind of man he was. He would have scorned to take refuge in a lie.'

I knew then that I had misjudged Lucien all along and that my father had known him better than I did and given him his trust. I realized now why he had died with Lucien's name on his lips.

'What will happen now?'

'We shall go through with it.'

'And Pierre?'

Lucien's face hardened. 'Pierre will do as I say.'

We climbed down the rocky path together. The horses, wet and nervous after the storm, were glad to see us. On the road home we met the Curé plodding along the track in his shabby black soutane, his thick ash stick in his hand. He put a hand on Lucien's bridle as we came abreast of him.

'Your stepfather called me to Villeroy,' he said. 'Is it all finished?'

'No, not yet. There is still tomorrow.'

'So it goes ahead.'

'Of course.'

'Good. I had not been sure.'

Lucien looked at me and grinned. Then he bent down towards the little priest. 'Father, do you think you could marry us?'

The Curé looked startled. 'Is this a time to think of marrying?'

Lucien laughed. 'As good a time as any and Emma Louise and I are weary of waiting.'

The Curé looked at me shrewdly. 'My dear children, our Catholic faith tells us that the sacrament of marriage is the exchange of vows between a man and a woman. The priest is merely a witness of the plighting of their troth. I hope I shall have the pleasure of being a witness at your marriage even though Mademoiselle Emma is a heretic.' He waved a hand in farewell before he plodded on.

'He knows who I am,' I exclaimed.

'He has always known,' said Lucien. 'He will see that your father is not thrown into the earth like a common criminal. He will have taken him into the church. Do you want to see him?'

'No. I want to remember him alive, not dead.'

'Good.' His hand closed over mine and we rode on together.

Chapter 15

We came back to Villeroy in the early evening, the sky like pearl and the air so soft you would never have believed there had been a storm except for the dust churned into mud under our horses' hooves, the branches ripped from the trees and the flowers beaten into the ground.

The pain was still there. It hurt to realize that I would never see my father again, never worry myself sick about him, never laugh with him, never hear his voice, half tender, half mocking. But the worst was over. I was sane again and Lucien had helped. He had made me see myself, he had turned me into a whole person, someone in my own right with my own life to live. The Lucien whom I had met in Paris was altogether different from the man I knew and loved now. I had feared the comparison with my father, but he had come through the test and not been found wanting. I had forgotten only one thing. He had stepped into my father's shoes and the element of danger that had been part of Jack Tremayne had shifted itself to Lucien. I was to be reminded of it all too soon.

When we returned, there was no one in the courtyard. Thankfully I went up to my room, stripping off my muddy riding skirt, dipping my face into cool water and changing into a clean muslin dress. It was not yet time for supper and presently I went downstairs. Martine was alone in the sitting-room, working at her embroidery. She looked up as I came in and I met her eyes. My heart overflowed. I ran across the room and fell on my knees beside her. Her arms went round me. We had both suffered the same bitter loss and there was no need for words. I think we were closer at that moment than we had ever been before. After a little she said gently, 'I am glad Lucien found you.'

'How did you know?'

'Joseph said Beauregard was not in the stable. I think Lucien guessed at once where you would have gone.'

'I wanted to die but he would not let me.'

She turned my face to look at her. 'Is it all right between you?'

'I love him, Martine.'

'I knew what he felt about you. I think I knew it from the very first day he brought you here. It is your feelings I've never been sure of, Emma.'

'You can be sure of them now.'

'Jacques and I and now you and Lucien. It seems so strange. I wish I knew what the end of it will be.'

'Listen, Martine. Lucien wanted me to keep it from you, but now I cannot. You know, don't you, that all along it has been he, not Pierre and not my father, who has been the leader?'

'I knew but I shut my eyes to it. I had to think of Henri. At first it was sheer necessity. We had to live. But Lucien is François de Fontenay's son and these last years he has been like someone chained. I knew he would have to break free. When Pierre decided to come back, it gave him his opportunity. He had a lieutenant who could carry out what he planned.'

And Pierre had resented his leadership just as he had resented my father. How blind I had been. I could see it all so clearly now. I was proud of Lucien and yet afraid for him too.

I said, 'Everything depends on tomorrow. If they succeed . . .'

'Ssh,' she put her finger warningly on my lips. 'Be careful. Someone may hear.'

'But who? There is no one here.'

'I don't know.' She passed a hand wearily over her face. 'Perhaps it is because today I am so . . . so *distraite* . . . but everything frightens me. What does Nicole know?'

'Nicole?' I repeated, astonished. 'Nothing. How should she?'

'Are you sure? Georges Montaud has been here all the afternoon. They were talking together for a long time. Why? She cares nothing for him.'

'Perhaps it is because of Armand. She wants to know when he will be released.'

Martine shook her head. 'It is not as simple as that. Guitry is not a man to do anything by halves. Jacques is dead, but that is not enough. He will hunt out every man, burn them out of their caves if he must so that he can present his master with a clean sheet. Only then will his failure be blotted out and his ambition given the reward he craves.'

She spoke so bitterly that I stared at her. 'How do you know that?'

'I know Guitry. He was savage this morning because the last clue still evades him. He suspects Lucien but he has no proof. He would like to do to him what he did to François.' She leaned forward whispering. 'Emma, whatever happens, take Lucien with you to England. Force him to go if he will not. Only then will I know him safe.' Then Henri de Labran came into the room and she sat up, saying lightly, 'Go up and say goodnight to Louis, Emma. He has been asking for you all day.'

Henri was kind. He came to me at once, taking my hand and asking how I felt.

'Thank you,' I said, 'I am quite recovered.' As soon as I could, I escaped upstairs to the child's room and found Lucien there sitting on the bed. The boy grinned up at me when I came in.

'Lucien has been telling me about England. He says they breed bulls there, bigger than ours and fatter, but they don't fight them, they eat them.' His disgusted face made us both smile, then suddenly he sat up, looking at me reproachfully. 'Where have you been, Emma? It's been a horrid day. There was a man in one of the downstairs rooms. I think he was dead. They said he was asleep and tried to keep me away, but I *saw* him. It was the man who gave me the dagger, a nice man, he made me laugh.'

A sad little epitaph from the boy he never knew was his. I couldn't trust myself to speak and Lucien answered for me.

'It was an accident, Louis. Try not to think of it any more.' He ruffled the child's hair. 'Now go to sleep otherwise Maman will be cross with Emma Louise and with me for keeping you awake.'

I bent and kissed him and went out with Lucien. Outside in the passage I clung to him in a sudden rush of tears.

'Don't go through with this. Please Lucien. It is too dangerous. I have been talking with your mother. Guitry knows too much.'

He put his arms round me, holding me against him, speaking soothingly. 'He knows nothing essential and by the time he does, it will be all over. We shall have made our capture.' He smiled. 'With a prize like General Bonaparte under my arm, think of how much I can demand for France from your British government.'

His jest succeeded in making me smile through my tears, but I found it hard to share his confidence. I no longer had any trust in what they were trying to do yet I knew it would be impossible to stop him. He laughed at danger just as my father had done.

He pushed back the hair from my forehead, looking deep into my eyes. 'I love you Emma, don't ever forget that.'

'Never, never again.' His kisses gave me courage. I thrust aside my fear. I made myself believe that all would go well.

The next morning I watched him ride up to the vineyards as usual. Louis wanted to go with him as he had done once or twice before. 'Not this time,' he said gaily, 'another day,' and only I knew that there never would be another time, that up in the hills Pierre and the others waited for him. As I turned to go back into the house Nicole came through the door dressed for riding.

'I am going to Tarascon to see Armand,' she said, casually pulling on her gloves and taking the reins from the stable boy.

'Is that permitted?'

'Of course. Monsieur Guitry gave me his promise.'

I watched her ride out with a chill foreboding. Nicole, so self contained, who did not want Lucien but hated me for taking him away from her, Nicole whose dearest love was reserved for her twin brother—how much did she know? The black eyes had never given anything away.

It was such an ordinary day. On the surface everything was as usual. I sat with Louis in the schoolroom and we read a simple English story together. We had been teaching Peppi to beg for biscuits. We laughed at his antics and I thought this is the last time I shall do this, the last time I shall go down to the kitchen fetching milk for Louis and coffee for myself, and I wished I could take my little half-brother with me to Trevira and tell him about the father I loved and he would never know.

It was all fixed. Some time late that evening I would slip out of the house. Mouton would be waiting for me and would take me across the marshes beyond Les Saintes Maries to where the *Sea Witch* waited. It was odd but I could hardly even remember what Victor looked like . . . I wondered what would happen if the boat wasn't there.

After luncheon I took Louis to the village and left him with the Curé, but I did not go into the church. My father's spirit had escaped into some other dimension; the coffin in front of the altar had nothing to do with him nor did I want to stay and see him put into the earth.

I was restless all the afternoon and could settle to nothing. I would have been easier if I could have gone with Lucien. I would not have minded danger so much as this endless waiting. It was early evening before Nicole came back. There was a curious air of suppressed excitement about her when she came into the room where I was sitting with Martine, my botched needlework on my lap, my hands idle. She threw her gloves and riding crop on the table.

'Very soon now Armand will be released,' she said.

'That's splendid news, but are you sure, my dear?' asked Martine.

'Yes. The Police Chief told me himself.'

'What has changed his mind? When your father spoke with him yesterday, he refused to give any promise.'

'Papa doesn't know everything. Things have changed since yesterday. Guitry told me nothing of course, but I got it out of Georges. He is as pleased as a cat with two tails, they all are.'

'Nicole, don't be so provoking,' said Martine sharply. 'Tell us what has happened.'

'Very well.' She perched on the edge of the table, swinging one small booted foot and smiling her small secret smile. 'Those traitors up in the hills have overreached themselves. They believe that Bonaparte intends a secret visit to Marseilles from St Rémy so they have a plan to murder him . . .'

'Murder him? Surely not.'

'I don't know why you should sound so surprised. It is not the first time they have murdered and anyhow it doesn't matter because they will not succeed.'

I was appalled. How had they found out? Who had betrayed every detail? 'What does Monsieur Guitry intend to do?' I asked striving to sound only casually interested.

'It's quite clever really. Everything will go as planned. They will see the horsemen approaching and they will believe it is Bonaparte, but when they ride down from the hills the tables will be turned against them. Jean will be there with his soldiers on one side and Guitry with his policemen on the other. They will have them caught between them like rats in a trap.'

'And when is all this going to happen?'

'Georges suddenly went dumb and wouldn't tell me any more,' said Nicole regretfully. 'I suppose he thought he had said too much. But I am certain it will be tonight. Thank goodness, it will soon all be over and Armand will be home again.'

The look of triumph on Nicole's face sickened me. Had we been careless, Lucien and I, and had Nicole put two and two together and sold us for the sake of her brother? I did not want to believe it, but true or false, I could not stop now to work it out. Somehow they must be warned, but how? I was not even sure of their meeting place. My mind raced while Martine asked more questions and Nicole answered with the same maddening unconcern. At last she went upstairs to change her dress and as she went past me, she paused for an instant leaning towards me and whispering.

'What a pity Lucien isn't here, Emma Louise. He would have been so interested. Don't you agree?'

I knew then that somehow or other she had guessed and this was her revenge. I hated her for condemning Lucien to death.

Alone with Martine, I said urgently, 'They have got to know about it. Someone has got to warn them.'

'What can we do? There is no one reliable whom we can send. Joseph has gone with Lucien.'

'There is the Curé,' I said. 'He may be able to help, or Mouton. There is just a chance that he may not have left yet.'

'I wish Henri were here. He would know what to do.'

But would he? Would Henri de Labran risk his own neck and that of his dearly loved son for Lucien who had caused him nothing but trouble?

'Supposing neither of them can be found?' said Martine.

'Then I shall go myself.'

'You cannot, Emma. It is many leagues from here and you do not know the road.'

'I can find it.' Desperation added edge to my voice. 'Don't you understand? I must try. It is Lucien's life. It is Pierre, Marius, all of them. If they are taken, they will be shot. You said so yourself. It is what Guitry has been waiting for.'

I was no longer sure of anything except that I could not sit back and do nothing and that it was best to go secretly. It was Martine who undertook to have Beauregard saddled and took him quietly down to the olive groves while I went up to my room to change into the breeches and jacket Armand had once given me with such gaiety and laughter. I might well need to ride hard and fast. I thanked God for my father's stern training and the long hours in the saddle at Trevira.

How oddly one's mind works at a time such as this. I could take nothing with me and yet just as I was about to go out of the room, I went back to pick up the silver coin Lucien had once tossed to me and as I took it from the drawer, I saw the ruby necklace. I knew now that Lucien had meant it as a pledge between us. I took it from its velvet case and slipped it into my breeches pocket. Then I was ready.

Martine had more foresight than I. She was waiting on the path holding the pony's bridle and in the saddle holster was one of her husband's pistols.

'I have never fired one in my life,' she said as I pulled it out weighing it in my hand doubtfully.

'I have, but not for a long time.'

'It may be useful if only as a threat. It is a rough road to Marseilles.'

We had grown very close in the last few hours. It was

hard to part and know I might never see her again. She leaned forward and kissed my cheek.

I swung myself into the saddle and watched her walk back to the house. It was not so long since I had seen her run down this same path into my father's arms and had known a bitter jealousy. She bore her loneliness and grief with a dignity that I envied. For an instant pain tore at me again, then I conquered it and turned Beauregard's head towards the village.

The Curé was not at home. 'He has been called away to someone who is sick,' said his housekeeper with a disapproving look at my breeches. 'He will not be back until tomorrow.'

I knew what that meant. He was away to the hills with the other rebels. He could not bear to be left out despite his lameness. I trotted on to the Camargue.

Mouton's little cabin was shut and locked. A dog barked furiously inside so I guessed he could not be out with the bulls. The big white dog went everywhere with him on the marshes. To hunt for him would waste too much valuable time. Now there was no help for it. Now I was really on my own.

I had seen the map on the table and the place Lucien had marked, but I had not studied it closely. I only knew that I had to follow the mountain road to where it turned south towards Marseilles. It took me nearly four hours to reach that point. Hours when I was forced to ask the way and still went wrong and had to retrace my steps. Hours when I stumbled up rough tracks and persuaded Beauregard to ford small streams dangerously swollen by the previous day's rain. I was tormented with anxiety as to whether I would get there in time and even if I did whether I would find them. The chance seemed so small; time and time again I nearly turned back, but the thought of Lucien murdered as my father had been murdered, gave me courage and drove me on. At one village a burly peasant pointed out the road to Marseilles.

'You'll not reach there tonight,' he said in his thick Provençal accent. 'Much better put up at an inn.' I shook my head and he went on warningly. 'There will be precious few out on the roads at night. Too dangerous. Best keep an eye to your purse and a hand on your pistol or your friends will find you plucked clean as a chicken and trussed up in a ditch!'

It was not a cheerful prospect, but I thanked him and went on. After a little, dense woods rose up on either side and the road divided. I had no notion which way to turn. My father would have tossed a coin and taken a chance so I did the same. Heads I go left; tails and it is the right. Tails it was and as I trotted on, chance, fate, destiny, call it what you will, came to my aid. I had not gone far when a figure stepped out of the scrub at the side of the road and halted me.

'You are riding late, young man,' he said. 'Where are you bound for?'

It was dark by now and the moon had not yet risen, but I was almost sure that it was Jean de Rennes. I caught a glimpse of the uniform hidden under the long black cloak and my heart leaped into my mouth in case he should recognize me. I roughened my voice praying that he could not see me too clearly in the shade of the slouch hat.

'You're right, I am late, Monsieur, and if you keep me here gossiping I shall be later still. I shall get a thrashing from my father.'

'Been cutting loose, have you, my young cockerel? Get along with you then.' He gave Beauregard a slap across the rump and the pony shot forward nearly unseating mc. I heard his laughter as I righted myself, but I didn't care. He had given me a clue. If there were soldiers hidden and waiting, then this must be the place. Lucien and his comrades must be concealed somewhere in the hills unaware of what was waiting for them.

The road in front of me twisted and turned. I waited till I had rounded a bend and then looked for a track on my right. I took a chance and plunged off the road into the woods. It was steep and stony; branches tore at me and creepers whipped across my face. Before I knew what was happening to me, I had blundered into the midst of them. They must have been strung out along the hillside. I was aware of horses, blackened faces were staring at me, whites of eyes gleaming. Silently I was lifted from my pony. Sounds were muffled, voices hushed. They pushed me forward. Then I was facing Pierre. I recognized him through his disguise.

He thrust back my hat and I saw the suprise. He gave a low whistle. 'Emma, by God! You make a pretty boy I must say.'

'Where is Lucien?'

'Why, my dear? Can't you bear to let him out of your sight even for a day?'

'I've not ridden twenty leagues to listen to jests,' I said angrily.

Someone else had pushed his way through to us. 'What is it? What is going on?'

'Lucien, thank God you're here. You must listen to me.'

He took my arm and drew me away from the others. 'What in God's name are you doing here, Emma? I thought it was all arranged.'

'You don't know what has happened. Guitry knows everything.'

'How? It is not possible.'

Breathlessly I poured out the whole story and Lucien listened, frowning.

'Damnation! Who could have betrayed us?'

Over his shoulder I could see Pierre's dark face. 'No one here, that's for sure,' he said dryly. 'Maybe your pretty little Nicole has been listening at keyholes.'

'What do you take me for? She could have learned nothing from us.' Lucien paused for a moment, his eyes narrowed. 'We must call it off at once.'

'Why? Guitry and his merry men are still only guessing. Georges would not have blabbed everything. You can be sure of that.'

'Jean de Rennes is here,' I said urgently. 'He stopped me not far along the road.'

'Jean? Are you sure of that, Emma?'

'She could be mistaken. It's black as Hades and in the dark one soldier looks very like another,' said Pierre easily. 'Probably some lad or other spending a night with his girl.'

'It was Jean,' I said stubbornly.

'If he is here, then Guitry is not far off. They have outwitted us.'

'What's wrong, Lucien? Are you afraid?'

'Damn you! You've no cause to say that.'

'After all it's your first time in action,' went on Pierre, lightly mocking. 'Best leave it to me.'

'No. There are good lives at stake. I am not going to see them thrown away for nothing.'

For an instant their eyes met, two wills battling with one another, then to my surprise Pierre gave in. He shrugged his shoulders. 'Have it your own way, but the men are scattered all along the ridge.'

'Get as many mounted as you can. Tell them why but do it quietly. We'll retreat through the hills. I'll go down to the road where the others are waiting and warn them.'

In the bustle that followed I think I was temporarily forgotten. Lucien was already on his horse. Someone brought Beauregard and helped me into the saddle. Then quite suddenly through the stillness of the night there came the call of an owl, clear, haunting, repeated three times.

'My God, it's too late. That is the signal. They have seen them coming and they will believe it is Bonaparte. Take the men back into the hills, Pierre. Go with them, Emma. I'll try and stop the others.'

But in the darkness and confusion only half the men had grasped what was happening. Some hesitated, but a great many went crashing down after Lucien though he shouted at them to keep back, and I went after them. There was no time to be afraid, no time to think of anything except that I must not lose sight of Lucien.

By the time I reached the road, a battle was raging. The moon had risen by now and in its pale light I saw the men swarming around a light carriage, but it was not Bonaparte in the dark green uniform but Charles Guitry himself who had climbed to the driver's seat. Lucien was shouting to his comrades to escape how they could. I was terrified and furiously angry at the same time. I pulled the pistol out of its holster with no clear idea as to what I could do with it. Then a figure loomed up beside me and a hand gripped my arm.

'Drop that, you young fool.'

It was Jean. I had lost my hat and my hair was blowing about my face. He peered at me and then burst out laughing. 'My God, it's Emma!' I tried to twist away from him but he held my arm tightly. 'A spitfire too. I always thought there was more in you than meets the eye.'

I had to stop him somehow. I swung the pistol with all the force I could muster. It hit him on the side of the head and jerked him back. 'You damned little bitch!' he exclaimed and lurched forward. In another minute he would have had me out of the saddle, but my bridle was seized and I was dragged away from him along the road.

Mouton said, 'You shouldn't be here, Mademoiselle.'

'Let me go. I'm not leaving.'

'Monsieur le Marquis ordered me to get you out of here.'

I looked back despairingly. Some of the men were already galloping up the road. I saw Lucien turn to follow them, then a shot rang out. His horse stumbled and he was pitched over its head. They closed in on him.

Guitry was standing on the box seat. He shouted, 'Get that girl,' and Mouton waited no longer.

'He will be killed. I must go back,' I cried out at him, but he had my reins firmly in his hold and we were galloping madly side by side. By the time the soldiers had forced themselves through and started after us, we had already got a good start, but Mouton was taking no chances.

'They could still come after us,' he said breathlessly. 'You'd be a prize worth capturing, Mademoiselle. There is one thing though. Those fools don't know the hills as I do.'

I still pleaded with him. 'Mouton, go back. You may be able to help him. I can go alone. I can find my own way to the boat.'

'No. He would not want it, besides I promised Monsieur Jacques that whatever happened I would see you safe away to England. Come on now. It will be rough going but we shall manage.'

He plunged off the road and through the trees, seeming to find his way by instinct. It was a journey of nightmare and sometimes I dream of it still. Every bone in my body ached and far worse than that was the thought of Lucien. Was he wounded? Was he killed? What would they do to him if he was captured? Of one thing I was sure, after this he could expect no mercy from Napoleon Bonaparte.

The first faint glimmer of dawn found us crossing a

desert so desolate, it was like a valley in some region of hell. A vast plain of grey stones broken only by solitary tamarisks bent and twisted into fantastic shapes by the mistral.

'What is this place?' I asked wearily.

'They call it the Crau and we must cross it quickly. There is little cover here and if we are seen . . .'

'Who would follow us here?'

'I don't know, Mademoiselle, but there has been treachery. We can't be sure how much is known. We cannot be too careful.'

By now I was so tired it took all my concentration to keep myself upright in the saddle. Once I swayed forward and was only saved by clutching at Beauregard's mane. Mouton glanced at me anxiously.

'You need not worry,' I said grimly. 'I shall not faint.'

By the time we reached the Camargue, the sky had turned pink and gold. All around us were the reeds fringing the marshes, whispering in the breeze. In an attempt to keep up my courage Mouton began to tell me of the creatures that lived in the swamps along with the bulls and the horses. There were serpents, he said, thick as a man's arm, badgers, hares and foxes. Sometimes when food ran short, they would trap and roast them. 'It's strong-tasting meat, Mademoiselle, but it goes down good when you're hungry and it keeps up the strength in your body.'

He went on talking. I scarcely listened. By now the sun had risen and beat down relentlessly. We were skirting the great lagoon. The marshy pools inflamed my thirst. I would have given anything to stop and dip my face into the brackish water, but Mouton was as pitiless as the sun. Beauregard gamely battled on, his coat dark with sweat. I began to think it would never end. We would ride on forever over these salt wastes, feverish and wretched. At last, when I was almost at the end of my strength, the huge black walls of a church rose up like a grim fortress amidst the clustered white huts and Mouton crossed himself reverently.

'The church of Les Saintes Maries,' he said. 'If we get through, I'll light a candle at the shrine. Take heart, Mademoiselle, we are nearly there.'

In another half an hour the horses were floundering in

deep soft sand. The dunes were all around us and beyond I had a glimpse of the sea rippling and shining, softly, lapping the shore. There was no sign of a ship or a boat anywhere. The beach stretched wide and empty under the sun. By this time I was a little light-headed from hunger and fatigue. How ridiculous, I thought, all this trouble to get here and it is all for nothing. Dreamily I let Beauregard carry me forward through the dunes when a man suddenly rose up between me and the sea. He held up his hand threateningly and I saw the gun. For a mad moment I thought, 'They have got here before us. We are lost, Mouton and I, as lost as Lucien.'

Then he spoke. 'Ah there you are at last. We've been waiting,' he said in deplorable French. 'Where in God's name are the others?'

Unbelievably it was Victor, still managing to look unmistakeably British despite his rough dress and seaman's cap. My hair was lank with sweat, my breeches filthy with dust and mud. I saw the astonishment in his face before I slid out of the saddle and felt my knees buckle under me. He caught me before I fell and lowered me gently to the sand.

'Emma, my dear, what has happened to you?' His concern was touching though I was almost too far gone to appreciate it. 'Where is your father?'

'He won't be coming.' Then to my shame, grief and weariness overtook me. My head swam, my throat choked. I hid my face in my hands and felt his hand on my shoulder. As the dizziness slowly receded, I heard him speaking in low tones to Mouton. Presently he came back to me, helping me to my feet, speaking soothingly.

'You needn't worry any more, my dear. It is all over. You are safe now. I am going to row you out to the ship.'

'No, no.' I tried to resist him as he half carried me through the sand to where the boat was hidden up one of the inlets from the sea. 'We must wait, Victor. We must wait for Lucien.'

'Lucien?'

'You don't understand. He should have come with us . . . in my father's place.'

'Yes, yes, I know, but first things first.' Another man waited in the boat. Together they lifted me into it. I said desperately, 'Mouton, listen to me. We will wait. I'll make them wait. Tell him.'

He nodded, but they had pushed the boat out and were rowing with slow even strokes. I saw Mouton outlined against the bright sun. He waved his hand and turned back to the horses.

The *Sea Witch* had only one small cabin which Victor handed over to me. 'I'm afraid I've nothing fit for you to wear,' he said when he took me there.

I smiled at his strong disapproval of my boy's breeches. 'It doesn't matter. Perhaps it's just as well that I am dressed like this.'

'My crew are all decent well-behaved fellows,' he said stiffly. 'You are exhausted, my dear. You should get some rest.'

He left me to wash and clean myself as best I could. The cabin was tiny but Victor's toilet articles were laid out meticulously, his dressing gown hung from a hook on the door. He made no concessions to being on a ship in the middle of a war. I was trying to brush the stickiness out of my hair with his silver-backed brush when there was a knock at the door. When I opened it, I stared at the wizened brown face beaming at me. It took me back to Trevira.

'Oh, Silas, how good it is to see you!'

'Good to see you too, Miss Emma. Been like a cat on 'ot bricks, the Cap'en 'as, these last few days.' He touched my hand as he gave me the tray he was carrying. 'Real sorry to 'ear about the master, Miss. We all are. Rare old times we always 'ad with 'im.'

Silas had been with my father for so long through bad days and good. It brought everything back so sharply that my eyes blurred and I put the tray down blindly. It was a moment before I could even see it—English tea with thin bread and butter and arrowroot biscuits. There could not have been anything more old-maidish or more typical of Victor. At any other time I might have laughed but not now. I was too grateful.

I could not remain in the cabin and lie down. A restless anxiety took me up to the deck as soon as I had drunk the tea. Victor was talking to one of the crew. After a few minutes he came and joined me at the rail.

'My dear Emma, I cannot tell you how grieved I am at the death of your father. I found that fellow back there difficult to follow. What exactly happened?'

'He was murdered.'

'Murdered?' he looked aghast. 'By whom?'

'He was the English spy, Victor. Six lives could have been forfeited for him so someone killed him first.'

'Damned rascals! But what else can you expect in a country like this. I always knew he should not have come back. I told him so more than once, but when did he ever listen to me? It was a foolhardy venture.'

'Perhaps, but it was a brave one. If it had succeeded, it might have saved Europe.'

'My dear child, I know how you feel but you must try and put it behind you.' His hand closed over mine. 'You will have me to look after you now.'

I withdrew my hand. 'Victor, how long can you stay before you sail?'

'Not long. They are growing suspicious already. The sooner we take the *Sea Witch* out of these waters, the better.'

'Can you wait a few hours?'

'Why?'

'There is just a chance that Lucien may escape and if he does, I think he will come here.'

'Who is Lucien?'

'Lucien de Fontenay. You must remember. You met him in Paris. We are going to be married.'

'Married to a Frenchman? But we are at war with this cursed country. You cannot mean it, Emma.'

'But I do.' I looked him fully in the face. 'We are engaged.'

'These things happen, and you have always been too impulsive,' he said indulgently. 'Don't think I blame you, my dear, but at a time like this I cannot risk your life and the ship's crew for an infatuation.'

'It is not an infatuation.' Somehow I had to make him understand. 'It is desperately important . . .' I looked away from him.

He stared at me for a long moment. 'I know you, Emma. You are trying to shock me, but I don't believe you.'

My hands tightened on the rail. 'I love him, Victor, very much . . .'

'I shall wait until the wind freshens, then we must sail,' he said stiffly. 'Lucien or no Lucien.'

I knew I had deeply hurt him and I was sorry but I had to make him realize what it meant to me and I could think of no other way. I stayed there on the deck gazing at the empty shore golden under the sun until my eyes dazzled and my head ached, but nothing stirred. Victor urged me to go below and rest but I would not. Then Silas fetched a chair and mechanically I ate the food he brought me. About five o'clock I felt the wind begin to blow and activity began on the deck. The sails were run up, blossoming into the sky like the white wings of seabirds. The anchor came up through the clear water dripping with emerald seaweed. I moved to the other side of the ship so that I could no longer see that desolate beach. The crew were shouting to one another, laughing and skylarking, happy to be on the move.

Soon, too soon, I would be back at Trevira. How desperately lonely it was going to be without my father, without gay Jack Tremayne who had said one April morning, 'Men have died from time to time and worms have eaten them but not for love,' and then had disproved those very words. If he had not believed Martine had need of him, he would never have come down out of the hills to meet his death. And now Lucien had gone with him and nothing remained, nothing. The pain rose up in me until I couldn't bear it any longer. I let my head drop on my clasped hands and felt the agonizing sobs choke in my throat. An arm came round my waist and a cheek was laid against mine. I thrust it away angrily.

'Don't Victor, please.'

'It is not Victor.'

It was so unbelievable that I hardly dared to turn around in case it was not true, but Lucien was standing beside me. I was staring at him through a mist of tears. The sea water ran down his face and his soaked shirt to gather in small pools at his bare feet. A long cut down one cheek was oozing blood. He put out a hand and touched my face.

'You are weeping, Emma. Why? Because it is I and not your father?'

'Oh Lucien, I thought . . .' I clutched at his hand as if to make sure he was real before I collapsed against him. He stroked my hair.

My face muffled in his wet shirt, I said, 'How did you get here?'

'I swam and I'm afraid I'm ruining Victor's spotless deck as well as soaking you.'

'Never mind about that. How did you escape?'

'I was lucky. They thought me dead so while they rounded up their men, I managed to crawl away. Some of the others had escaped too. One of them had a horse. It was a devilish journey. I thought I would never get here.'

I saw how exhausted he looked and I touched his cheek tenderly. 'You must take off these wet clothes . . .'

'In a moment.' He held me away from him, looking into my face. 'Emma, I want you to realize something first. I'm not deserting France. The fight will go on.'

'I know.' I think I'd always known. There had been my father and now there would be Lucien. It was my fate and I accepted it. I put my hand on his arm. 'Lucien, who was it who informed against you? Was it Nicole?'

'No,' he smiled wryly. 'I don't think she would have minded exchanging me for Armand, but I don't believe she was ever quite sure.' He paused. 'It was Pierre.'

'Pierre? But how? Why?'

'It's not easy to tell you. He is my uncle after all.'

'Was it he who betrayed your father?'

'Yes. I believe it happened just as your father said, but Pierre was never able to forget what he had done and he hated your father because he knew and yet did nothing about it. It was the one mistake your father made. He forgot that some men cannot endure generosity in others. It belittles them too much in their own eyes. So out of jealousy and bitterness, Pierre killed him.'

For an instant the whole scene swam before my eyes, the dark shed, the lurking figure and my father coming unexpectedly to meet his love. 'When did you first realize it was Pierre?'

'It was during the evening while we were waiting in the

hills. Something he said about your father's death, something he could not have known, but I didn't want to believe it. Then you came and quite suddenly I was certain.'

'Does your mother know?'

'I think she guesses. She knew him better than anyone but she could never quite forget that he was the little brother she had once loved. I can still only make a guess at what he did. I believe that he could see no way out for himself but to take the credit for the murder and submit to Bonaparte. So he sent an anonymous letter betraying our plan and thought he could pull himself out of it at the last moment. I honestly don't believe that he meant us all to die, but it all happened quicker than he expected.'

'Has he escaped?'

'I don't know, but the Pierres of this world usually manage to keep themselves afloat. That is why I have to go on fighting them if your British government will let me. I have something here that will please them,' he patted his pocket, 'if the sea has not ruined them. The papers your father captured on the night of the garden party.'

'But first we will go to Trevira . . . you will like it there, Lucien.'

'Shall I?'

'It will be like Fontenay,' and suddenly in spite of grief and weariness, joy bubbled up in me. 'I don't know what we shall live on but I still have the coin you gave me, and I have these . . .' I pulled the rubies out of my pocket.

Lucien smiled. 'Clever girl. We can sell them.'

'We shall do nothing of the sort. I want to wear them as the Marquise de Fontenay and there are always pawnshops. My father said once that I was a very poor bargain with nothing but a ramshackle house, a few acres of bog and half a share in a tin mine for a dowry.'

'It's a great deal more than I have any right to expect,' said Lucien looking down ruefully at himself. 'We are fools, aren't we? A scarecrow . . .'

'And a scrubby stable boy . . .'

'With lovely eyes.' He pulled me to him. His kisses tasted of the sea. Then I drew back.

'Lucien, hadn't we better tell Victor you are here?'

'He knows. He hauled me over the side.'

'Poor Victor.'

'Poor dear Victor,' agreed Lucien. 'How he must dislike me.' He shivered as he linked his arm in mine. 'Do you think he will throw me back in the sea if I borrow one of his shirts?'

About the Author

CONSTANCE HEAVEN was born in London in 1911, the daughter of a naturalized British citizen from Germany. An accomplished actress, Ms. Heaven turned to writing after the death of her husband in 1958, and is the author of historical novels, biographies, and romantic suspense fiction—for which she is most famous—published in the United States and in Great Britain.

Currently a lecturer at the City Literary Institute in London, Constance Heaven now makes her home in Teddington, a riverside suburb of Middlesex.

More SIGNET Bestsellers You'll Enjoy Reading